Take the Monkeys and Run

A Barbara Marr Murder Mystery

Karen Cantwell

Take the Monkeys and Run

Acknowledgments

There are so many people to thank – people who have encouraged me, helped me, stood by me. My parents, my husband, my children, my friends. Thank you so much.

For *Take the Monkeys and Run*, a few people were instrumental in its inception, and I know you would not be reading this book if it were not for them: Ellie Camarda for sharing her own true monkey story; Jeri Thomas, who read every single page of my first draft, and laughed even when some of those "funny" lines still needed work; Julia Sullivan who granted me the right to use the term House of Many Bones; Misha Crews and LB Gschwandtner for always believing in me and standing by me even in the tough times. Thank you.

Cover Art by Shauna Callahan

Chapter One

The sky was black, my toes were numb and I was a lunatic.

Forgetting that our recent October nights had turned colder, I had set out on my mission barefoot. I had no idea what the thermometer said, but the ice cold brick beneath my unprotected feet told me plenty. And my worn-thin-through-the-years knit jammies were certainly no match against the biting air. Evidently I had left my brains in the house along with my shoes and down-filled parka. Indiana Jones, our orange Tabby, followed me and purred while he rubbed against my legs, offering a tinge of warmth at best.

I squinted into the darkness. "Three thirty in the morning. Am I totally insane, Indy?"

"Mew."

"Thanks for the vote of confidence."

Yes, I'm a grown woman and I talk to my cat. What's the big deal? My cousin Samson the psychiatrist tells the family I'm delusional and should be medicated. Pshaw I say. Samson has a psychiatrist of his own as well as a far more disturbing obsession with large farm animals, so I severely doubt his legitimacy. As long as Indiana Jones talks to me, I'll keep talking to him.

My name is Barbara Marr. I'm not a lady coroner, bounty hunter or crime scene investigator. I don't fight vampires, werewolves or flesh-eating zombies destined to destroy humanity. Even worse, I don't knit, sew, bake gourmet goodies for sweet English ladies or refinish houses then flip them for a profit. In fact, I lack a veritable encyclopedia of talents and accomplishments. I have managed to give birth to three children, but when my teenage daughter looks at me like I'm an alien from the planet Freak, I wonder at my parenting abilities.

Then of course there is my marriage. Not long ago I would have bragged to anyone about our solid bond. True love. True fidelity and commitment. That was before Howard dropped the bomb and moved out. So perpetuating matrimony can be added to the list of things I don't do.

When reviewing the list of lifetime achievements for which I am proud, being mother to my three girls sits at the very top, followed by the time I saw Yul Brenner in a convenience store and discreetly let him know he had ketchup on his chin. He was so thankful that he autographed a bag of Fritos for me.

And most recently I got familiar with the video camera again and shot a music video with my daughters. We called it *Four White Girls Do Madonna.* I posted it on You-Tube and got over twenty-five views. It was very exciting. Still, I'm not exactly setting the world on fire.

So when Howard left, I decided it was time to resurrect my dream and write about movies. I love the movies. Old movies, new movies, musicals, dramas, comedies, westerns, action, science-fiction, and anything starring Meryl Streep. Some years ago, in between changing diapers and potty training, I had bought a domain name, ChickAtTheFlix.com, with the intention of building a movie review website. I kept the domain name, but got side-tracked by little things like ear infections, strep throat, pre-school, elementary school and baby number three. Now, with my life deteriorating before my eyes, the time had come to take the bull by the proverbial horns and start anew.

After putting the girls to bed, I needed a way to keep my mind off Howard. I plotted and planned a grand design. The website would contain reviews of current release movies as well as DVD releases of older classics. I would also have a weekly blog where I waxed enthusiastic on different subjects of the cinema. Since I had just recently watched a Men of Mystery Film Festival on the Classic Movie Channel, my first blog title would be, "Charlie Chan or Sherlock Holmes? Whodunnit Better?"

At two a.m., I was too tired to think about the website, but too upset about my marriage to sleep, so I turned on the TV. Movie fare included *The First Wives Club*, *A Bill of Divorcement*, *An Unmarried Woman* and *The Breakup* on HBO. Disgusted, I turned off the TV, turned out the lights and contemplated learning voodoo so I could hex Howard with a festering urinary tract infection.

By three a.m., I had been crying for at least twenty minutes when I heard the rumble of a truck outside my bedroom window. Suddenly, I had something else to occupy my frazzled mind. The truck was back at House of Many Bones.

And that was how I ended up outside on a cold, fall night with no shoes on.

Howard hadn't changed the porch light bulb before skipping out, so I was resigned to forging ahead with my crackpot scheme sans illumination to guide me. I'd give him a piece of my mind the next time I saw him. Not that I knew when that would be.

With teeth chattering, I crossed my arms and shuffled forward blindly down the brick walk from my front door, intent on catching a glimpse of the activity next door at House of Many Bones.

"Come on boy," I said to my cat. "You can protect me."

Indiana trailed behind, but I detected trepidation in his gait.

Nine Hundred White Willow Circle, dubbed by me as House of Many Bones, was the neighboring house to my left, and the current source of my midnight madness. A contemporary style home with avocado green painted siding and beige trim, it camouflaged nicely with its wooded lot and appeared to be like any other house in our quaint and quiet town.

But appearances can be deceiving.

This particular house had been vacant for nearly thirty years Even stranger, none of the retired couples who had lived on our street long enough to have some knowledge of its history would talk squat about it. They'd talk about the weather, how much their new roof cost, or the woes of their latest hip replacement, but they wouldn't give up one itsy bitsy little word about the strangely vacant house. In my twisted mind, there could be only one reason a place stays uninhabited that long: skeletons. Be they literal or figurative, I was sure that house just had to be full of skeletons.

I had developed my skeleton theory and coined the nickname five years ago – not long after we moved into the neighborhood. Every Tuesday, rain or shine, I observed a rusty El Camino pull into the driveway of Nine Hundred White Willow Circle at one o'clock sharp. One hunched-over, arthritic man would crawl out of the car, do various jobs around the place then leave. After a few weeks, being the neighborly sort I am, I attempted contact. He had just finished mowing the lawn. The meeting remains vivid in my memory.

"Hi there!" I remember saying, offering my hand for a friendly shake and smiling my friendliest smile. "I'm Barb. Barbara Marr. We just moved in next door."

He didn't return my smile. Instead, my hand lingered awkwardly mid-air. I pretended to swat at a fly instead, just to avoid looking foolish. I highly doubt that I accomplished that goal.

Undeterred by his silence, I bumbled forth. "So, I notice you don't actually live here. Do you own the place, Mr . ."

Mr. Whoever-He-Was just stood there staring. Bent, wrinkled and mute. As the silent seconds ticked by, I started getting nervous like a dog that doesn't like eye contact. If I'd had a flea to scratch, I would have scratched it. He broke the stare by pulling a hanky from his back pocket and wiping the sweat off his face. Then he blew his nose. I cringed.

"So," he said finally, replacing the hanky. "You like your life?"

"Excuse me?" I covered my mouth, trying not to gag. That whole, blow-your-snot-into-a-piece-of-cloth-then-cram-it-in-your-pants thing has disgusted since I was five and saw Grandpa Joe blow a loogie the size of Texas into a dinner napkin thinking it was his trusty, crusty nose cloth. I still turn green remembering.

"It ain't a trick question, Toots. Do you like your life?" He pointed a gnarled finger in my face.

"Yes," I gulped, a little disturbed by his manner, but also surprised to hear someone actually say "Toots." I was sure only criminals in 1940's gangster flicks used that word. "Yes," I coughed. "I do like my life."

"Then don't come over here again askin' questions. Very simple. Stay away from me. Stay away from this house." He moved off, pushing the lawnmower to the garage.

Needless to say, that was the beginning and the end of our relationship. And that's when I decided there was probably a whole lot more in that house than dust and cobwebs. Who knew what madness lingered in the mind of Grumpy Lawnmower Guy? Maybe years ago he chopped up more with that lawnmower than just blades of grass, and now only the bones lay hidden within the walls of that house just waiting to tell their sad story.

So at three o'clock in the morning, nearly five years later when I heard a truck with muffler issues rumbling into the driveway next door for the second night in a row, my curiosity was piqued. Ubur-piqued. Grumpy Lawnmower Guy was scary, but he was predictable to a fault. Middle-of-the-night errands were not his style. Not at all. Something was definitely up in my generally calm little corner of Rustic Woods, Virginia and I wanted to know what. And Lord knew I needed a diversion from masterminding painful plots on Howard's well-being. Hence my frigid barefoot foray into the cricket infested dark night. Truth be told, I was probably also channeling a bit of the Chan-man after watching that Men of Mystery Film Festival.

Regardless the reason, I was moving forward and the only question really was, should I keep going? Reaching my driveway, I realized that acquiring a reasonable view of the house or the mysterious truck was going to be harder than I thought. First, the black of night was a major impediment. With no moon or streetlights to help, I was like a bat with radar malfunction. Secondly, the significant distance between the two houses and the fact that they were separated by a line of dense trees and shrubbery meant I would have to walk out into the middle of the street to really see anything of worth.

"What do you think, Indy," I whispered. "Out to the street or back to our house?"

He didn't answer. He purred and rubbed, but he was keeping mum.

"The street is cold and the house is warm, and at least I was able to see the top of the truck from my bedroom window. And one of the girls could wake up and get scared if they don't find me in bed. Whadaya say?" I was weighing the pros and cons with my hands moving up and down like the Scales of Justice. "Street? House? Street? House?"

"Mew."

"Great minds think alike."

The cat and I agreed that a warm and toasty house was a far better alternative to a frigid and fruitless expedition. Turning back toward the front walk, I stopped when my eyes caught a hint of light glowing through the trees between my property and House of Many Bones. Based on the location of the light and how low to the ground it was, I had to assume it was coming from one or more of its basement windows near the rear. *Aha*, thought I. Maybe there was something to see inside that window. The gears of my curious mind were turning again.

"Look at that," I whispered again. "Maybe we should just take a gander over to those trees, peek through and . ."

"Out for a nighttime stroll?"

With a jump, I grabbed my pounding chest and stifled a scream that, left un-stifled, might have aroused the entire neighborhood. Luckily, it was just my neighbor and friend Roz, who had sneaked up from behind, nearly causing me a major myocardial meltdown.

"Don't scare me like that."

Roz Walker lived in the house on my other side. She was smart. She was wearing shoes. Fleece lined. And a puffy coat over a flannel robe. Playboy wouldn't be calling her anytime soon, but she was warm.

"Sorry." She handed me a flash light. "You look like you could use this."

I turned on the flashlight. "Thanks. How partial are you to those shoes?"

"You're spying aren't you?"

"You didn't answer my question."

"You first."

"Of course I'm spying. So are you. Your turn." I shined the light onto her shoes for emphasis.

"Keeping the shoes. Not necessarily partial to them, but I like my feet. You can keep the flashlight though. I won it in a raffle."

"What are you doing awake at this hour?" I tucked the flashlight under my arm so I could blow warm air into my icy hands.

"The truck woke me up. You?"

"Never fell asleep."

"Howard?"

"Instead of counting sheep, I tried counting my blessings. When that didn't work, I tried counting ways to hurt my hideous husband."

"Did that help?"

"I'm awake, aren't I?" With fingers warmed enough to function again, I shined some light onto my lawn illuminating a maze of carved pumpkins and Styrofoam tombstones. "Can you see the truck from your house?"

Roz shook her head. "Barely. I could see you real good though." She tugged at my sleeve. "Did you know your pajamas glow in the dark?"

"They're Halloween pjs – those are little ghosts." I pointed to the glowing white figures on my top. "I'm trying to stay festive despite the sad state of my life." I shined the light toward House of Many Bones. "Do you think it's a moving truck?"

"Could be. Small one." Roz's breath was visible when she talked.

"Did you see Grumpy Lawnmower Guy?" I started bouncing to get my blood flowing.

"I didn't see anybody. Maybe the house has been rented or sold and someone's moving in."

"At three thirty in the morning?"

"Actually, it's after four now. You should go back inside and try to get some sleep."

My ears detected a faint noise from next door.

"Wait!" I stopped bouncing. "Did you hear that?"

"What?"

"That." I turned my ear. "You don't hear it? It sounds like . . . hmm."

"What?"

"It kind of sounds like a monkey."

"It's your cat."

"No. No it's not." Reaching down, I picked up Indiana Jones and held him under one arm. The noise was still there. Almost a vibration. Barely audible, but definitely from House of Many Bones.

"I'm going a little closer. I'm sure I hear something."

"Well you're on your own. Peter made me promise to come out just long enough to give you the flashlight and find out what you were up to."

"Then give me your shoes."

"No way. I have to walk through sticker vines to get back to my house. Come by tomorrow for coffee. Or lunch, depending on when you wake up." She flicked on her own flashlight and stepped gingerly away, leaving Indy and me alone to fend for ourselves.

Stepping out onto the frosty grass, I had second thoughts. The icy blades felt like millions of needles pricking the bottoms of my nearly gangrenous feet. Damn! At the very least, I was going to need a pair of shoes if I was going to attempt a peek through those trees. The minor noise had faded anyway. And maybe Roz was right. Maybe this was as simple as new neighbors moving in. Neighbors who worked odd hours. A bartender perhaps. A bartender bringing a few things by after his shift ended at two.

Reason trumped wild imagination. I took two steps backward onto the driveway and put the cat back down.

"Let's go, Indy. We're not cut out for adventure after all."

I hadn't even turned back toward my own house when out of the blue, piercing the dead still of the night, a high pitched howl stopped me in my tracks and sent my heart rate racing at breakneck speed. This was no vague sound drifting through the crisp night air. This was loud, sharp and painful to the ears. Sort of a man-beast howl. Hard to describe, but every decibel was chilling to the bone. Seconds later, I heard a door at the rear of the house swoosh open followed a flurry of activity on the ground behind House of Many Bones. Leaves rustled wildly and there was a pounding of footsteps. I couldn't see what was happening, but it didn't sound good. It seemed that something very violent was going down. I looked back for Roz, but she was long gone.

Forgetting my feet altogether, I flew up the driveway, across the walk and up to my front door. Indiana had beat me there and was clawing to get in. As my hand landed on the door knob and turned, I heard a man yell from the backyard.

"Toes!" he screamed.

Wow, that was one mad bartender.

Indiana and I leapt across the threshold. We were inside, but not yet safe in my mind. Just before the door slammed shut, I heard the man yell again.

"Toes, you chickenshit fuck! Get back here!"

Chapter 2

After checking all windows and doors for secured locks, I ran upstairs and checked on all three girls to make sure they were safe and sound. Like the angels they were, I found each one sleeping peacefully, completely oblivious to the wild goings-on outside. In my bedroom, I peeked out the window one more time. The van was still there, but no maniacs or other oddities that I could see. The idea of calling the police crossed my mind, but I decided against it. Maybe it had been a simple quarrel or dispute. Then I would be embarrassed.

Somewhat calmed, I crawled into bed, pulled the coves up to my chin and flicked on the TV for added company. Woody Allen's *Take the Money and Run* had just started on The Comedy Movie Channel. I texted Roz to ask if she had heard the ruckus, and while waiting for a reply with the cell phone still in my hand, I laid my head down on the pillow, closing my eyes just for a minute. It had been a long, hard day, and the rest felt good. The phone rang, and assuming it was Roz, I answered without checking the caller I.D.

"Hey," I mumbled. "Did you get my text?"

"Barbara? Is this Barbara Marr?" asked male a voice on the other end.

"Yes . . . this is Barbara," I replied cautiously. "Who's this?"

"Steven Spielberg."

I happen to think Steven Spielberg is a very sexy man. Wisdom, sensitivity and creative genius light my fire. Steven has 'em all. He also frequents my dreams on a regular basis.

"Am I dreaming?" I asked, just to be sure.

"Yes. Yes you are."

Oh well, at least it was better than the nightmare of my waking life.

"Okay, I'll play," I said.

"Did I catch you at a bad time?"

"I'm asleep, and there's a wild man outside my house very concerned about his toes, but no, I guess it's not really a bad time."

"I just visited ChickAtTheFlix.com. Fantastic website you've got there. Your review, '*Jurassic Park: Not Just for Dinosaur Lovers*,' was amazing. You really saw what I was going for. You understand me."

"I'm glad you liked it."

"No, I didn't like it. I LOVED it. Listen, I'll get right to the point. I want you to direct a movie for me. I'll produce. It will be great."

I coughed. "Me? Why me?"

Actually, I did play director with the video camera a little more than the average bear, editing little masterpieces here and there. Like the recent music video on You Tube.

"That video!" said Steven, his voice shrill with excitement. "It's brilliant. You're a genius. Raw, natural talent. Hollywood needs a fresh voice like yours."

I smiled. That was the one. It was a personal favorite. Catchy, upbeat, and original. *Material Girl*, after all, did provide a deep, ironic springboard from which to showcase my talent.

After some discussion of casting (Orlando Bloom) and money (ten million), I agreed to direct *Terminated Mission to Die Hardly*.

Steven explained the premise. "It's an intense action, thriller with a little comedy thrown in. We'll have monkeys."

"Monkeys?" I asked, hearing chattering on the other end. It started low and grew louder. Laughing monkeys.

"Steven?" I hollered over the din. "Are you there?"

He didn't answer. All I could hear were monkeys. I looked at my cell phone. It had turned into a banana. I started eating it then remembered I was dreaming. When my eyes opened slowly I found myself sprawled out face down on the pillow, drooling on my cell phone.

Rolling over on my large, lonely bed, I saw that the night had passed and a soft morning light was filtering through my windows. I choked back the recently familiar desire to cry. Daylight meant another day of facing what my life had become. The TV was still on, so I found the remote and clicked it off. Staring at my ceiling, I wished for a retreat back into my silly Steven Spielberg dream. I squeezed my eyes shut for a minute, then opened them again hoping for the best. No Steven Spielberg. Just harsh reality and the sound of wind screaming through the trees, followed by the familiar plink, plink, plink of acorns bouncing off my roof. Fall had come to Rustic Woods, Virginia and my life had to go on.

While contemplating the rigors of metaphorically putting one foot in front of the other just to get through the day, I became aware that animals were scampering on my roof. Nothing unusual really. Squirrels roamed my yard as frequently as Tiger Woods dated cocktail waitresses. These did sound larger than my typical squirrels however. Quite a bit larger. The scampering turned into a sort of thumping that increased in intensity until finally peaking with an orgasmic-like crescendo of high pitched squeals. Lovely, I thought. Teenage Mutant Ninja Squirrels making whoopy on my house. Well, at least someone was having sex.

Thinking of sex, or rather the lack of sex, made me think of Howard. Thinking of Howard made me want to stop thinking.

No need to worry. I was a mother. The tell-tale shuffle of small, slippered feet in the hall outside my door indicated the end of adult thinking time.

"Mo-ommy!"

Within seconds the door flew open and a delightful fairy wannabe, adorned with wings and lace, hovered over me on the bed, taking in a serious inspection. Her chubby little fingers gingerly caressed my face while her sweet breath warmed my cheeks.

"Mommy," said Amber, "why are your eyes all red?" Amber was the youngest and most whimsical of my three children.

"Oh, I guess it's just allergies," I said with a sniff. "Or something."

"You mean, like my allergy to milk?" she asked.

"Yeah, something like that."

"Well, frankly, Mommy," she said in her honest way, "you don't look so good. You should stay away from whatever makes you look like that."

I pulled my weary body out of bed and skulked across to the dressing mirror. She was right. I looked like crap. I felt like crap. My life was crap. I stared at the reflection staring back at me. Was this really what my life had come to? Was I destined to be a marital failure? The years had started to make their impression on my face. My once fair complexion was succumbing to gravity and cheap skin-care products. The dark circles under my eyes were proof that sleep had not been a recent friend, and my mousy-brown curly hair – sadly turning mousy gray – was smooshed upwards giving me a sort of Don-King-finds-his-long-lost-white-sister look.

I looked back at Amber. Her fiery red hair bounced in ringlets all around her perfectly alabaster six year old face. She still smiled at me lovingly, revealing that one little blank space in front where her tooth had fallen out the day before. I couldn't help but smile back, thinking of my baby losing her first tooth . . . Damn! Frozen where I stood, I realized I had done the unthinkable – the thing every mother fears worse than a bill from the orthodontist. I had forgotten my tooth fairy duty.

I thought back through the events of the previous evening. Despite every desire to just disappear into my bed for the rest of eternity, I had managed to make supper. Then, after reading *Little Women* to Bethany and *Peter Pan* to Amber, I listened while Amber prayed to God and the tooth fairy to take care of her tooth and also to be generous with monetary compensation. Once the tooth was stowed safely under her pillow, I kissed her goodnight then lumbered to my own room where I flopped onto my bed and fought back the urge to cry while I tackled the idea of creating that new website.

My intention was to get back up when I knew she was asleep and put some coins under her pillow. I really, really did mean to do that. I just got side-tracked by the hours trying to forget my misery. Then, of course, there was the truck at House of Many Bones and the loud man desperately seeking his toes.

"Look Mommy, what the tooth fairy left me!" Amber said, holding up a beautifully stitched red and purple oriental pouch.

"What's that?" I didn't know if I should be scared or relieved. Only one thing was for sure – I hadn't left it there.

"It's a goodie bag from the tooth fairy. I found it under my pillow and it has all kinds of pretty things in it. Look!" She dumped the bag out on my bed. Four different Japanese coins, various pieces of Japanese candy of differing sizes and colors, and a necklace with Japanese letters. It didn't take a Japanese rocket scientist to figure out who in my house had been the bearer of these good tidings

"Mommy, do you think the tooth fairy is Japanese?" she asked.

I tousled her head of curls. "Sweetie, I'm positively certain she must be. Now, do me a favor, go wake up Bethany and you two fix yourselves some cereal. I'll be down in a few minutes."

It was time to go find myself a tooth fairy.

"Hey there Sugar Bear," I said to Callie, sitting on the edge of her bed. She pretended to be asleep. "What's up Buttercup? How's it shakin' Francis Bacon? What's the score Dinah Shore?" I tickled her for emphasis, but I wasn't getting a reaction. She was a rock. "What's the news, doggy doo?" She still wasn't budging. "Okay, I'm running out of cute here, and I'm trying really hard to be up-beat. Play along, will ya?" She slowly pulled the covers off of her head, but she didn't say a word.

"Thank you for saving my butt," I said.

"You're welcome."

"Your sister, The Jabberwocky Fairy, is now going to tell half the civilized world that the tooth fairy is Japanese. How do you think Santa Claus and the Easter Bunny will handle this news?" I tickled her again. She forced a half-smile.

"Otanjou-bi Omedetou Gozaimasu," she said. A Sophomore at Forest Glen High School, Callie had taken to her beginning Japanese language class with unexpected enthusiasm.

"Wow, that's a mouthful," I said. "Please tell me that doesn't mean 'May you die naked in a bamboo grove.'"

"No," she giggled, finally, "It means Happy Birthday."

I gave my forehead a slap. She had just reminded me of something else I didn't want to think about – my birthday.

"Mamasan Marr turns forty-five. You should have let me forget," I said smiling.

Callie turned to her side, crooked her elbow and held her head up with her hand. She was a younger, prettier version of her father to be sure. Brown hair the color of dark chocolate, thick and wavy. Perfect nose. Penetrating, almost black eyes and flawless skin, even at fifteen. I should have been so lucky at her age.

"Mom," she said, "is this the end?"

"Egad! I hope not. I really wanted to live to see forty-six."

"No! You know what I mean – will he come back here, or is it over? You know, for good?" She wasn't smiling.

"Schweet-heart," I said, doing my best Bogart, "It ain't over till the fat lady sings."

While the girls wrestled up some semblance of a breakfast, I got to work on changing my attitude. And fixing my scary hair. Today was my forty-fifth birthday. Impending old age and a problem marriage were staring me in the face. Not a good place to be. I figured that right now, I had two choices – crawl out of the pit or wallow and die. To wallow or not to wallow? That was the question. Look at Scarlett O'Hara. Did she cry and whine when Rhett walked out the door not giving a damn? Well, okay, she did. But not for long I'll bet. Not Scarlett. Same story here, baby, same story here.

After dressing, wetting my freaky 'fro and crunching the curls into a more presentable do, I stood in front of my mirror and looked myself in the eye. It was time to give myself a good pep talk. Hands on my hips, I started out stern.

"Barb," I said. "Get a grip."

I was about to expand on the whole getting-a-grip idea, but was distracted by the squirrels on my roof, back for an apparent second round. I decided to try again.

"Barb . . . get a . . ."

Thump, thwack, bump! I couldn't concentrate. Womp, scramble, scramble, flump! Holy cow, those squirrels were big. And noisy. Kind of like they were talking to each other in some shrieky animal way. I'd never heard such vocal squirrels. In fact, the closer I listened, the less they sounded like squirrels . . . and the more they sounded like . . . monkeys.

Chapter 3

Pulling back the curtains of one bedroom window and then the other, I scanned my yard for signs of life. Two average sized squirrels scampered up one tree and a zealous woodpecker worked away on another, but nothing out of the ordinary.

Our forested suburb of Rustic Woods, Virginia sits nestled just twenty miles outside of Washington, DC. Designed in the 1960's, the plan for Rustic Woods was to remain natural, seemingly untouched by man. People don't cut trees down in Rustic Woods or the tree-police will come a-knockin' on your door. Big fines, and even worse – people start talking behind your back. "Psst – did ya hear? George Finkel cut down two trees. Did it in the middle of the night. Tsk, tsk, tsk." As a result, Rustic Woods teems with wildlife – deer, raccoon, squirrels-a-million, fox, beaver, and even a bear once. Monkeys, however, were not on the Nature Center's list of native critters.

Certainly, the lack of sleep was having an effect on my senses, causing me to hear things that just weren't there. Mr. Zealous Woodpecker flew off and the two squirrels disappeared into a nest far up in their tree. I made a mental note that the driveway at House of Many Bones was void of trucks or other vehicles, emergency or otherwise. Maybe I had imagined the danger of the previous night after all. In the light of day, it seemed logical that I could have blown the whole thing out of proportion.

I was about to close my curtains and breathe a sigh of relief when a new problem pulled up into my driveway. Needing to intercept certain disaster, I ran out of my room and downstairs in a flash.

Figuring I had about ninety seconds from the time my feet hit the foyer floor, I rounded the corner to my kitchen where the three girls munched loudly over bowls of cereal at our sadly dilapidated oak table. "Okay, girls," I said. "I want your attention. It's time we faced reality. Daddy is gone. He's not gone forever. He's just a little. . . well, he's got some kinks to work out. I guess. Whatever. But we have a bigger problem now. Grandma's on her way in and she can't find out."

"Why?" asked Bethany, her mouth full of milk and cereal.

"This is Grandma we're talking about," I said.

Bethany swallowed. "Good point."

"You want us to lie?" Amber whispered.

"Not lie. No. I would never want you to lie, Sweetie. Just . . . avoid the truth."

Callie rolled her eyes.

The front door opened.

"Quick," I said. "Act natural." The girls continued munching, but looked at me like I was a crazy lady. Which I was. The last thing I needed right now was unsolicited advice from my mother, the woman of many trades. She had an answer for everything, but in my many years of experience, it was usually the wrong answer.

I had just plopped my behind in an empty chair between Amber and Bethany and opened a book lying on the table when my mother breezed into the kitchen.

"Mom! What a surprise," I said, looking up as if I'd been reading for hours.

She looked with interest at the book in my hand. "What are you're reading?" she asked.

"Hmm?" Since I hadn't actually been reading the book, I was stumped for an answer. Thank goodness Bethany was quick on her feet.

"*The Secret Garden*," she answered for me. "It's my book and I liked it so much, she decided to read it."

"I never liked that book much myself," my mother replied. "You know, I wrote a children's book once."

Amber's eyes lit up. "You did? Can I read it, Grandma?"

"Oh, it's in the bottom of a drawer somewhere. I almost had it published once, but realized it was far too ahead of its time. It's meant for . . . more advanced children."

Amber blinked, not getting my mother's meaning. I sighed and stood up. I needed a cup of coffee. Actually, I needed a Harvey Wallbanger, heavy on the Harvey, but coffee would have to suffice.

"What are you doing here, mother?" I asked, pulling the can of Folgers from the cupboard.

"What do you mean? Your birthday of course," she said, grabbing me for a grand bear hug. My mother commands quite a presence. She towers over my five foot eight inch frame. She's a freakishly tall, big boned woman. Not fat, just big. Everything she does is big – she dresses lavishly, she walks big, she talks big. I felt dwarfed by her character as a young girl, only thankful that I didn't inherit her monstrously large physical frame.

"As a birthday present, I'm taking you and Howard and the girls out to dinner tonight." That was my mother. She never questioned that things wouldn't occur exactly as she decided they would. Consequently, she always got her way.

"Where is Howard, by the way?" she asked.

"Work," I said, throwing old grounds into the trash. Technically, I wasn't lying – he might have been at work.

"On a Saturday morning?"

"Emergency." Again, not technically a lie – if he was at work, it would have been due to an emergency. Probably. Maybe. While I didn't like to admit it, I didn't know much about Howard's job.

"I don't understand the kind of work that man does. An engineer who always seems to have emergencies. Your father was an engineer and he never worked odd hours or had emergencies. Bless his dear soul." My sweet father, who was a small man compared to most, died in his sleep three years ago, supposedly of sleep apnea. I always suspected that maybe my mother accidentally rolled on top of him in the middle of the night, smothering the life out of him.

"It is what it is, mom," I sighed, turning on the Mr. Coffee. It was very hard to please my mother.

"Well, I have to run. I'm going to the gym. Did I tell you I'm training for a marathon? I'll call you later today and arrange a time– we'll do Fiorenza's." She yelled the last bit over her shoulder while flying out the front door. I stood in the middle of my kitchen, trying to imagine my flappy-skinned giant of a mother running a marathon. She'd probably scare off half the competition. Of course, who was I to throw stones? I got winded just looking at the treadmill.

As I grabbed a mug from the dishwasher, the phone rang. I checked the caller ID, half-hoping it would be Howard, but pretty sure it wasn't Steven Spielberg. I was only a bit let down when I saw that it was Roz. I picked up the receiver, anxious to find out if she had heard any of the previous night's raucous at House of Many Bones.

"Hey, Roz."

"Did you get any sleep last night?"

"A couple of hours I think. Hey, did you . . ."

Amber was pulling on my sleeve.

"Not now, Amber, I'm on the . . ."

"Mommy, can we keep them?"

Every mother knows this axiom: the minute you get on the phone, a child will find a reason to interrupt you. My patience was wearing thin. "Amber, I'm on the . . . ."

I noticed Bethany and Callie staring out our window, seemingly transfixed.

"Mommy!" Amber wasn't giving up. "Please, can we keep them?"

Bethany looked at me with a particularly queer expression on her face, then back out the window.

"Sorry, Roz. Hang on a minute. Amber wants me to see something."

"They could live in our basement! Please, Mommy, please! They're so cuuuuuute!" She was pulling me to the window by the sleeve while I talked in the receiver to Roz.

"Anyway, I wanted to know if you heard . . ." Out of my kitchen window I did see something moving around in the branches of my trees. I stopped talking. I blinked. Amber squealed in delight. I blinked again, sure that my contact lenses were just foggy, causing a strange optical illusion. Amber was jumping up and down and pointing while Bethany joined in with claps of delight. My jaw had fallen to my knees. I hadn't been hearing things after all. I was both relieved and bewildered.

"Mom . . . ," Callie said focused in disbelief on the same vision. "Do you see what I see?"

Holy cow.

"Roz," I said. "I have to call you back. I've got monkeys in my trees."

Chapter 4

The girls had run outside faster than I could say "rabies," so I dashed out after them, phone in my hand dialing the Fairfax County Police.

"Hello," I said more calmly than one might think, "I have monkeys in my trees. Can you send someone to catch them?"

A moment of silence made me wonder if I'd been disconnected.

"Is this a prank?" a woman on the other end finally asked.

"No, this isn't a prank. My name is Barbara Marr and I live at 902 White Willow Circle in Rustic Woods. There are monkeys in my trees."

"Are you sure they aren't squirrels? You have some very big squirrels in Rustic Woods."

I detected that she was patronizing me. I wasn't sure. I felt patronized.

"Well, unless they evolved overnight and acquired the ability to swing from limb to limb with arms longer than their tails, I'm thinking these aren't squirrels. There are definitely, unequivocally three monkeys . . . make that four monkeys in my trees. And the fourth one just pooped on my mums."

"Ma'am, I hear a lot of screaming in the background, is anyone hurt?" she asked.

I looked around my yard. The gaggle of my three girls had grown as Roz and her three kids joined in my yard, followed by another neighbor, Maxine, and her yapping poodle, Puddles. Maxine, who lived just one street over, was an aging hippie-widow with past-her-bottom straight, gray hair and an affinity for huarache sandals and hemp. I liked Maxine a lot, but that poodle of hers was the yappiest damn animal I ever met.

"No, no one is hurt – just excited. We don't get monkeys around here too often you know," I said. "Listen, is there something you can do here?"

"Can you describe the monkeys?"

"They're brown. Long tails. Long arms."

"Do you know what kind of monkeys they are?

"Sorry, I don't have my Wonderful World of Monkeys Reference Volume handy right now. They're monkeys. Bigger than a bread box."

"There's no need to be rude, Ma'am, I'm trying to be helpful here. This usually isn't our area, but I'll send a squad car anyway and contact animal control."

Roz and Maxine were standing next to me in my side yard holding themselves tight to keep warm. I gave a quick scan around the rest of my yard, just to make sure a stray monkey or two hadn't come down from the branches to check out life on land. Fake foam and resin tombstones and a hideously tacky inflatable witch decorated our lawn in anticipation of Halloween, just five days away, while handmade ghosts hung from my dwarf Japanese Maple. The inflatable witch was erected against my wishes by an insistent Amber and her relenting father, who decided to hit the high road shortly thereafter. Yup, plenty of Halloween on the ground, but luckily no monkeys.

While it had just turned colder in the last couple of days, Northern Virginia had been experiencing a doozy of an Indian Summer, giving every blade of grass in my lawn plenty of reason to grow knee high, despite the light layer of leaves that had already fallen to the ground. Sadly, my yard had the appearance of a long forgotten graveyard. Too much longer, and some pesky old man wearing three inch thick glasses and carrying a clip board would announce himself at my doorstep as a board member of the Rustic Woods Homeowners Association, and slap me with a hefty fine.

"Who were you talking to?" Roz asked.

"The police," I said.

"How about animal control?" she asked.

"The dispatcher said she'd contact them. Do you think we should make the kids get in the house?" I asked. "Who knows if they have rabies."

"Let the kids enjoy it. Those monkeys don't look like they're coming down any time soon. Hey, speaking of monkeys, the PTA meeting is Thursday and Peter has to work. Can Callie baby-sit?"

Roz was the PTA president at Tulip Tree Elementary School. She was wonder woman. Mother of two boys and a girl, each just a year apart in age, PTA President, den leader for Cub Scouts and volunteer at the local retirement home.

A person could always recognize Roz, even from a distance. Only about five foot three and thin as a rail, with thick blonde hair cut Dorothy Hamill style, her standard uniform was a calf-length, floral rayon dress with comfortable tan loafers. She must have had thirty of those dresses. She was also a devoted friend, and the only person who knew that Howard had moved out. She'd been my shoulder to cry on for the last few days.

While we shivered and gawked at the primates playing, a breeze blew through dropping acorns all around us. The wind seemed to have an effect on the monkeys too. The four of them all stopped moving for a minute, sitting on branches in two different trees. One crossed his arms as if he was cold too. After a moment of silence, they started chattering and climbing again.

"The dispatcher on the phone asked me what kind of monkeys they are – what do you think?" I asked the ladies.

"They're definitely not chimpanzees. Too big for spider monkeys." Roz offered.

"They have cute faces, eh?" Maxine grew up in Canada and even though she lived in Rustic Woods for over a quarter of a century, she still liked to say 'eh?' every once in a while.

"Where do you think they came from?" Roz wondered.

Suddenly I remembered the previous night's adventure. "That's it!" I shouted.

"That's what?" Maxine asked.

"Last night – remember, Roz? I did hear a monkey. I'm not crazy after all."

"That's still to be determined." Roz stated matter-of-factly.

Roz explained to Maxine, who looked puzzled. "A van pulled into the driveway of the vacant house over there last night . . ."

"Three o'clock in the morning," I corrected her.

". . . and Nancy Drew here came outside trying to see who it was. She claims she heard a monkey."

"Right," I agreed. "And after you went inside and there was this horrible howl and even though I didn't see anyone, I heard some guy storm out of the back screaming something about toes."

Maxine shook her head. "You young people sure have wild imaginations."

"I didn't imagine it. I heard a monkey and now look in my trees. How is that imagination? That's plain freaky-weird is what that is."

Chuckling, Maxine gave a tug on the leash. "Well, this has been fun girls, but Puddles and I have errands to run," Maxine said as she turned to leave. "Let me know how this turns out, eh? And let me know if you find the crazy man with no toes." As she started up the street trying to quiet Puddles, she pulled a cell phone out of her coat pocket and put it to her ear. She was probably calling her many widow friends to tell them about the crazy neighbor with monkeys in her trees.

As Maxine disappeared, a police cruiser turned onto White Willow Circle. It pulled just past my driveway and parked on the street.

"Are you sure you heard a man screaming?" Roz asked.

"Trust me, there was a whole lot more than screaming going on in that house. I'm sure of it." A moment later, a very handsome, nicely proportioned policeman was standing in front of me asking for the owner of the home.

"That would be her," Roz said smiling, pointing to me and winking.

"And your name, Ma'am?" he asked. He was all business.

"Barbara Marr."

"You have an animal problem here? Monkeys . . ." he gave me a sideways glance.

"Look for yourself," I said pointing to the trees. "Holy cow, Roz, is that another one?"

"Yes it is. That would be number five. They're multiplying before our very eyes! Boys! Don't touch the monkey poop! Yucky!"

Mr. Policeman looked concerned. "Ma'am, I suggest we get the children into the house until animal control has taken possession. We don't know if they have rabies."

I gave Roz my best I-told-you-so grin.

"Fine," I said. "But first I have to ask you to stop calling me Ma'am – I turned forty-five today and I don't need anymore reminders that years are passing me faster than light particles. Call me Barb." I could see Mr. Policeman struggle not to smile, but he lost the battle and looked down at his feet while he regained a more stoic attitude. While Roz rounded up her kids to leave, she whispered in my ear.

"He's cute," she said. I agreed. He was cute. Stop it Barb, I told myself. You can't think another man is cute. Not yet.

"Girls!" I shouted across the lawn. "Back in the house please." My demand drew three frowns and lots of groans. "Hey, don't blame me – the police officer here said so."

I smiled at my new uniformed friend. "Sorry to do that, but I'm tired of always being the bad guy."

"I'm used to it." The barest hint of a grin appeared on one side of his mouth. The promise of a dimple looked possible if he would have allowed himself a full-out smile. He was looking better and better, this man of the law. He had a sort of Brad Pitt thing going there with his sandy blonde hair and all.

As it turned out, the time to consider the sex appeal of another man – Brad Pitt sexy or not – would have to wait. Howard's Camry was pulling into the driveway.

Now, my husband Howard, more recently known as Howard-the-creep, looks a little like George Clooney – everyone says so. Same dark hair, a little less chin, slightly softer features. I had to admit, he was supremely handsome as husbands go, despite the fact that if a magic Jeannie were to grant me three wishes, the first would be that he suffer thirty consecutive days of passing golf-ball sized kidney stones.

I took a moment to consider the circumstances – Brad Pitt the policeman beside me, George Clooney the renegade husband walking up my driveway, and monkeys in my trees. Hmmm. Give me a Matt Damon look-alike from Animal Control and I might think I was at a read-through for *Ocean's Fourteen.*

Howard had more than a slightly concerned look on his face as he eyeballed the police car parked in front of our house. He walked briskly across the front lawn landing just behind me and the uniformed stud.

"What's going on here?" he asked. "Are the girls okay?"

"The girls are fine," I said through clenched teeth. "Do you care about my well-being, oh by the way? Or maybe what I'm up to these days? Did you know I started working on my movie review website again? Are you interested in hearing about that? Oh, of course you're not. That's why you left. Come for more of your things?"

Howard dropped his shoulders and threw up his arms, knowing this was a lose-lose conversation.

"Officer," I said. "This is my husband, Howard, but he doesn't know about the monkeys because he moved out this week."

"Monkeys?" Howard asked, ignoring my sarcasm.

"In your trees sir," said Officer Brad, looking relieved that animal control had arrived just in time to rescue him from a potential domestic disturbance.

"What happened?" Howard asked looking up. "Jesus! Where did they come from?"

I crossed my arms over my chest and raised my brows. "Why are you here?"

"I wanted to see the girls for a few minutes and to see if you had calmed down enough to talk about things."

"Things?"

"Barb, come on," he whined. "I'm trying here."

Damn! He even whined liked George Clooney. I had a hard time being mad at him as I looked into his sumptuous, deep brown eyes. Those were the eyes I got lost in when I met him at college. Now his perfect nearly-black hair had these super sexy silver streaks running through at the temples. I could just take a big bite of him. No time for reminiscing or getting all hot and bothered though. Time to show him I didn't give a hoot.

"Trying? You're trying?" I shook my head. "I don't think so. Just go in and see the girls. I've got a house to take care of here . . . and . . . monkeys to catch." I stomped off to talk to animal control whose second van had just arrived.

An hour later, animal control and the monkeys were gone. Officer Brad Pitt Look-a-like too. Sure that the monkeys were related to the strange goings-on at House of Many Bones, I gave him a full account of what I had witnessed the night before. He nodded politely, semi-interested, but was dispatched to another emergency, so I didn't get a warm and fuzzy that the police would be looking into it anytime soon. He did leave me his card though, in case I saw "anything else suspicious." Turned out he had a real name – Eric LaMon. *Nice name*, I thought. *Nice butt.*

Howard was on the phone in the kitchen when I came back into the house after bidding the Fairfax County contingent farewell.

"Yeah Mom," he was saying, "we'll see about Thanksgiving. I love you too." And he hung up. He had a guilty look on his face. "I called her from here so it would show on her caller ID."

"You didn't tell her?"

"No." He was looking down, tapping his fingers on the counter. He couldn't look me in the eyes.

"Thanksgiving?" I inquired. "What's that all about?"

Howard was acting more uncomfortable than ever.

"I'll tell you later. I'll call you – maybe we can meet somewhere and talk things out. Calmly. I gotta go."

He was pushing all of my buttons. "You 'gotta go'? What do you 'gotta do'?" I was on a roll, shoving finger quotes in the air in front of his face and everything. "It's Saturday for crying out loud. You certainly don't have the yard to take care of. I guess that's my job now, huh?" Sarcasm appeared to be my weapon of choice. He was either oblivious or immune to it by now, because he just looked at me, kissed me on the forehead, and started to leave.

Noticing a piece of paper by the phone I picked it up. "Is this yours?" Reading what was on the note, I stopped. Scribbled in pencil was the name Marjorie Smith and a phone number with a local area code. Howard snatched it out of my hand.

"Who's Marjorie?" I asked, stunned. The room started to spin a little.

"A woman at work," he said shoving the paper into the breast pocket of his Boston Fog.

"Why do you need her phone number?"

"She's selling me a couch."

"Why do you need a couch?"

"To sit on. I'll call." He was gone. Out the door. I looked around the empty room, seething and perplexed.

I had absolutely no idea what Howard was doing – or more frightfully WHO he was doing. But now I had a name. Marjorie Smith. Selling him a couch. Every time I even barely let myself go there — to consider that he might be having a affair — I turned into a sobbing mess. I didn't want to cry anymore. Wimpy women cry.

Taking a moment to get my mental bearings, I thought about the girls. I wasn't going to let them see me be weak. They deserved better. I was going to be a rock. A brick wall. A lighthouse in the storm. I was going to be like Sigourney Weaver in Alien. Lieutenant Ripley. Now there was a strong woman to admire. Buff bitch who took no shit. If that woman could survive man-eating aliens, I could survive a little marital mishap. I needed to go to the gym though, if I was going to look like Sigourney's Lieutenant Ripley.

Figuring the girls were upstairs playing or on computers, I decided to check the mail. The mailman had arrived just as Animal Control was slamming their last van door shut. Striding out the door, I whispered a little mantra to myself. *She's selling him a couch. She's selling him a couch. She's selling him a couch.* I was hoping that if I said it over and over again, I'd come to believe it. In my driveway, I was surprised to see Howard standing on the front lawn of House of Many Bones, talking on his cell phone. When he saw me, he flipped the phone shut and walked my way.

"What were you doing?" I asked, eyeing him suspiciously.

"Just checking the place out. What did you say you heard last night?"

"Did I tell you about that?"

"Didn't you tell me about that?"

"I don't remember . . ."

His cell rang and he looked at it, but didn't answer. "Look, I've got to get back to work. We'll talk about . . . well . . . look . . . nevermind. Just . . . be careful." He slipped into his Camry, backed out fast and sped away, just in time for my friend Peggy to pull up in her blue Honda Odyssey. My house was beginning to feel like Grand Central Station

"Ciao, baby!" she hailed, stepping onto the drive. Peggy was a pasty-skinned, red-headed, stout lady of obvious Irish lineage who converted to Judaism before she married and then to Italian-ism after she married. For their honeymoon, she and her husband, Simon, spent an entire month in Italy. Ever since, she has talked Italian, walked Italian, cooked Italian and often forgotten that her maiden name was O'Malley, not Minnelli.

"Hey, Peggy," I said. I was glad to see Peggy – she had a way of making people happy.

She noticed I was watching House of Many Bones. "Whatcha lookin' for-a Signora?" she asked. "More monkeys?"

Word had already spread.

"Talked to Roz, huh?" I asked. "You should have been here – it was wild. But no, I'm not looking for more monkeys. I'm trying to figure out why

Howard was just . . ." I shook my head and looked back at House of Many Bones. "Something very strange is going on here I tell you."

"I'm so sorry about Howard." She touched my arm and gave me that yes-Roz-told-me face. There were many people in this world who I did not want to have knowledge of my current personal dilemma, but Peggy was not one of them. I was actually glad Roz told her so I wouldn't be forced to recount the gory details another time.

"Thanks," I said. "He stopped by. But he left again."

"So," she picked her words carefully, leaning against her van, "was this mutual?"

"Nope. He just told me one night, and he moved out the next day. I don't even know where he is. He won't tell me." I felt another cry coming on, but choked it back. Lieutenant Ripley would have been proud.

"Mama Mia. Did he say why?" she asked.

"Hmmm, what were his exact words . . . oh yes, they're etched in my memory forever: 'I need space.'"

"Oh, that one," she nodded. "Joanna Spelling's husband told her he needed space too. Turned out the space he needed was a condo in Leesburg for boinking their nanny. In fact," she said, pointing a knowing finger in my direction, "I hear babysitters are the leading cause of divorce next to the secretary. Any nannies in your past?"

"Not a one. And he doesn't have a secretary." I didn't mention Marjorie Smith. Saying it out loud would be like admitting the possibility that Howard was with another woman.

"My cousin's husband, Steve, left her — he needed 'to find himself'— so she decided she would find out who he was finding himself with. She would follow him after he left work, stuff like that. Turns out Steve had a friend all right – a BOY friend. That was a long time ago. Steve is Stephanie now. And he only has one arm. My cousin chopped off the other one."

Peggy never ceased to amaze me. She knew everybody on the planet, and she always had a story. Truthfully, I really didn't feel like talking about Howard anymore. My attention kept straying to House of Many Bones and what had happened the night before. I knew I hadn't imagined it like Maxine said. Surely there was a screaming man and surely those monkeys were involved somehow. I took off across my yard.

"Where are you going?" Peggy sounded surprised.

Stopping, I turned to her. "She's selling him a couch!" I yelled.

"What?"

"Nevermind." I marched away again. "I'm going to House of Many Bones. I think those monkeys are connected to what happened there last night."

"What happened there last night?"

"Roz didn't tell you?"

Peggy's cell phone rang. "Look! Speak of the devil." She answered. "We were just talking about you. I'm following Barb to her Boney House. She's babbling about monkeys and something that happened last night?" After a second, she flipped her phone closed. "She's coming over. She said I should watch you and make sure you don't get into any trouble."

House of Many Bones was two stories with long, tall, slitty windows in the front, and small windows positioned way up high in the back. Several large evergreens and two overgrown rhododendron bushes generally obscured my view of the house, with the exception of a small opening between two of the bushes, which revealed a singular basement window. The infamous lighted window from the previous night.

Roz was outside in a flash, joining me and a reluctant Peggy on the impromptu sleuthing adventure. Conveniently for us, people weren't out and about, so no one saw us slipping through the trees and into the backyard.

"So Barb," Roz said, "I owe you an apology – you may not be crazy after all."

"How's that?"

"After I took the kids home, I found a message on my answering machine from Maria Nichols."

"Who's Maria Nichols?" asked Peggy.

"That's her house back there." Roz pointed to the back of a house some twenty yards or so from where we were standing. "She lives on Green Ash Lane – she can see this back yard from her kitchen window. You know her, right Barb?" I nodded. The Nichols' were new to the neighborhood and their youngest girl played with Bethany.

"Well," she continued, "she called me to see what all the commotion was over here with the police and animal control and this, that, and the other, and did I see the man sneaking around behind the empty house?"

"What?" my ears perked up.

"That's what I said! So I called her back. She says she saw some guy dressed in black, walking around back here, being very sneaky and acting peculiarly suspicious." She slapped her hand on her leg for emphasis. "Same time as monkey time!"

"Maybe she just saw one of the animal control people looking around for other monkeys or something," Peggy said.

"I had the same thought, but Maria says this guy was wearing a long black wool coat – dressed a little too nice for doing outdoor work. She says he parked his very sleek Towncar on her street, practically in front of her house, and went through the woods to get here."

"So what are we looking for now?" asked Peggy.

"Anything we can find."

We searched the ground for footprints or other signs of life. The area was so significantly shaded that grass couldn't grow. It was basically a backyard of dirt and leaves. There was no patio to speak of, just a small cement slab at the door, wide enough for a doormat, if one were so inclined. My heart rate moved into the aerobic range. Peggy carefully scanned the area of ground nearest to the concrete slab and door.

"I'm not seeing anything here," she said.

Roz decided to look farther out into the yard where Maria Nichols had mentioned seeing a cloaked mystery man lurking about. I tried to look into the house through the glass panes of the door, fairly certain that I had heard the door open last night after the horrible man-beast howl They were covered in dirt and grime, and since I didn't come equipped with my nosy neighbor cleaning kit, I used my sweatshirt sleeve. I wiped away just enough dirt to see that the panes had been covered up from the inside with cardboard.

"Roz, you finding anything over there?" I asked.

"Not a thing," she answered. "Maria swore she saw someone walking around over here, but I don't see one sign of it. You'd think we'd see something, it's just dirt over here."

Peggy wandered around to the other side of the house. A moment later she came back with a prize.

"Look at this!" she held up a brand new broom. Brand new except it had obviously been used on the dirt, because the bristles were covered in it. I looked closer at the ground at my feet. Sure enough, it had been swept over – long bristle marks were etched in the dirt.

"Someone has been covering up their tracks!" I cried. The hair on my neck stood on end. We weren't just barking up an empty tree – we were really onto something. Someone REALLY had been at this house and didn't want people to know.

In our excitement, we all started poking around the house and looking into windows. I tried the doorknob to no avail. Then I went around to the low basement window where I had seen the light, realizing that might be our best bet. Roz and Peggy followed. I got down on my knees for a better look. The mud-covered, aluminum window appeared to be the type that slid back and forth to open and close. If there had been a screen, it was gone now. I pulled at the window with my hand, and much to my surprise, it opened like a breeze. I sat on my bottom, dumbfounded, and stared up at Roz and Peggy.

"What do I do now?" I asked.

"Geez, I don't know," said Peggy.

"If we go in, it would be breaking and entering, right?" asked Roz.

"Probably," I said.

We were silent for a good minute. A strong, autumn breeze blew through and chilled us all a bit, although I'm not sure the chill was so much the cool air as much as the moderate to major amount of fear racing through our veins. Poor Roz and Peggy had the same look on their faces as a squirrel I saw the day before, frozen in the road staring into the headlights of an oncoming SUV.

"Well," proposed Peggy, "maybe it's only breaking and entering if we get caught."

"Oh, right. And what if we do get caught, Peggy?" sniped Roz. "Let's face it, this is fun and all, but going in – that's another thing altogether."

"Okay," I said, "Roz is basically right. On the other hand, while we're here, and while the window is open, why don't I just stick my head in – just my head? I'll do it fast, no one will know. Then we'll run the hell out of here." I was feeling very gutsy and very sleuthy.

"Admit it Roz," teased Peggy, "you're as curious as we are."

"Fine, fine, fine," she snapped. "I'm curious. I'm very curious. I'm seriously curious. Just stick your head in a little." She motioned toward the window. "But make it quick. Our luck is going to run out soon and someone is going to see us."

I got back on my knees and asked them to hold my legs, just in case. I didn't want to fall in – then I'd have problems. Probably couldn't skirt the whole breaking and entering issue on a technicality if that happened. I put my hands on the ground and moved my head in through the narrow opening. It was still dark and my eyes took a moment to adjust.

"Do you see anything?" asked Peggy.

"Not yet."

I blinked a couple of times. It was horribly musty and dust swam right up my nose. I brought my hand in to rub my nose in an attempt to stifle a sneeze. Then I noticed a smell far worse than musty. It was strong and had a sweet sort of aroma, but not a good sweet. The scent was familiar, but I couldn't place it immediately. My eyes were just beginning to adjust to the dark when it hit me – the smell. It was just like the time I found the dead chipmunk in my pantry. . . I started feeling not so good about the whole enterprise when I caught sight of something on the floor. I blinked once more to focus clearly. Suddenly, the situation went from "Hmm-this-is-interesting" to "Holy-Mother-of-God-what-do-I-do-now?" Because, as it turned out, I was looking straight down into the rotting eye sockets of a very dead face. Problem was, there was no body. Just a head. The head was dead.

Then everything went black.

Chapter 5

My eyes opened and I found that my head was in Peggy's lap. I couldn't remember why I was on the ground. I remembered it was my birthday and thought this was a strange way to celebrate . . . . then it all came back. The dark room, the smell, the head. I struggled to sit up.

"What happened? Where's Roz?" I asked, my mouth barely able to form the words.

"You fainted. Well, you screamed first. Then you fainted. My cell phone died so Roz went to call 911. I was so scared! We could barely hold you – you went limp. Limp as a rag doll. A heavy rag doll. It was awful! Awful!" Peggy's arms were flying in all directions as she rambled on about the events after my blackout. She was bouncing around so violently, my head nearly flew out of her lap. "I was sure we were going to drop you," she continued. "You were so heavy. Dead weight. It was awful. Man, how much do you weigh?"

"I got it – I need to lose a few pounds. Geez." I rubbed my head. "Did you see it?"

"It? Oh, God. There's an IT? We were afraid to look. I'm a wuss. The smell says enough. Please tell me it's a dead animal."

Roz was running back carrying a bottle of water and something else I couldn't make out. Just as she reached us, I heard sirens in the distance, the sound growing louder.

"Are you okay? Is she okay?" She was looking back and forth between us.

"I'm fine," I answered. "My head is starting to pound though."

"Oh, here," she said handing over the items she had brought. "A bottle of water and Tylenol. Please tell me it's a dead animal."

"It's not a dead animal," I said.

"Is it dead?" asked Peggy.

"Oh, it's dead. What's left of it."

Peggy and Roz clamped their hands over their mouths at the same time. Just about then, two uniformed bodies rounded the corner. I had finally managed to pull myself up to a sitting position – when I looked up, I saw that one of the two people was my Brad Pitt-handsome policeman friend. I tried to remember his real name from the card he had given me. No such luck. He'd just have to be Officer Brad. He probably wished he'd clocked out after his first call to our neighborhood. This time around, Officer Brad was accompanied by a squat female officer who appeared stiff and uber-serious. Neither of them said a word as they stared down at us, so I felt compelled to start the conversation.

"So, you again," I said, being a little too flip for the occasion. Not necessarily being accustomed to finding dead heads in neighborhood basements, I wasn't exactly sure how this was going to go down. Would I be wearing gray by the end of the day, curled up on a cot singing the jailhouse blues?

"I was just about to say the same thing," he replied, definitely not smiling. He wasn't happy. I figured that he was about to get a lot less happy too.

"I'm afraid there's a dead head in this basement here. I found it by accident."

Officer Brad didn't blink a blink. There were several seconds of uncomfortable silence. Even the lady cop was starting to sweat. Eventually, I detected a twitch on his lip that I couldn't quite read. Hard to tell if it was an angry twitch or a sympathetic twitch. I was praying for sympathetic.

"By a dead head, ma'am," he finally said, "do you mean a person, such as a rock band groupie?"

"No, I mean a head. The head of a dead human. The rest of him isn't there. Well, at least not on the floor." Unfortunately I pictured the decaying head again while talking and started to feel nauseous. "Excuse me, I think

I'm going to throw up." And then I did. I sprayed chunks all over Officer Brad's shiny black shoes.

As more cars arrived and Officer Brad cleaned off his shoes, the burly lady cop quickly took over, moving the three of us away from the house to the street out front. White Willow Circle was starting to glow with the throbbing of red flashing lights. The shrill of sirens filled the air.

A paramedic named Chaz arrived and seemed disappointed that I didn't have a telephone pole through my guts like a grisly scene in an episode of ER. I figured it was his first day. He did give me a warm blanket and oxygen though, since I was shivering in massive spasms. While he took my blood pressure, Roz told me that Peter had scooped up my girls and taken them to their house. He would watch them until things settled down. Thank God for Peter.

I found myself wishing Howard were there holding me, keeping me warm. And then, just as if he read my mind, I saw his car turn onto White Willow. He couldn't get past the police cars so he parked at the corner and ran up the street. His dark eyes were darker than usual, contrasting his ashen white face. He looked terrible and that made me happy. He was worried. Now if he'd just remember it was my birthday, then he'd be perfect. When he finally reached me, he took me in for a long, strong hug. He smelled so good. I didn't want to let go. Suddenly, with him holding me like that, comforting me, the reality of my discovery became overwhelming and I started shivering uncontrollably again.

"Are you okay?" he asked.

I nodded, fighting back an urge to cry. It stuck like a lump in my throat and prevented me from speaking, but I was sticking to my oath – I wasn't going to be a wimpy woman. Sigourney's Lieutenant Ripley didn't cry when she found that dead guy in the space ship. Neither would I. Tears fought to find open air, but I shut down those ducts tight.

"Where are the girls?" he asked me.

Peggy chimed in, realizing, I think, that I might be having trouble talking. "They're at Roz and Peter's," she answered. It occurred to me as we stood there that his arrival didn't appear to be casual in nature. He drove up fast, like he knew ahead of time that there was a problem.

"Did Roz call you?" I was finally able to ask. He shook his head no, while observing the growing activity at House of Many Bones. It was hard to tell, but it seemed that he was avoiding the question.

"Who? Peter?" I queried further.

"So, are you ready to tell me what happened here?" he asked, changing the subject. His avoidance of the question wasn't lost on me, but I was too freaked to force the issue. I gave him the whole story – the truck, the screaming man, the call from Maria Nichols, and our idea to conduct our own investigation of sorts, figuring there was really no harm, and maybe we'd be helping out if we discovered some intruder, yada, yada, yada. I thought I was stretching it a bit, saying we were trying to "help," but I guess, all things told, we probably did help. I mean, we found a dead body. Or, rather, we found part of a dead body.

I was very proud of Howard. He listened to my whole story without interrupting me or rolling his eyes once. I was fearful of the eye roll. He's pretty good at that. Howard is generally, a very calm, collected guy who never loses his temper. He doesn't yell and he doesn't throw things, but he knows how to give a mean eye roll. I thought that was a woman-thing, but he's damn good at it. In fact, not only did he keep his eyes friendly on my story, but he actually seemed interested in and asked me several pertinent questions.

His interest caused me to think. Maybe what our marriage lacked was intrigue. Mystery. Something fun to talk about. Maybe, I thought, he really was seeing another woman. Possibly someone more intriguing than me. Someone sexy, sultry and beguiling like Lauren Bacall in *To Have and Have Not*. Someone enigmatic and maybe even dangerous. Damn! My mind was dreaming up crazy ideas. Shut it out, Barb. Shut it out. Luckily, I was rescued. Officer Brad, whose real name I was doomed to forget, walked over, ready to take statements from Roz, Peggy and myself. He talked to me first.

"So, Ma'am. . ." he began. I had to interrupt.

"Grant an old lady a wish, and call me Barb, remember?" I pleaded, hoping that maybe a little playfulness would soften the encounter a bit.

"Okay, Barb," he said, finally cracking a smile. "Tell me how you were able to see inside the house."

"The truth?" I asked crinkling my nose.

"That's always best in these situations," he answered. "And by the way, I don't think you're an old lady. I'm forty-four myself. Do I look old to you?"

Geez. Was he flirting with me?

"Oh no! You don't look a day over Brad Pitt – I mean thirty-four!" I stumbled over my words. I was pretty sure I was flirting back. He smiled, looked at his shoes a moment, and I knew I'd better get on to the matter at hand.

"Well, about the house . . ." I began, "it's kind of like this – I don't know if you know this or not, but this house has been vacant for something like thirty years or so."

"Twenty-nine," he corrected me instantly. Hmmm, he did know. I wondered what else he knew?

"Right" I said surprised. "A long time. And I told you earlier about the strange truck last night. Well, I saw a light in a window – that one right there. Then another woman we know saw some man snooping around the backyard today when that whole monkey hoopla was going on, and well, we were, well, you know, concerned, because it's our neighborhood, and there's this grumpy lawn-mower guy that more or less threatened me five years ago." I was rambling purposely and hoping that maybe he had missed the fact that I didn't really answer his question about how I managed to come upon the rotting head in a house that I didn't have legal access to. Turns out, Officer Brad wasn't only good looking, he was smart too. He didn't miss a thing.

"Yes, but how did you see inside the house."

"Oh, that." I was in a pickle. Okay. Well, they say the truth will set you free. "We decided, to, you know, go take a look around for ourselves, make sure the house hadn't been broken into or anything, because you know, we have kids, and we wouldn't want strangers around here breaking into houses, because, you know, as mothers – mothers who shouldn't go to jail or anything – we were concerned, and so I accidentally opened the window and stuck my head in. I didn't go in all the way, honest! If my friends had dropped me, well then, I might have, you know, fallen in and then my whole body would be in, but I didn't. I think, technically, you might say I just looked in, wouldn't you?"

"Accidentally?" Boy, that guy didn't miss a trick.

"Hmm?" I tried to act innocent.

"You said you 'accidentally' opened the window. How did you 'accidentally' open the window?"

"Oh . . ." I said, stalling. Think! "Well . . . . it was dirty. Mm hmm, and so I had to wipe it off to look in you know," and remembering that I had wiped off another window, I held up my sleeve and showed him the dirt. "And when I went to wipe it, it slid open quite easily – almost on its own really." I knew this was lame, but I was determined to stay out of jail. I imagined the network news teaser: "A mother from Rustic Woods does time in the big house after discovering a dead head in an empty house – what will become of her kids? Details at ten."

Suddenly, I started to feel nauseous again. The mixture of fear, excitement, and adrenaline added to shivering in the chilly October air for over an hour was wearing me out.

"You know, I think I'm feeling sick again . . ."

Officer Brad, not wanting to have to clean his shoes a second time, moved off hastily.

I walked over to Peggy and Roz and hugged them both, while Howard talked to the policeman. My two friends looked as sick as I felt. Peggy's husband, Simon, had come over to give her some moral support. When Howard was done talking to the police, he put his arms around me and walked me into our house while the frenzy continued.

"You want something?" he asked as he walked to the kitchen.

"A cup of tea would be nice. With a whiskey chaser. Make that a whiskey, forget the tea. Make it a double."

"You don't drink whiskey."

"Oh. I forgot. Just tea then." I shivered. "And a warm blanket." I sat down in my nice big, overstuffed, comfy chair in the family room, curled my feet under my bottom, and laid my head down on the soft chenille pillow.

I must have fallen asleep, because the next thing I knew my eyes opened to darkness and I was covered in our red electric blanket. My body felt like I'd just run a marathon – not that I'd ever run a marathon, but I have a good imagination. I moaned, pulling my body out of the chair, and hobbled to the kitchen, turning the light on.

There was a big note scribbled in crayon taped to the microwave: TOOK THE GIRLS OUT TO DINNER. WE'LL BRING SOMETHING BACK. HOWARD. PS: HAPPY BIRTHDAY. I smiled. He didn't forget my birthday. Or – my smile faded – maybe he DID forget, and the girls reminded him. More likely the latter.

The clock said ten after six. I had slept a long time. Howard and the girls would probably be back soon. I was hoping they'd bring me my favorite – soft tacos with extra cheese from Taco Loco. Soft tacos would really hit the spot. I opened a couple of cupboards, but nothing compared to a soft taco, so I pulled two small Almond Joys from the Halloween candy bowl. At least I was getting some protein. Isn't coconut a fruit? I contemplated going upstairs for a shower to wash away the stress and grime, when the phone rang. Caller ID told me it was Roz. I picked up.

"Hey," I said.

"How are you doing?"

"I'm feeling better. Still creeped out though. You?"

"Well, I'm okay, but boy, did I have to calm Peter down. He was furious at me. Said I was a busybody."

"Busybody? Does anybody really say that anymore?"

"Just Peter, the old fogey. He's settled down now though. But that's not why I'm calling. You left before the good stuff happened!"

"Something else happened?" I was stunned. I couldn't believe the day I had been having. The birthday from hell.

"Oh yeah, something else happened. A black, very official-looking car pulled up followed by a big white van. Two guys in suits and sunglasses got out of the car and flashed badges around to the police at the scene. Guess who it was."

"Will Smith and Tommy Lee Jones?"

"Who?" She asked. Evidently, Roz wasn't a fan of the *Men in Black* movies. Poor Roz.

"Nevermind. Who was it?"

"They were from Meadowland Labs."

"What's that?" I asked. I wasn't understanding her fascination or the connection.

"Meadowland – the animal testing lab in Loudoun County."

"I don't get it."

"Turns out, there wasn't just a dead human head in that house."

"What else?" I asked, even though I was starting to follow her and was thinking I might know the answer.

"Monkeys."

"Live monkeys or dead monkeys?" I cringed when I asked the question.

"Three of them. Dead, dead, and dead."

Chapter 6

Dead people. Dead monkeys. It was all just too far out of my league as a suburban soccer mom. On the other hand, it certainly did have a very exciting, CSI-ish sort of appeal. Evidently, Rustic Woods wasn't as sleepy as it appeared on the surface.

Roz was forced to get off the phone and handle her kids who were bouncing off the walls like monkeys themselves after Peter's dinner of Spaghettios, fruit loops, and Coca Cola. I proceeded upstairs, showered until the steam was so thick I couldn't see my toes, and pulled myself into my softest, warmest periwinkle fleece jammies. I was set in for the night. All I needed now was a mammoth mug of hot chocolate. With marshmallows. Lots of them. I padded my comfy self back downstairs, cooked up a delectable pot, poured it into a mug, padded back into the living room, flicked on the TV, then settled back into the overstuffed chair all warm and ready to do nothing but relax into a complete vegetative state.

Steam curled up from the Mickey Mouse mug that filled both of my hands, warming them gently. My lips were perched over the brim, ready for a tentative taste test, when a light knock sounded on the front door. My heart went into overdrive. After the day I'd had, an unexpected nighttime knock at the door didn't exactly give me the warm and fuzzies. Certainly, it wasn't Howard and the girls. They would have just let themselves in – loudly. I put my mug down on the side table, tiptoed quietly to the front door and put my ear against it for a listen, while contemplating if I should answer. Maybe it was the maniac mutilator of bodies, coming to chop me up next.

There was no security chain on the door to protect me if I cracked it open for a peek. If my uninvited guest was, say, The Merchant of Death, he'd slam that door off its hinges the minute he had a chance, making me funeral home-ready in about two seconds flat. With my ear still at the door, I noticed that the unidentified someone on the other side was trying the doorknob. My heart kicked out of overdrive and stalled. Luckily, the door was locked. I pulled my ear away and moved back. The doorknob stopped jiggling. I tried to breathe. That wasn't going so well. I heard scuffling, a bang and a clank, then a key going into the lock. Holy crap. I pictured Howard and the girls coming home, only to find my head lying on the foyer floor, my body stolen by some sicko head-less body stealer.

Frantically, I began scanning the room for a blunt object. Realizing that running was probably a smarter option, since the only two things in my house at the moment worth protecting were Indiana Jones the cat and my own body, I scooped up Indy and turned on my heels to make the mad dash. Too late. The doorknob turned and my door swung open hard and fast.

I screamed so loud that Indiana Jones howled and jumped out of my arms, scratching me on his way down. My scream and Indy's howl were immediately followed by a louder scream and a crash. The louder scream came from the massive intruder standing in my doorway – my mother – and the crash came from the cooking pot previously filled with what appeared to be vegetable soup that now covered my foyer floor and half the walls. My heart started pumping again. I was breathing like a horse on the last lap of the Kentucky Derby and I was seething mad.

"Mother!" I screamed. "What the hell are you doing? Don't you ever knock?"

"I did knock!" She screamed back.

Oh yeah. She did.

"Barbara Nancy Pettingford Marr, you nearly gave me a heart attack!" Even at forty-five, my mother knew how to scold me using all of my names. "And look what you made me do," she added, pointing at the soup stained floor. Indiana Jones, evidently assessing that the situation at hand was safe, returned to begin lapping up the warm liquid. My mother had succeeded in pinning this disaster on me and consequently took the wind right out of my angry sails. The woman was a marvel. I'm sure even Chuck Norris would cower like a dog if confronted by her towering presence and those piercing, beady eyes.

"You know," I said, trying to regain some semblance of self-respect, "I'm here alone and I wasn't expecting you, so it only seems fair of you to realize that I may have been a little concerned that someone was letting themselves into my house. Where did you get the key from anyway?"

"The flower pot where you keep it. And don't talk to me in that tone – I'm your mother. Why are you alone anyway? Where are Howard and the girls?"

"He took them out to dinner." I had gone to the kitchen for paper towels and had returned, getting on my knees, to start cleaning up the mess. "Why are you here?" I picked up a small brown bean. "What is this stuff anyway?"

"I called earlier to arrange a time for your birthday dinner. Howard said you were asleep and felt like you were getting a cold, so I thought I would bring over this chicken, lentil, vegetable soup I discovered on the shopping channel. It's supposed to turn a cold around in just one day. The secret ingredient is a Chinese herb that is supposed to revitalize your immune system."

With all of the excitement, I had definitely forgotten about the birthday dinner. "Did you tell Howard you were coming over?" I asked.

"Of course not. I didn't decide to bring the soup until after I talked to him. Why would I?"

"It's just that some advance warning would be nice sometimes. Prevents little things, like . . . scaring the hell out of me. Jesus! This stuff smells like dirty socks."

"My heart is warmed by your gratitude." She walked to the kitchen removing her coat. "Look at me, I'm a mess. I need to clean off my coat." Helping to clean my floor and walls did not appear to be on her agenda.

I had just finished picking up the last lentil bean when my mother swept back into the foyer, the coat draped over one arm. She scooped up her pot. "I have to be going now. I have a training date with Master Kyo."

"Who?"

"Master Kyo – I'm training for my black belt. I'm sure I told you that. The great Korean art of Tae Kwon Do."

"I thought you were training for a marathon."

"Of course. I'm doing both. I'm expanding my horizons and accepting great, new challenges. You really should think of taking on a challenge or two yourself you know. It relieves stress and calms the nerves. You'll never be sick again. Take my word." Without thinking I might have a response, my mother opened the door with vigor ready to fly out dramatically, only to find Howard in her face. He looked as surprised as she did.

"Oh," he said, trying to hide the terror I knew he felt. "Hi, Diane. How are you?"

"I'm better than my daughter, evidently. Fancy finding you here – it's such a rare treat to actually find you at your own home, Howard. Maybe if you were around more, Barbara could find time to take care of herself. I had to bring her soup to get her well again." She put him in his place fast. I had to admit, I hated it when my mother scolded me, but it was fun to watch her tear into Howard. He looked to me for help, but I just shrugged. "You're on your own dude."

"Soup?" he asked. "Was it good?"

"Ask Indiana – he's the only one that got a taste," I said.

Howard gave me a questioning look while my mother excused herself from the scene.

"Good bye Barbara." She slipped by Howard to leave.

"Grandma!" yelled Bethany, "Did Mommy tell you that monkeys came to our house to play?"

I cringed.

"Monkeys?" my mother's voice trailed off. I wasn't up for the explanation.

"We were playing imaginary games, Mom. She's still having fun with it. Say Goodbye to Grandma now, girls. She needs to go now."

Bethany protested my imagination claim. "But Mommy . . ."

"Bethany, come in. It's getting cold. Bye Mom! Go knock 'em dead." Seeming a little bewildered, my mother wandered past the girls and left. The girls stepped in behind Howard.

"What was all that about?" he asked.

"My mother, amazing marathon runner, slash master of martial arts, decided to take a stab at being a stealth Martha Stewart. Except she wasn't so stealth – she scared the shit out of me letting herself in the front door and I ended up with beans on my walls."

"Sounds like just another day with Diane," he said, smiling. I smiled too. You had to love my mother, even when you wanted to kill her.

"Thank you for not bringing up today's excitement – my discovery." I was being vague, around the girls. "There's no way I want to explain that one to her."

"Me either," he smiled. "I'm sure she'd find a way to blame it on me."

Once they were all in and the door was closed, I noticed that they were acting suspiciously happy and were holding bags behind their backs. Bethany giggled and broke the silence.

"Hi Mommy!" she squealed, "Look what we got you!" She shoved a large, brightly colored bag in my face. "Presents!" In fact, all three girls and Howard were bearing gift bags and boxes. I felt a lump in my throat and the urge to sniffle.

We moved to the living room where I could sit and enjoy opening my birthday stash. I took them one at a time, starting with Amber since she's the youngest and most persistent. I was saving Howard's present for last, not quite sure if I was going to love him for it or hit him over the head with it. In the bright pink and yellow and purple daisy designed bag from Amber I found not one, but two pairs of positively perfect fleece jammies very similar to the ones I was wearing. Next to chocolate and peace on earth, warm pajamas is what I wish for every birthday and Christmas. Soft and warm matching fleece socks are another favorite, which is what I found in the black, white and red kitty cat bag from Bethany – five fantastic pairs in different colors. "Boy, am I going to be warm this winter!" I gushed. Callie handed me her bag with a smile and a preface: "Action for a super mom," she said. I looked into her very simple, but refined striped bag to find several DVDs: *Die Hard*, *Armageddon*, *Con-Air*, *Mission Impossible*, *Terminator I* and *II*, and yes, *Alien* to replace my antiquated VHS collection.

"Okay girls, you sure know me." I hugged each of them. "I'm just an old woman who likes to curl up warm and toasty in front of a good action flick."

I turned my attention to Howard. "So what do you have there? A hot chocolate machine?" I was joking of course, because his bag wasn't that big. It also was too small to hold a robe, which is what he usually got me, so my curiosity meter was reading high. He rocked back and forth on his heels and smiled in that way that let me know he was very proud of himself. He was looking especially handsome in a weathered sort of way – it looked like he hadn't shaved in a day or two and the little flecks of gray peppered around the growth was looking mighty sexy. His wavy hair had a wind-blown look to it that would even make George Clooney jealous. The little lines were showing around his smiling eyes. I wasn't going to smile back though, because I didn't want him to think everything was hunky dory. Damn straight. He wasn't going to just breeze in like nothing was wrong, bringing me presents and a pearly white smile and think I was going to fall into his arms. Wimpy women do that. Not Sigourney-Weaver-from-Aliens-women.

I set my mouth straight and firm, crossed my arms over my chest, and put forth my best sarcastic tone. "So, are you going to give it to me, or are you just going to stand there grinning like a goon?" He kept smiling. Okay. He was calling my bluff.

"Mommy!" chided Amber. "That's bad manners." She was right. Bad Mommy. I guess even Sigourney had to mind her manners in front of young children.

"I'm sorry baby," I said. "You're right." I looked back at Howard, who was now looking even more proud of himself – did he coach her? Hmm.

"Daddy," I corrected myself, "are you going to give me my present sometime today, please?" Okay, so, just a little sarcasm – with a smile. I actually was getting very anxious to open the mysteriously small package. Jewelry came in small packages.

"Yes, mommy," he continued playing the game, "I'll give you the package, but you have to give me a kiss first." Amber squealed, Bethany giggled, and Callie pretended to gag herself with her finger. I stared him down, unblinking. Just what kind of game was he playing? I thought women were supposed to be the complicated ones.

"What are you thinking?" he asked.

"I'm thinking, no kiss." I said, with a frown. I wasn't about to back down now.

"No present," he said, still grinning like a silly Cheshire. We both stared at each other. Actually, I glared, he grinned. I glared some more, he continued grinning. It was a real showdown. Minutes seemed to tick by. The girls quieted down and looked back and forth between us. Who would draw first? Finally, I got up out of my chair, walked to the kitchen, shoved my hand into the Halloween candy jar, and pulled out my ammo. I walked back, and stood in front of Howard.

"Put your hand out," I said.

"What?"

"Just put it out." He put his hand out and I very precisely placed one, single Hershey's Kiss into his hand.

"Checkmate," I said. The girls all giggled again, except Callie who was too much of a teenager for all of the gross grown-up banter. She just rolled her eyes. She'd learned it from her father. Howard, conceding he'd lost the battle, handed over the bag. Now it was my turn to smile. I would consider giving him a real kiss if the gift was made of real gold. I grabbed the bag and pulled out a small box that could, in theory, hold a pair of earrings. Or maybe a bracelet. If I dared to dream big. . . maybe a diamond necklace. Probably a bracelet, I reasoned – the box was a little too big for earrings and too small for a necklace. The anticipation was electric. I slowly pulled off the shiny blue box top. Damn! It wasn't a bracelet. It wasn't earrings. It wasn't gold. In fact, I didn't know WHAT it was. It was black and blue and squiggly shaped and looked like it belonged in the twenty third century.

"What is it?" I asked, pulling it from the box.

"It's a bluetooth!"

"A WHAT?"

"A bluetooth. For your cell phone. Isn't it great? You're always complaining that it's too dangerous to talk on your phone while you're driving. Now you can go hands-free." He was too damned happy. What is it with men and gadgets? I should have known a zebra doesn't change its stripes. When did Howard ever buy me jewelry? Had I forgotten the time he bought me a box cutter for our anniversary?

"What do I do with it?" I asked. I already had some options in mind that involved his posterior and a lot of shoving.

"You put it on your ear."

I thought sticking it IN his ear would be more fun. The urge to cry was sneaking up on me. But I took a vow. Thou shalt not be a wimp. I couldn't slip. No crying. I also couldn't go off on a ranting rampage since the girls were in the room with us. Basically I couldn't be a wimp or a bitch, so I had to suck it up and act like this alien-device was the next best thing to a diamond pendant. Which I did. I did a little oohing and aahing and gave the girls hugs again while Howard spent quality time with my cell phone and new bluetooth. Bethany and Amber brought me my bag of dinner – not one, but two soft tacos, a large coke and nachos with cheese from Taco Loco. A feast fit for a queen. Callie popped *Die Hard*– my favorite Christmas movie – into the DVD player and the girls cuddled on the couch with hot chocolate while I munched down my mexi-meal.

When Howard had finished with my cell phone, he asked me to come to the dining room table so he could give me a hands-on demonstration. Yippee. I plopped down in a chair across from him, arms crossed in a definite attempt to project with my posture that I was not a happy camper. He got it.

"You're not very happy with me, are you?" he asked.

"Oh, you think?"

"I was hoping we would have a nice night together."

"Were you planning on staying?"

The silent response was deafening.

"Thought so. Well, I'll just put this beautiful bluetooth in bed next to me so I can be reminded of you and how hard you tried to make this such a nice night. Together."

More silence. Howard stared at me through somber eyes. There was a hint of darkness under them, which made me think he hadn't been sleeping well. I realized, as we sat quietly watching each other, that there was a sadness in him that I had never seen before. A vulnerability that was unlike him. I started to feel guilty for being so hard on him. Maybe he did just need a little space. Maybe if I just gave him some time, he'd figure this all out. It didn't make sense to me, but maybe it didn't have to. Of course, I thought even further, maybe the space he needed involved sleeping space with another woman. Maybe he needed time to decide between me and some sleazy, trampy bimbo skank named Marjorie Smith. I went from feeling guilty to feeling homicidal. I got up from the table so fast and hard, I knocked over my chair. I pointed to my new birthday present.

"Does that thing have instructions with it?" I asked

Howard nodded.

"Fine. Leave them. I can read. I'll figure it out myself. I am capable, you know." I stomped back to the living room and crawled back in with the girls to finish watching the movie.

Howard disappeared upstairs, only to reappear a few minutes later with an arm full of clothes. Lovely. Just shove that knife into my heart a little further then turn. He stopped and looked at us on the couch. Amber jumped off the couch, spilling her hot chocolate, as she ran to hug him.

"Don't go Daddy! Stay! It's Mommy's birthday."

"I'm sorry, sweetie. I'll come back another time," he said. "I promise."

"When?" she asked

"Soon."

"Let him go Amber," I said. "Daddy probably has better places to be. Like with his girlfriend." Damn! That was not a good thing to say in front of the girls. I couldn't help myself. Female hormones. They'll strip me of control every time.

Howard froze. With eyes as dark as a moonless night, a glare from Howard could be a scary thing. He was motionless. I'd hit a nerve. Which nerve was questionable, but it was a nerve. Was it the girlfriend nerve?

"Do you have a girlfriend, Daddy?" cried Bethany.

"No!" he shot back at her. "I do NOT have a girlfriend."

"Well that's good," sighed Amber, "Because you already have a wife. That could be awkward."

I nearly choked on my nachos.

"Yes, that would be," said Howard. He glared at me again. "Can we talk? Outside?"

"Nope." I didn't feel up for a confrontation. Even if I did start it. "It's cold outside," I said. "And it's my birthday." He rolled the ol' eyes, turned and walked out, slamming the door behind him.

"Great way to scare him off, Mom," said Callie, storming off to her room. Just what I was thinking. But, of course, I justified to myself, HE was the one that left. Not me. Shouldn't I be the one slamming doors?

I stayed on the couch trying to watch the movie with Bethany and Amber until they fell asleep. Trying was the operative word because I couldn't keep my mind off the fight with Howard. Finally, the girls drifted to sleepy land. I covered Bethany with several blankets, carried Amber to her room, then crawled into my own, achingly empty bed, making a determined effort to get some restful sleep myself. Alas, my effort was never fully achieved. I tossed all night coming in and out of dreams about Howard and various nameless, faceless sleazy, trampy bimbo skanks.

Oddly enough, when my eyes popped open at 7:41 the next morning, I wasn't thinking about Howard. I was thinking about monkeys. What was the deal with monkeys anyway? With animal testing labs added to the mix, my concerns rose. I had watched that movie *Outbreak* with Dustin Hoffman. It taught me all I needed to know about monkeys and deadly epidemic disease. The fate of mankind was possibly in serious jeopardy.

I wanted answers, but how was I going to get them? Think, think, think. The only common denominator to the monkeys and the dead guy was the house. I needed to know more about that house. The problem was that I didn't even know who owned the place. Even worse, I didn't have the foggiest idea how to find out. That's when I had it – the beautiful "Aha!" moment.

I scrambled downstairs to the family computer and booted it up, praying for some time before the girls woke up. It would be easier to do this without them around. Finally, after what seemed like hours, the computer was on and ready to go. I went to my file of addresses and phone numbers. I remembered the good ol' days when I had them in a little book and I'd have found the number and have it dialed already. So much for technology. I grabbed the phone and dialed the number I saw on the screen in front of me. I wasn't a private investigator, but I was about to enlist the help of one. A deliciously adorable one at that. This simple phone call would do more than help me decipher the mystery of House of Many Bones. It was also going to send Howard off the deep end.

Chapter 7

The phone rang once. The phone rang twice. Three times. By the sixth ring my palms were sweaty and I was hoping to get the answering machine. Ring eight had me in a panic – should I really be making this call? I was considering hanging up when smack dab in the middle of the ninth ring, the phone picked up. Whether I had reached human or machine, however, was questionable, because the answer was not immediate. Finally, a sound nearly animal in nature crossed the line.

"Yeah?" came the dim, gravelly, groan.

"Colt?" I asked, praying now, that I had the wrong number.

"Yeah – who the hell is this?" He didn't sound well.

"It's Barb. Are you okay? Is this a bad time?" I really wished I had hung up on ring eight.

"Barb? Of course it's a bad time. It's – wait a minute, let me look – Jesus Barb! It's five o'clock in the fucking morning. On a Sunday. "

I slapped my head. My bad.

"Colt, I'm sorry! I forgot about the time difference. I'm sooooo sorry."

Colt Baron was a dear friend who currently resided in Santa Monica, California. He also served double duty as my ex-boyfriend and Howard's ex-best friend. Howard, Colt, and I had been fast friends at college in San Diego. I'd started dating Howard during our sophomore year, but we broke up the beginning of our senior year. Then Colt asked me out for more than just burritos at The Burrito Shack and he turned out to be a pretty fun boyfriend too. Thinking guys were usually cool with those kinds of things, I assumed Howard would be fine with the new relationship. Not so much. He stopped talking to both of us. After graduation, we went our separate ways – Howard to an engineering job in Washington, DC; Colt two hours north to better surfing beaches ; while I stayed in sunny San Diego hoping for an upwardly mobile job in the not-so-exciting world of publishing.

I had majored in Film and Television and minored in Literature, the dream being I'd make it big in Hollywood someday writing and directing my own films. I suffered, however, from super-sized, monstrously massive self-doubt reinforced by my parents' continual declarations that I should come back down to earth and concentrate on a "more realistic" career. Hence, I found myself editing other people's dreams at a local San Diego publishing house.

Three years later, Howard and I met again at a friend's wedding in Palos Verdes. I couldn't resist those midnight eyes, wavy locks, and killer smile. He was just too yummy. We reconciled really nice that night, and somehow managed a long-distance romance for about six months until I finally packed up and moved to Arlington, Virginia, to be closer to my honey. Meanwhile, I had stayed friends with Colt the surfer man, who rambled through different jobs up and down the California coast.

Colt's current profession was, conveniently for me, that of private investigator. I wasn't exactly sure how he came upon this line of work – did he need to be licensed? What was the training involved? Did he just hang up a shingle and call himself a PI? Those were things I just didn't know.

When I thought of private investigators, two images came to mind: Humphrey Bogart's Phillip Marlowe and Tom Selleck's Magnum. Marlowe wasn't Colt's style, but Magnum was. I imagined Colt as a flaky sort of PI only shorter and without the mustache. Knowing Colt though, he probably did hit the Santa Monica scene in a zippy little red Ferrari.

I felt bad for waking him up, but I have to admit, I was having fun picturing him in bed. I knew for a fact that he slept in his birthday suit. "Colt, I'm sorry, I'll call you back later . . ."

"No, no. It's fine. Just give me a minute," he moaned. "Is everything okay?"

"Yes. Sort of. I mean, no one is sick or dead or anything. Well, someone is dead. I just don't know who."

"What?" That woke him up. I visualized him sitting on the edge of his bed, very concerned about me. Nice image – still picturing the birthday suit. Nice birthday suit, from what I remembered.

"What's going on?" he asked. "Tell me."

I relayed the whole miserable tale – the night of howls at House of Many Bones, the live monkeys, the rotting head, the dead monkeys, the officials sporting badges from Meadowland Labs. I was hesitant to tell him that Howard had moved out, but my need for sympathy was at peak levels, so I finally succumbed to the need for a "poor baby" and spilled the beans on that subject as well.

He was quiet when I finished, but I could hear breathing on the other end. "Wow," he said finally. He was a man of many words.

"Wow? Is that all you have to say?"

"Yeah, I think so."

"Can you help me?" I asked.

"With the monkeys, the dead guy, or Howard? I'd be glad to come out there and give him the ol' one-two."

"The dead guy?"

"Howard."

I smiled. He still cared. I felt really guilty calling Colt like this. But I needed to know someone still loved me. And I really, really wanted help un-boggling my mind-boggling dead-things-in-the-creepy-house dilemma. REALLY.

"No," I said. "I don't want you to beat up Howard." Well, maybe just a little roughing up would be okay . . . "I want to know more about where these monkeys came from and why there are dead body parts in my neighborhood. It's a wee-bit disconcerting, as you can imagine. I was hoping you could give me some pointers on how to do a little amateur investigating."

"A 'wee-bit'? What are you, a leprechaun?"

"Will you help me or not?"

"Okay, here's what I think," he said. "I think you should stay out of it. It stinks."

"The smell was awful."

"No. I mean the whole thing stinks of something bad. Something you shouldn't be getting involved in, Curly. Stay out of it."

The problem was, my decision was made. One thing about me, when I make a decision to do something, I do it. True enough, my decisions may be slow in coming, but once I've made one – watch out. I'm a pit bull. Besides, my motive was largely selfish – if I kept busy enough, I wouldn't think about Howard every waking minute of the day. Colt, knowing my stubborn side the way he did, figured this out as soon as I went silent.

"You're going to do this anyway, aren't you?" he asked.

"Yep."

"Okay, well, I'd better lead you in the right direction then. What are you looking for?"

I spent nearly an hour on the phone with Colt while he listed ways I could locate relevant information. It actually didn't appear all that hard and might even be fun given my more-than-average knack for nosiness. The last thing Colt said before hanging up was, "Tell Howard he'd better watch out. I may come out there and steal you for myself."

I laughed. Colt didn't.

The first item on my list was gathering more information on Nine Hundred White Willow Circle. Colt agreed it was very strange and probably not coincidental that the house had been vacant for so long. This meant real estate research on the internet and possibly a trip to the county court house to determine ownership. He said the details would be fairly easy to find through tax records.

He also recommended talking to others in surrounding streets to find out what they knew, since the neighbors on my street either didn't know or wouldn't talk. Did anyone around town know the owner? Did they know

Grumpy Lawnmower Guy? Stuff like that. Colt said to do the preliminary research and then call him back. After I collected some good information about the house, we'd start looking into the testing lab. He thought it was possible some of the information about the house might lead us to the labs anyway. I wasn't sure how he connected those dots, but he was the pro, not me.

It was Sunday, and as eager as I was to get started, I had promised the girls a fun day in Washington, DC, so the investigative work would have to wait. Talking to Colt had lifted my spirits as well as boosted my confidence to tackle this little endeavor, so I decided to call it a day on that job, and put in some hours on the Mom-job.

Visiting the museums and monuments in Washington D.C is a real treat. Driving in DC is not. I liken it to riding a roller coaster while on Quaaludes. Still, having vast amounts of American history and culture at your fingertips is a treasure and makes the hell-ride worth every scary turn. The museums are my favorite. The girls love the museum gift shops. So, over the years, we have come to a workable arrangement – they don't complain about the museums if I don't complain about how much money we spend afterwards. Howard hates museums and won't go with me, so I take what I can get.

After rounding up the girls and taking a vote, it was decided, rather un-unanimously, that we would go to the International Spy Museum. That's because Callie wanted to see the Japanese American Memorial instead, while Bethany wanted the Museum of Modern Art, and Amber wanted the Museum of Natural History (for the hundredth time). My vote for the International Spy Museum carried the day when we let Indiana Jones act as the tie-breaker – he agreed with me. The International Spy Museum. Besides, if I was going into spy mode, it seemed appropriate that I should get psyched up.

Bethany and Amber were still shoving their way into shoes and coats when my front door flew open. It was my mother, presenting herself in her usual grand Endora-from-Bewitched manner.

"Mom, what are you doing here?"

"Checking in on you, of course. How's that cold of yours?"

I had forgotten about my fictitious cold. I sniffled once or twice. "Oh, you know, it comes and goes," I said.

She started stripping off her coat and gloves as the girls were piling theirs on.

"Mom," I whined, "can't you see we're leaving? Why didn't you call first?"

"I was out and about anyway. Besides, I'm your mother, do I need an invitation?" The question must have been rhetorical because she continued to blabber on. "Do you like my new gloves?" She rubbed them against my face. "Feel that – cashmere. Do you want some? I can order you a pair."

"Shopping channel?"

"Daily special. I'll order you a pair. Do you want Cranberry Red or Camel?"

"I don't want new gloves."

"How about a coat? Tomorrow's special is spectacular – lamb's wool, full length, and it comes with a matching hat."

"I don't need a coat."

"Of course you do. Look at that thing you're wearing. It's falling apart.

"It's brand new."

"That's a shame. Really, you should check out the shopping channel – their merchandise doesn't wear so quickly. And they'll take anything back at anytime, no questions asked."

"Mom!" She was wearing me out. "We are leaving now," I said throwing my purse over my shoulder.

She looked at us as if she had only then realized that we were dressing up for outdoor weather. "Oh! Where are you going? I'll go with you."

"You wouldn't enjoy yourself. We're going to the International Spy Museum."

"Are you kidding? That's right up my alley. I was a spy once."

"Mom, you were never a spy."

She shook her head, dismissing my comment. "It was brief. Before I met your father. Very exciting time of my life." Everything my mother claimed to have done in her life, including getting drunk with Ernest Hemingway, happened before she met my father. Since she would never confess to her real age, I figured she was either a very precocious teenager, or she met my father when she was sixty. Which would make her about . . . a hundred.

As it turned out, the museum was a hit – the girls marveled at the James Bond car with its nifty spy gadgets, while my mother told the story of how she was once considered for a role as a Bond Girl. This was, of course, before she met my father. As luck would have it, I knew my Bond movie trivia. I had her.

"Mom, *Dr. No* was the first James Bond movie and it came out in 1962 and you were married to Dad in 1962."

"Your point dear?"

"I think you're making this up."

"Well Miss Smarty Pants, 1962 is when the first Bond movie FINALLY came out. What you don't know is that a little known movie producer by the name of Harry Schmenck tried to make a James Bond movie seven years before *Dr. No.* Do you know what the name of THAT movie would have been? Hmm?" She was looking down at me very haughty and pleased to know something I did not. "*Casino Royale* – the name of the first novel by Mr. Fleming introducing the James Bond character to the world. THAT was the movie I was considered for."

How did she do it? The girls giggled while I tried not to appear embarrassed. I'd get her yet. Most likely, this Harry fellow was a shy accountant with an 8mm who once speculated to her that someone should make *Casino Royale* into a movie.

After wandering through most of the exhibits, we stopped for lunch at the museum café, which was a real treat, since a person practically had to take out a second mortgage or sell a kidney to afford the exorbitant prices.

Anyway, I used a credit card, deciding to let Howard pay the bill. Revenge is sweet.

The younger girls got pizza, Callie and my mother had chef salads, and I splurged on two very greasy chilidogs with cheese – and onions.

"You aren't exactly setting a good example for your girls eating a meal like that," chided my mother.

"Mom, I'm a grown woman. I can eat what I want."

"Okay. I'm just saying . . . "

"Mom! I got it!" A small part of me – okay, a large part of me – okay, most of me – knew she was right, but I wasn't going to give her the satisfaction of agreeing, and besides, today I was indulging. I had just turned forty-five, my husband had moved out of the house, I was finding body parts in neighborhood houses and potentially diseased monkeys were running rampant through Northern Virginia. I really, really deserved those chilidogs. Really. Every delectable bite. I chased them with an icy cold Coke. Regular. Bring on the calories baby. Bring 'em on.

"Mommy, can I get something at the gift shop?" Amber mumbled through a mouthful of pizza.

"Sure! Here's a twenty – go wild!" I gave each girl twenty dollars and off they trotted. Probably not wise to be so nonchalant about money now that my husband was playing Mr. Single-guy, but I was looking forward to "accidentally" leaving the receipt in the middle of the table next time he came over. It was another personality flaw of mine – finding ways to purposely piss people off when they've made me mad. Like the time in college when my male roommate's new girlfriend threw away all of my plants, claiming she thought they were dead. They were a little brown maybe; limp and droopy, but not dead. Her name was Michah. So I started calling her "Minah" – like the bird. "Hey Minah, can you turn the TV down?" "Minah, is that your toilet over-flowing?" "Yo, Minah, I think someone is towing your car." I thought it was a hoot. Minah, Minah, Minah. She practically turned purple each time I said it. Of course, I learned the hard way that you can't go around purposely irritating people too much, or it comes back to haunt you. Because, shortly afterwards my pet rabbit, Mel Gibson, mysteriously found his way out of his cage and into the condo complex pool – without a life preserver. Poor Mel Gibson. Of course, I knew Michah was the culprit – mostly because of the tell-tale note tied around Mel's little neck that said, "My name is Michah!" I said it was a personality flaw. Thank goodness Mel responded to CPR and went on to live a healthy life.

One would think after nearly losing little Mel I would have learned my lesson not to goad people who made me mad. While I pondered my obsession to rile Howard, my stomach grumbled. I rubbed my tummy. "Shhhh, tummy," I said. "We're in public." My stomach answered back with a bit of a gurgle. I was starting to feel somewhat on the gassy side. Hmm, this isn't good, I thought. Better get home.

We all crowded back into my white Grand Caravan, the girls with their packages from the gift shop, my mom with her new gloves, and me with a growing sense of gastric urgency.

Shortly after turning onto Constitution Avenue heading toward I-66, my body sent me a strong message. The message wasn't good. The chili, the dogs, the cheese and the onions were waging a war somewhere between my small and my large intestines.

Okay, I thought, I can make this. It was only twenty minutes until we got home. Well, maybe thirty. That was if there was no traffic. Sweat was starting to form on my brow.

Bethany and Amber were singing songs. Callie asked me a question, which I didn't hear because all five senses had shut down instinctively to prevent outside stimuli from distracting me. Concentration was the key. Get home.

"Mom! Didn't you hear what I said?" she moaned.

"What?" I asked. "Sorry. I have . . . a problem." I shifted in my seat to make things a little more comfortable, putting my pedal to the metal.

My mother gripped her armrest. "Barbara, don't you think you're going a bit too fast?"

"Not now, Mom," I said through clenched teeth.

"Barbara, what's wrong?" my mother asked.

Now there was sweat on my upper lip. From the rearview mirror, I could see Callie giving me that look teenagers give their parents when they've decided we're all really the stupidest people alive and they know everything.

"Mom," Callie said in her new condescending tone, "you're acting very weird."

"What's wrong with mommy?" cried Amber from the back, cluing into the activity up front.

"Nothing's wrong, Sweety," I said, "I just have to go to the bathroom, that's all. I'll be okay."

My mother clicked her tongue. "I told you so . . ." she sang, shaking her head. Click, click, click. The woman could make the most annoying tongue clicking noises ever.

"What?!" I screamed.

"Those chilidogs . . . "

"You're supposed to go to the bathroom *before* we get in the car," Bethany sing-songed. "That's what you always tell us."

In my misery, I could only mentally acknowledge Bethany's statement of truth. Certainly I did not follow my own rules, and was suffering the consequences.

"Mommy," cried Amber, "are you sure you're okay, 'cuz you don't look so good!"

"I'm fine!" My knuckles were white on the wheel, my eyes focused on staying safe while speeding forth. "Really! I'm fine, just . . . just keep it down so I can concentrate," I said.

"Concentrate on what?" asked Bethany.

I chose not to answer that question.

As we neared Rustic Woods, the discomfort grew worse. I flew down Purple Poplar Road, the final leg of our trip. My rate of acceleration was far exceeding the posted limit. I probably only had ten minutes to go, provided I hit all green lights. Maybe I could roll through a red if no one was around.

My eyes were fixed on the road. They weren't, however, fixed on the police cruiser I passed going, if I had to take a guess, oh, sixty in a forty mile an hour zone. The lights shone in my rearview mirror. Oh man! I was going to have to stop. This could get real ugly. I pulled slowly to the side of the road, wiped the sweat off my face, and rolled down my window. I couldn't believe my eyes when I looked into the rearview mirror and saw who was sauntering up to my van. Officer Brad. Damn!

He stepped up to the car and looked in. His head tilted in recognition. He almost smiled. "Ma'am," he said. "Nice to see you again." Then he rambled on about speeding, safety on the road, and some other vehicular nonsense – all things that were not registering since my mind was on other matters.

"Shit," I said. "Shit, shit, shit." I was muttering, half crazed.

"What was that, Ma'am?" he frowned.

"Mommy has to poop!" screamed Amber from the backseat. "Can't you see she's all sweaty?"

Officer Brad looked horrified, losing his stoic policeman's composure for only a nanosecond. He took a good long look at me. My face flushed red. It was burning like lava. If someone had put a white sickle and hammer in front of me I could have passed for the communist flag.

"Sir," my mother interjected, crossing her body in front of mine to get a better view of Officer Brad. "My daughter here made a poor dietary choice and ate some chilidogs that appear to have disagreed with her. She now has a serious need to use the restroom." She whispered the word "restroom" as if they were a communicable disease. "Of course, I told her she should eat something more healthy, but you know children never want to listen to their parents. Do you think you could let us go just this once?" Officer Brad's face did not change expression. "Please," he said. "Go."

"Are you sure?" I said, even though I was already moving away at a good clip. "Thank you!" I yelled as I sped toward home.

"You see that," said my mother, "You should be glad you had me along. I used to be involved in law enforcement."

I made it home in the nick of time, throwing my keys onto the floor while pulling my pants down while running to the bathroom. Not graceful, but definitely efficient. I remained in the bathroom for a while, contemplating the obvious parallels between my life and the crapper. My mother called out that she had to get home and change for Tae Kwon Do. Something about not being late for the new instructor. Thank God for small mercies. As I crawled out of the bathroom to face the rest of my Sunday, the doorbell rang.

Amber, who has two speeds – stop and go – was at the door in record time. By the time I reached her, the door was open and I was greeted by a pimple faced, curly headed boy of about sixteen, uniformed in gray and blue. He was holding a long, large box wrapped with a red, velvet ribbon. It looked suspiciously like . . . flowers! I peeked quick at the boy's name tag: Alex. Beneath his name: Rustic Woods Floral Center. They WERE flowers! My Howard had come through – he felt guilty and sad and horrible. How wonderful! I grabbed the box while Amber announced loudly throughout the house that I got flowers. I tore off the red ribbon and threw off the top. Red Roses! He'd never sent me red roses before.

I grabbed the small envelope and started to pull out the note, a smile as wide as the Mississippi shining on my face. I stopped short, though, as a memory flooded in. I HAD been given red roses before. But not from Howard. My smile faded and my stomach gurgled again – from nerves, not chili dogs. Only one person had ever given me red roses, and he had done it more than once. It was his signature – his MO. I read the note silently. *Happy Birthday, Curly. They say Virginia is for lovers. I thought I'd find out for myself.*

Holy cow. What had I done?

Chapter 8

The delivery boy took my signature with an embarrassed smile and moved on quickly. I stood frozen on my front door stoop, staring at the card like an idiot. Colt was there – I could see him in my peripheral vision as he walked around the corner of my house. Emotions of sweet joy and utter guilt played ping pong with my heart.

"What's a guy gotta do to get a hug in this town?"

I smiled in spite of myself. Geezie Louisie he was cute. Colt Baron was one of those men who definitely aged with grace. In college he was a blonde, trim and muscular surfer boy. Today, he was still blonde, trim and muscular, but he was all man. Little lines that grow around the eyes might make a woman look old, but on Colt they were like butter cream frosting – the proverbial icing on the cake. Whereas Howard had a significant amount of gray, Colt had hardly any, and what little there was remained nearly hidden in a full, feathery blonde head of hair. In fact, I'd have killed to have hair like his – soft and wispy. Perfect to run your fingers through. At five foot ten inches, he was just barely taller than me. He was still dressed for California weather – a brown, faded Dos Equis t-shirt, khaki cargo shorts and well-worn leather sandals. A black computer case hung from his left shoulder. The muscle bulge showing through his t-shirt was quite pleasing to the eyes. My eyes wandered lower – his calves weren't bad either.

"How did you get here so fast?" I finally tore myself away long enough to ask.

"Caught the first plane out of town, gorgeous. You think I'm going to let you go through this alone?" By "this" I wasn't sure if he meant my dead monkey problem or my Howard problem. I looked at my watch. It was 5:05 pm. It's a four or five hour flight from LA non-stop. He moved fast.

"You can't just pick up and leave town like that," I said.

"Maybe you can't, but I can. Right now, there's nothing I need to do there that I can't do here." He held up an olive duffle bag that looked like it had been through both world wars. "Can you put me up?"

That was Colt. Spunk and spontaneity. Always the can-do attitude. This wasn't the first time he had just shown up on our doorstep unannounced. Some fifteen years earlier, soon after Callie was born and long before we moved to our house on White Willow Circle, we were roused out of bed one morning by his loud knocking on our apartment door. That time, he had been bicycling up the East Coast from South Carolina with his paramour du jour. They had stopped in Northern Virginia – her to see a brother in Leesburg, and him to stir up the pot in the new Marr household. The thing was, I always loved to see Colt. Howard, who did not, would stew like a chicken in a pressure cooker. Turn up the heat to high with Colt staying over, and we might find Howard splattered on the ceiling. Therefore, the question was not COULD I put him up, but SHOULD I put him up. Colt sensed my hesitation.

"You know," he said, "it will really piss off the How-boy. This could be a good thing."

"Yeah, or it could be a bad thing," I replied, thinking that good or bad, I didn't need Howard's permission to invite anyone to stay at my house.

"What the hell," I said, throwing my hands in the air. "Everything's bad these days anyway." And with that, Colt moved in. Holy cow.

Colt had visited us in our White Willow house once before – he had visited two years earlier when he came to DC for some private investigator's conference something or other. Remembering the way now, he went straight to the guest room then returned downstairs in a minute's time unencumbered by his travel gear. He quickly made himself at home by looking for something to eat in the kitchen while the girls circled around him asking questions and acting very girly. All girls loved Colt, no matter the age. He had actually bought them "I LOVE L.A." t-shirts at the airport before getting on the plane. I smiled while I sipped tea at the kitchen table and watched. Then, when the sky turned very dark, I rounded the girls up to get them to showers and baths and bed.

"Let's go, girls," I said, sad to be breaking up their fun. "Tomorrow is a school day." They responded with the usual "Do we have to?" and "Just five more minutes." Since I was actually looking forward to grown-up talk with my old friend, I remained firm.

"Nope, let's get a move on. Colt will be here tomorrow." They grudgingly slumped their disappointed way upstairs.

"The remote for the TV is in a basket next to the couch," I reminded Colt. "We keep beer in the basement fridge. Help yourself. I'll be back down after I get the girls to bed."

"I can't wait." He smiled.

The bedtime routine was rather long, with hair brushing, book reading, and kiss giving, so I didn't make it downstairs again for a good hour or more. I went to the family room first, expecting to find Colt drinking a beer and watching football, but no such luck. I called out his name.

"Colt?"

"I'm here!" His voice came from the bathroom. "I'm fixing your toilet."

"You didn't have to do that," I said as I rounded the hallway to peek in. Stopping suddenly, I caught my breath and cringed. Oops. The spectacle was too comical for words. It could best be described as a He-man Stand-off. Evidently, while I was upstairs, Howard had come into the house and unexpectedly discovered Colt involved in a handyman activity. Colt and Howard were now faced-off, head to head, mano a mano, over my guest-bath toilet. The top was off, the seat was up. Howard gripped a plunger in his hands with purposeful intensity. Colt had a wrench in one hand and something that appeared to be the guts of my toilet in the other. I didn't know if my toilet was being repaired, or sacrificed to the great God of Macho. My first instinct was to laugh. My second instinct was to run. Howard looked ready to kill.

"What's going on?" I finally asked, deciding not to laugh or run.

"Your toilet was running, so I decided to help you out and fix it," Colt said, staring Howard down.

"OUR toilet doesn't run. YOU must have done something to it," Howard countered, teeth clenched, brow furrowed.

"Um," I interjected with a hesitant wince, "actually, Howard, it has been running for a few days now. I have to keep jiggling the handle to get it to stop." I made a tiny little jiggling motion with my hand, pinching my fingers together and smiling sweetly, hoping the obvious cuteness of my action would temper the temper. Howard's eyes turned toward me ever so slowly. My sweet smile was not reciprocated. In fact, he was looking a little like Jack Nicholson in *The Shining*. Thank goodness he didn't have an axe. Cute, it seemed, wasn't getting me very far.

Colt grinned. "See, Howie ol' man? If you'd stick around, like a good husband, you'd know a thing or two about your own house."

Ouch! Boy, things were going from bad to really, really, really bad. Howard was not the hitting sort, but I would have bet big Las Vegas dollars that Colt was about to take one across the kisser with that plunger.

Howard focused a nasty stare on Colt. Silence. Staring. Silence. More staring. Only the tick, tick, ticking of the kitchen clock through the thick, masculine air proved that time, was not in fact, standing still. My heart raced, awaiting some sort of resolution to this testosterone charged dilemma. I decided to back my way out altogether, figuring it best to just let boys be boy, but Howard had different plans.

He spoke choppy and staccato like Captain Kirk having a bad day. "Can - I - talk - to - you? Please? Upstairs?" Then he turned to Colt and with emphasis, said, "IN OUR BEDROOM?" I didn't have a choice really, because he grabbed me by the elbow and guided me, not so gently, down the hall and up the stairs.

Colt called after us, "Don't worry about me! I'll just be fixing your toilet!"

Howard closed the bedroom door and sat down on the bed. He was taking deep breaths with his eyes closed, his head in his hands. I felt bad for him although I didn't know why. I should have felt good that he felt bad. Hadn't he been jerking me around for the last week? But still, something down deep told me something more was going on. I sat down next to him and put my hand on his leg for comfort.

"I'm sorry," I said.

"No. I'm sorry. This is my fault. I guess," he said. A few more deep breaths.

"Truth?" I said. "There's no guessing about it. It is your fault." It felt good, at least to get that off my chest. He looked like a sad puppy dog – the creep.

"Why is he here?" He knew how to get to a girl with those sad eyes.

"It's sort of a . . . well, it's really a long story. It's not what you think."

"What do I think?"

"I suppose you think I'm trying to get back at you by asking him here."

"That's what I think. Why didn't you tell me the toilet was running?"

"Didn't think of it," I said. "It's not really something that's weighing on my mind right now, you know?"

He nodded in an understanding sort of way. We were both quiet for a moment. He looked at me and now his sad puppy dog eyes had turned dark and dreamy. I was melting. He leaned in and kissed me softly on the lips. It was the kiss that won me over on our first date, and again when we met years later at the wedding. Soft. Long. Sweet. He pulled back. We looked at each other for what seemed like hours. Part of me wanted another kiss. The other part of me wanted to grab his cheating little neck and choke the life right out of him. He finally broke the silence. "What do you mean it's a long story?" he asked.

I couldn't believe my ears. "Is that all you have to say?"

"What?"

"You come in here, act all mad, then you go all puppy-dog sad, then you kiss me, THEN you want to interrogate me?!" I was on a rampage.

"Well, you bring HIM into our house for some reason that is a 'long story' and you don't think I have a right to ask?" He was shouting now also. So much for soft, sweet kisses. "And I wasn't interrogating! Trust me, you don't want to see me interrogating!" We both stopped shouting and blinked at each other for a second. That was a strange thing to say.

"What did you say?"

"What?" He shrugged. He was playing stupid and I snapped.

"Get out!" I shouted.

"What?"

"Get out! I'm sick of this. Either poop or get off the pot, Mister! Why the hell did you come anyway? You move out for God knows what reason, but you keep coming around." My arms were flying every which way and my face was red hot.

"It's my house too. I wanted to see the girls."

"I don't care. You chose to leave with your little two-second, half-assed 'I need space' explanation. Give me a break. We all know what that means. Listen up, and listen good: don't come around here anymore until you decide what it is you want. Well, except, maybe could you come mow the lawn and rake the leaves tomorrow? It needs it bad."

"No!"

"No?"

"No!"

"Fine!" I said, "Then I'll just ask Colt to do it!"

"Fine!" and he stomped out.

"Fine!" I shouted down the hall. "Fine!" I almost started crying until I remembered I wasn't supposed to do that anymore. I stopped myself mid-sniffle. Thankfully, most of the shouting had occurred in our bedroom, so hopefully we hadn't woken Bethany or Amber. I was sure Callie was probably still awake, which meant she probably heard it – I would have to deal with that later.

My marriage appeared to be flat-lining with the introduction of the Colt complication. Life was just peachy. I made it downstairs just in time to hear

Howard slamming the front door. I found Colt in the family room sitting on the couch, as I had expected earlier, drinking a beer and watching football. He looked up when I walked in. "That went well," he said.

"Oh, shut up. This is all your fault," I said.

He covered his heart with his hand. "I'm hurt! After I came all this way to fix your toilet and everything! So ungrateful." He was shaking his head in mock sadness.

"Okay, you're right. It's not your fault. It's . . . it's just crummy. Plain crummy. And I'm not going to cry!" I shook my finger at him to make my point.

"That's good, because I don't want you to cry. Do you want a hug anyway?" he asked.

"Sure." And we sat on my couch and I cuddled him like he was a big, comfortable teddy bear. That's how I fell asleep.

The next thing I knew, the sun was up and the kitchen was apparently ablaze with activity. Pans were clanging, dishes were banging and girls were giggling. I was covered with the big blue down comforter from my bed and my pillow was under my head. For the first time in days, I felt almost well rested. Finally, a decent night's sleep. I got up and padded my way to the kitchen to see what all the ruckus was about. Colt was bouncing around with a spatula and a spoon conjuring some creation at the stove. The girls were all dressed for school and setting the table. Wow. Things were never this organized in the morning when I ran the show. I always seemed to be two steps behind where I should have been and yelling for everyone to move faster.

"Mornin', Curly!" Colt said when he saw me. "Primo java for the sleepy one." And he handed me a jumbo mug of hot coffee. "Cream and sugar, just the way you like it," he said, with a bow. Boy, was he pouring on the schmaltz. I smiled anyway. What woman doesn't like to be treated like royalty?

"Sit down Mommy!" said Bethany. "We made breakfast for you! Your favorite – banana and chocolate chip pancakes!" Bethany pulled out a chair for me as Amber wobbled over with a platter of pancakes so big she could barely see over them. I held my breath, sure she was going to tumble right over, pancakes, platter and all. Callie swooped in at the last minute and helped her lower the platter down to the table gracefully.

"This is so wonderful!" I cried, rubbing my hands together in anticipation of a yummy breakfast. It had been a long time since anyone had fixed ME breakfast. Especially banana and chocolate chip pancakes. I was pretty sure Howard didn't even know how to use a pan, much less whip up my favorite breakfast in one.

We all ate joyfully and then the girls, all on their very own, trekked off at their various times to the bus stop – Callie first since her bus came earlier, then Bethany and Amber a little while later. When the house was quiet again, Colt and I sat in silence at the table, enjoying more coffee and some reflection time. After many quiet sips, Colt spoke up.

"Sorry about last night – that thing with Howie," he said. "Wish I knew what's up with that dude."

"You and me both," I sighed.

"He's being a real asshole."

"Yeah, well, he's my asshole. We'll work it out. I guess." I didn't sound convincing, even to myself.

"Do you mind if I ask a personal question?"

"Shoot."

He leaned a bit over the table. "Have you two been having problems for a long time?"

"I didn't even know we were having problems! Honest." I put my hand up as if taking an oath. "This came out of the blue. One day he says he's moving out and BOOM – he's gone."

Colt contemplated my answer for a moment, while rubbing his chin, then asked, "How was the sex?"

"Okay – that's too personal."

"Well, you know, these things are important to a man."

"The sex was FINE."

"You know, we like it pretty often . . . "

"Three times a week good enough for you?" He was getting my goat. And I might have been exaggerating about the three times a week. Just a little.

"That's a start . . ."

"I'm telling you that the sex was GREAT and we seemed happy as clams, the next day he says he needs space and he moves out. Got it?" While I considered Colt a very good friend, the topic of sex was a little too friendly.

"Got it. You want me to talk to him for you?" he asked.

"No. That would definitely make things worse."

We sat in silence again, contemplating my sad marital state.

"So," Colt finally said, changing the subject. "Contrary to popular belief, I did not come here to assist you in your plumbing needs. I'm here to talk you out of this cockamamie scheme of yours. Possibly we can find you another hobby. Scrapbooking perhaps? Or how about curling. I mean, the Canadians love it and they're pretty cool, so it must be good."

I crunched my brow and crossed my arms. "Scrapbooking?"

"Don't forget the curling. Another attractive option."

Sighing, I fiddled with a fork on the table. "Actually," I smiled, "I have started working on a website – remember the movie review website I talked about a few years ago?"

He snapped his fingers trying to remember. "FlickChick . . . FilmChick . . . TicTac . . ."

"ChickAtTheFlix."

"Dot com. Right." He sat up straight in his chair. "Now that's what I'm talking about. Great idea, lots of potential. Here, I'll go get my computer and you can show me."

"But," I said, stopping him. "I'm still doing this."

"By this, you mean the house, the monkeys . . ."

I nodded.

"I can't talk you out of it? There's always archery. You could pretend the target was Howard. The bull's-eye could be his balls."

While that was an interesting option, I still shook my head.

Colt stood up. "Well then," he said, "We have some work to do today. Do you have your list?"

"You're really going to help me?" I asked.

"You think I'm going to let you have all the fun? I'm nice, but I'm not THAT nice."

"Yes! You're wonderful!" I stood up to kiss him on the cheek. "I'm going to take a shower and get dressed. Then we can get started."

"You in the shower. I like that image."

"Stop that now," I said, shaking my finger at him

He put his hands innocently in the air. "Hey, I have an active imagination, what can I say? Remember, I HAVE seen you naked before."

"You'd better go take a cold shower, buddy. Besides, it's been twenty-five years since you've seen this body naked. Things are drooping that I didn't know could droop. Put that in your active imagination," I said walking off toward my bedroom. Once I arrived, I locked the door behind me. Colt, in a playful mood, was capable of just about anything. And quite frankly, the way I was feeling, I didn't know if I was capable of resisting a playful Colt.

After showering it took me longer than usual to dress. I wanted to look good, but not too good. Of course, I didn't want to LOOK like I was trying to look good, but not too good. I didn't want to dress down either. Because I did want to look good. I finally decided on jeans – not the baggy ones, but the Calvins that fit just right. I added a long sleeved tee that hugged my curves rather nicely, if I do say so myself, and went down just low enough, but not too low. And it was a simple green, which did bring out my eyes, but wasn't dressy enough to look like I picked it out on purpose. It was a tightly choreographed outfit that didn't look planned at all. At least, that's what I hoped.

Then there was the makeup – just a bit. A little mascara because I looked like the walking dead without it. Some foundation under the eyes to hide the circles still hanging around from many sleepless nights. A tad bit of rouge to wake up my face. Some clear gloss on the lips. There. Beautiful, but not obviously so. Man. Being a woman was a lot of work.

I finally made it downstairs about 9:30. Colt was at my front door, talking to some woman that I didn't recognize. The layout of our neighborhood – no sidewalks and houses set far apart on large lots – wasn't naturally inviting to door-to-door sales, so I wasn't accustomed to strangers knocking on my door. My suspicion antennae went up.

Colt stepped back when he saw me come downstairs.

"Hey, Curly, this nice woman just came by to talk with you." He was acting a little strange, even for Colt, and I swear he tried to wink at me when he had his back to her.

"To me?" I said.

"Yes," said the stern looking lady. She was strikingly tall – nearly six feet. Dark hair pulled back tight against her head. No makeup. She wore black jeans, black hiking boots and a purple fleece vest over a black turtleneck. Her demeanor was all business, although I hadn't figured out what business that might be. She didn't have a bible in her hand, so I was ruling out any saving of my soul. She extended her rough, worn hand for a shake and introduction.

"My name is Patricia Webber," she said. "I'd like to speak with you if you don't mind."

"Well," I hesitated. "I guess that depends on what you want to speak about."

"I'm with PETA," she said matter-of-factly.

"PETA?" I asked. Colt answered before she could.

"People for the Ethical Treatment of ANIMALS," he said. Then he did it again, and I knew I had seen it right this time. That dirty devil winked at me.

Chapter 9

Colt intercepted the conversation. "Excuse me," he said to the lady, "we'll be right back." Then he closed the door on poor Ms. Webber's frowny pinched face.

"Well that was kind of rude," I said.

"Yeah, whatever. Now listen. This woman thinks she's going to get information from us, but what she doesn't realize is that we're going to get what we need from HER. Let her ask her questions, and you go ahead and answer – unless I give you a signal. If I give you a signal, don't say anything and let me do the talking. You understand?"

"Not really. What kind of information would she have for us?"

"Who's the PI here?" Roger that.

"What's the signal?" I asked.

"Um, okay, let's see . . . I'll kick you."

"No you won't!"

"Yeah, you're right, that's too obvious. I'll . . . cough. That's it. If I cough, you let me take over. Got it?"

"I guess. You're the pro." Although, increasingly I was losing confidence in that fact.

"In more ways than you know." Colt winked again before opening the door to Patricia, who looked none too happy.

"I'm so sorry," I said. "My friend here was just, uh, a little concerned – you know, a strange person coming and asking me questions. He's a little over protective." I tried to act as apologetic as possible without being obsequious.

"I'm not strange," she stated rather emphatically. By the looks of her, I wasn't so sure.

"I'm sure you're not," I said. "Won't you come in? Can I get you something? Some tea? Coffee? Water?"

"Nothing, thank you. I won't take much of your time."

I guided her to the living room where she chose to sit in one of my high-backed wing chairs. She had a rather large, black bag slung over her shoulder, which she laid on the floor at her feet. She pulled out a red spiral notebook and a pen. Colt and I sat on the couch. "I suppose you know why I'm here," she said.

"Probably," I said. "Monkeys?"

"Precisely. Monkeys. Do you know what kind of monkeys those were in your trees, Mrs. Marr?" Wow, this woman knew my name and everything. I was guessing she knew what kind of monkeys those were too. Colt coughed. Geez! I didn't even get to answer the first question?

"Actually. . . . Ms. Webber, was it? She does know what kind of Monkeys those were," he said.

I cocked my head toward him in confusion. I was quite sure that I didn't know what kind of monkeys they were.

"What she wants to know," he continued, "is how did you come upon the news that she had monkeys in her trees?"

Ms. Webber pursed her thin, colorless lips. "We have our ways, Mr. . . I'm sorry, I didn't get your name . . ."

"That's because I didn't give it to you," he said. Ms. Webber's lips pursed together even tighter. She looked like she had eaten a lemon while being constipated. She blinked a couple of times, straightened her back then turned her attention back to me.

"Mrs. Marr, I came here to see if you could be of any help to us with important information. Are you at all interested in answering my questions today?"

Colt coughed.

Geez! I turned to him. "Can't I answer one lousy question?"

"What?" he said, giving us the innocent act. "I coughed. I might be coming down with something." He coughed again then got up to leave the room, tripping over Ms. Webber's bag on his way out. I gave him an irritated glare then returned my attention back to the testy Ms. Webber.

"I'm sorry. Please. Ask away."

She questioned me mainly on the topic of the monkeys on my property. Where did I first see the monkeys? How many did I see? Did anyone else see the monkeys? Who did I call when I discovered them? Yada, yada, yada. They were actually some very obvious and un-inspired questions. I thought I could have done better. She scribbled notes periodically as I gave my answers. It was all very benign. Oddly, she didn't ask me about the three dead monkeys found in House of Many Bones. I was certainly expecting a question or two about those sad little creatures. Not that I could have relayed much information since I hadn't actually seen them myself. Yet, certainly, since they were dead, she should be more interested in them. I would think they probably weren't treated very ethically, after all. Maybe she didn't know about them. I considered bringing up the subject, but stopped myself. Colt was adamant that we only get information from her, not vice versa.

Her final question was a little odd and seemingly non sequitur. "Mrs. Marr, I was wondering, do you know anything about a man named Tito Buttaro?"

"Tito Buttaro?" I laughed. "Sounds like a character from The Godfather. Why? Is he a monkey-smuggler or something?"

She blinked and pursed those sourpuss lips again. "Can I take that as a 'No', then?" she asked.

"As far as I am aware, I do not know anyone by that name."

"Thank you for your time, Mrs. Marr," she said, standing up and throwing her bag back over her shoulder. She nearly threw my arm out of its socket with her vigorous, good-bye shake. Still no smile. She made her way briskly and stiffly to the front door and let herself out. Colt came back into the living room when she was gone. He was munching on a newly ripe banana.

"Boy, those PETA people sure are a lively bunch, huh? I'll bet she's a real hoot at parties," I said.

"She's not PETA." Masticated banana slurred his words.

"What?"

"She's not PETA. She's a Fed. FBI baby!" Colt was bouncing around me, fake punching like he was a heavy-weight. Half-eaten banana in one hand. He was obviously very proud of himself. Still a kid at heart.

"FBI? Do you think so?" I asked.

"Don't think so. Know so." He stopped doing his Rocky imitation long enough to lick his fingers.

"How?"

"I saw her badge." The bouncing recommenced. Bounce, bounce, punch. The air was getting a real beating.

"When?" I couldn't believe it.

"Man, Curly, what the hell have you gotten yourself into here? You've got Feds coming in posing as PETA guys. I mean, there's something rotten in the State of Denmark if they're not willing to identify themselves as FBI." My head was swirling with this information.

"When did you see her badge?" I asked again.

"Oh, that piece of investigative work?" He bounded to the kitchen with the banana peel, telling his story more loudly as he went. "That's when I tripped over her bag. No accident." I heard the trashcan lid drop. "She didn't even notice because I was so slick." He returned with a self-satisfied smile on his boyish face. "That's what you can call me now – Slick. Slick Baron." He plopped on the couch.

"Oh, and her name isn't Patricia," he added. "It's Marjorie."

Chapter 10

"What?" I felt as if someone had pulled a rug out from under me. I grabbed the wing chair for support.

"Curly, you look bad."

"What did you say her name was?"

"Marjorie. Why?"

Suddenly feeling very sick, I grabbed my stomach and groaned. "How do you know that? Was it on her badge? Was there a last name?"

"No, it was embossed on her wallet. First name only. While I AM good at what I do, I have to say, she's not a very good agent. She should have closed that bag up better."

I groaned again.

"Am I missing something here?" Colt asked.

Feeling weak in the knees, I moved to the couch. "I have to sit."

"Tell me what's going on."

"Maybe she didn't care about the monkeys at all," I pondered out loud.

"Do you think it's about the dead guy?"

"Not the dead guy either. I think it's about Howard. But it just doesn't make sense. Why would he leave me for her? I mean, I know I'm not very objective, but I don't really think she was very good looking, do you?"

"What in the world are you talking about?"

"Certainly she's not brimming over with personality…"

"Curly, you're worrying me here."

I told Colt about finding the paper with Marjorie Smith's name and phone number and expressed my fears that he wasn't buying a couch, but was actually embroiled in a passionate love affair.

"Why didn't you tell me about this earlier?"

"Because saying it out loud makes it feel more real."

"Well," he answered in reply, "it's been a long time since Howdy Doody and I have been buddy-buddy, but I've got to say, I just don't think she's his type. Give me a break. Her over you?" He shook his head. "Nope. I think you're barking up the wrong tree here. The name thing is a coincidence. He's probably out buying that couch from Marjorie Smith right now, while FBI Marjorie dreams up another undercover persona."

I wasn't convinced. In my wild imagination, Marjorie Smith and FBI Marjorie were one and same. She was checking me out. Howard told her about the monkeys in my trees so she used that as an opportunity to scope out the scene. She was figuring out how to wear me down – get me out of the picture. She was FBI – she had a gun.

I ran my theory by Colt. "Think about it, she could snuff me out in a snap and hide the evidence easy. Plausible, right?" I asked.

"Plausible, not. Listen," he said, sitting next to me on the couch and putting his arm around me, "you're getting way too paranoid here. Howie The Boy Scout would never have an affair. He loves you too much. Shit. I was there the first time he laid eyes on you – he fell in love with you then and he never stopped loving you. Not for a minute."

"You think so? You never told me that."

"Yeah? Well, there's a reason."

"Why?"

"Because he wasn't the only one that fell in love with you that night."

Awkward moment of silence. Colt quietly picked at a straying thread on his jeans. I watched him pick, not sure what to say next. His words made me happy and sad at the same time. Truthfully, I had my feelings for Colt too, but I loved my husband, despite everything.

"Thank you," I said, finally.

"For what?"

"Everything."

Something suddenly occurred to me. "Why were you peeking in her bag to begin with? What were you looking for?"

"I thought you'd never ask! I had my doubts about her from the minute I opened the door. Take PETA – those boys are all over the internet. They've got guys on the inside – whistleblowers, decoys, the whole nine yards. They're pretty much in the know. Especially about Meadowland. They have whole web pages dedicated to Meadowland monkey abuse. It just didn't seem like they'd bother to send someone out here, even if they do know about the little guys swinging around here in your cozy little woods – which they probably do." He shook his head. "They've got bigger fish to fry. Plus, that chick just looked to me like she was trying too hard to look PETA, you know? Boy, I'm still hungry. Do you have any apples?"

"In the fridge." We got up and moved our way to the kitchen.

"By the way," he said, "we do know what kind of monkeys they were – Rhesus Macaque." He opened the refrigerator door, pulled an apple out of the crisper and crunched into it before continuing. "They're called "Old World" monkeys – they're used for testing across the board – psycho-pharmaceuticals, AIDS drugs, vaccines, you name it – because they're the primate most closely related to humans. Here, take a look." He grabbed his laptop from the corner of the dining room where he had it plugged in. It turned out that while I was asleep, Colt had gotten a head start on the investigating. Callie had taken a cell phone photo of the monkeys, and she showed it to him, so he used that to compare to images on the internet. I had to admit, he was good.

He showed me a website with a picture of the same kind of monkey as those that had been in my trees. Only this monkey was tied down and hooked up to wires. The story related horrors of hideous experiments perpetrated on the poor little creatures. One story in particular went into great detail about researchers opening up the skulls of monkeys, then inserting implants with electrodes into their brains, taking "measurements" the whole while. Another described a psychiatric experiment where the primates were tortured and abused to the point of complete and utter mental upset, then given different doses of anti-psychotic drugs to test the drugs' "effectiveness." It was all just too horrible and nauseating.

After viewing several different websites, I had to stop reading. I was certainly starting to see that Meadowland Labs had something to hide. I wasn't making the FBI connection though. It actually would have made more sense to me if the creepy lady had been from PETA.

"Why did you suspect she was a Fed?" I asked, although the word "Fed" sounded alien coming out of my mouth. They only say cool in-the-know-words like that in the movies and spy novels. I felt way out of my domestic element.

"I didn't think she was an agent! Are you kidding me? But I thought she was suspicious. I'll tell you what – it's very obvious that whatever is going on here is *muy, muy grande*. How long did you say that house has been vacant?"

"The policeman said twenty-nine years."

"Do you think any of your neighbors around here have been here that long or longer?" he asked.

I laughed. "Are you kidding me? When people move to Rustic Woods, they die in Rustic Woods. They never leave. Most of the people on our street are retirees."

"Great!" he said, clapping his hands. "Let's go talk to some old people."

"But I already told you, no one talks about that house."

"They don't talk to YOU about that house," he smiled. "But let's see what we learn applying a bit of the ol' Colt Baron charm."

White Willow Circle, like many residential streets in Rustic Woods, ended in a cul-de-sac. The Perkins lived next to Roz in a two-story brick front colonial. They were a nice couple, whose children were grown with children of their own. They were a cute, short little pair bordering on the rotund. Mr. Perkins looked about five foot three at most, and Mrs. Perkins was at least three or four inches shorter. Whenever I saw them, I was reminded of the Weebles toys that my brother used to play with as a toddler – Weebles wobble but they don't fall down.

Mr. Perkins had been a career civilian working for the Navy. He retired shortly after we moved into the neighborhood five years ago. They've always been friendly and helpful to Howard and me, so I had no reservations in pressing them further regarding House of Many Bones. Colt and I walked out the door and right into Roz, who was coming for a mid-morning visit. I suspected that she was aware of a strange man staying at my house and was on a fact-finding mission of her own.

"Hi there!" she said, smiling at Colt. "Who's this? Find a replacement for Howard already?"

"Hey, Roz," I said. "This is Colt Baron – my friend from California." Roz smiled as recognition of the name lit up her face. I had mentioned Colt more than once, and she knew our history. She also knew Howard didn't care for him a whole lot.

"Oh! Hello! I know ALL about you!" she said. Colt grinned his boyish grin. He liked being infamous.

"I hear that all the time," he said.

I made my introductions. "Colt, Roz Walker. She lives in that house there." I turned to Colt. "Roz was with me when I was snooping around the vacant house – that one over there."

"You told him?" asked Roz.

"Told him everything – he's here to help," I said

"Oh! That's right – you're a Dick."

"Roz!" I screamed.

"Well, that's what they call you guys, right? A private Dick?" she explained.

Colt laughed. "I think that was in the days of Bogart and Cagney films," he said. "Curly, here, is a little worried, so I came to offer professional and emotional support. Do you know the Perkins too? We're going over to talk to them now."

"Curly, huh? We have pet names." She slid me a sideways glance. "Interesting . . . well, yes, I do know the Perkins. Mind if I come along?"

"Not at all – in fact, you two are the neighbors here. You can introduce me, then just step back and let me work my magic."

We started across my front yard toward the Perkins' house. Roz was smiling and looking at Colt's butt, which did look delicious in his faded jeans. "He's cute," she whispered in my ear. "Where do you find these guys? His hair is perfect!"

"He's just a friend," I whispered back. Colt was walking just slightly in front of us. "I can hear you," he said playfully. I knew him. Even though I couldn't see his face, I knew he was smiling like a Cheshire cat and thoroughly enjoying the attention.

"I wish I had friends like yours," she smiled with a hint of jealousy.

I knocked on my neighbors' door. I was pretty sure they were home – Mrs. Perkins' spotless burgundy Impala was in the driveway. We stood for several seconds, expecting someone to open the door, but it didn't happen. I knocked again.

"Maybe they're not home." Colt said.

"Nah – her car is in the driveway," said Roz. "They're home."

Poor Mr. Perkins had failing eyesight which forced him to give up the joy of driving two or three years back, hence, their only car was the new Impala which Mrs. Perkins drove like she was in the Indy 500. I often thought that it was probably a good thing Mr. Perkins couldn't see so well, figuring he might suffer a heart attack if he could actually observe even half of the traffic rules she broke while transporting him around town.

"Maybe they're taking a nap or something. I don't want to bother them," I said.

Roz thought we should try one more time, so I knocked again, louder this time. This time we heard shuffling behind the door. They didn't own any pets, so we knew at least one person was in the house.

"Mrs. Perkins?" I shouted. "Mr. Perkins? It's Barb and Roz!" More shuffling, but the door didn't open.

"Maybe we caught them in the middle of a little afternoon delight," Colt proposed.

Roz and I scrunched up our faces at that thought. Reaching past me, Roz rapped again and called out. "Hello! Hello! Is anyone home?" Finally, the door opened a crack – just enough to expose a small portion of Mrs. Perkins' tiny, round spectacled face and nothing more.

"Hey, Mrs. Perkins. How are you?" Roz said as she looked way down at the little lady behind the door. "We didn't catch you in the middle of anything did we?"

"Noo . . . ," Mrs. Perkins said, hesitating in a very obvious way.

"We were wondering if we could ask you a couple of questions," I said.

"About what?" She was still hiding half behind the door. Any day of the week, squatty Mrs. Perkins was the very definition of the friendly neighbor. Always smiling when she greeted people – always ready to stop and chitchat. She's even been known to drop by with a plate full of freshly baked chocolate chip cookies or a yummy batch of lemon bars. Now she stood cowering behind her door with a suspicious scowl. It didn't appear that an offer of cookies or lemon bars was forthcoming. I was perplexed and bewildered. What had happened to this sweet woman?

I continued, despite her scowl. "About the vacant house," I said. "I suppose you saw the activity over there a couple of days ago – my friend here . . ." I was about to introduce Colt, but she cut me off at the pass.

"Why can't you just leave well enough alone!" she shouted. I was taken aback. "You should never have gone snooping over there you nosy. . . nosy . . . ," she was shaking and stuttering and looking most suspiciously at Colt. Then she looked me in the eye. "You nosy little slut! You have no idea what you're getting yourself into. Just stop! You'll ruin it for us all!" She slammed the door in our faces. We heard the dead bolt turn and snap.

"She called me a slut!" My feelings were hurt. "How does being nosy make me a slut?" I turned to Roz accusingly. "Did you tell her that Howard moved out?"

"No!" she said crossing her heart. "I swear."

Colt put his arm around my shoulder. "I wouldn't take it personally, Curly," he said. "She was obviously upset. It probably didn't have anything to do with you. However – we must be on the right track. These people obviously know SOMETHING." I was still stewing over being called a slut. I didn't think that was necessary. All I did was look in an empty house, find a rotting human head, and faint. I didn't have an orgy in there. Geez! Roz, however, seemed to be enjoying herself, and since no one had called her a slut, she felt like moving right along.

"Maybe if the Perkins know something," she said, "someone else does too. We can probably find someone willing to talk. How about the MacMillans?" They lived next to the Perkins.

"They're out of town," I said, still sulking.

"Since when?" she asked.

"Since yesterday morning. I saw them pack up their RV and drive off."

Roz put her hands on her hips and a queried look crossed her face. "That's strange, they usually let me know when they're leaving and ask me to pick up their papers."

Just then, we saw Maxine, huarache sandals and all, being towed down the street by Puddles the poodle. Maxine lived one street over on Red Maple Leaf Lane. According to Maxine, she and her now deceased husband had been the first to build a house on their street over thirty years ago. Roz and I looked at each other. Maxine knew everything there was to know about anything in this neighborhood. She smiled when she saw us and stopped – we introduced her to Colt.

"I see you are monkey-free today, eh?" she said with a smile. "Monkeys in Rustic Woods – I've seen it all now."

We questioned her about House of Many Bones while Puddles yapped and tugged in an attempt to move on. With all of his ten pounds of gray, curly-furred fury, he was going nowhere fast and let everyone know as much. Maxine said she had no idea who owned the house, but she had heard about our little fiasco and she was quick to give us an answer about why the Perkins wouldn't talk, why the MacMillans suddenly left town, and why no one else on White Willow Circle would cough up information. She shook her head at us. "Girls, girls, girls. You are stirring up some very old and very scary history here."

"Scary, like, ghost scary?" I asked.

"No, honey," she yanked on Puddles leash. "Scary, like, anyone talks, they get kneecapped scary," she said. The three of us took turns looking bug-eyed at each other.

"Are you saying what I think you're saying?" asked Colt.

"You ever see that movie. . . what was it called . . . ?" She was sniffing the air to remember the word. "Oh, it had that handsome Robert DeNiro . . . Good People? Good Men?"

"Goodfellas?" I offered. I knew my Robert DeNiro movies.

Maxine shot her arm in the air. "That's it! Well, think along those lines. Capishie?"

"Are you saying," Roz said, "That people are afraid of the Mafia? In Rustic Woods, Virginia?"

"You said it, honey, not me!"

Chapter 11

Roz and I stood there with our jaws hanging like droopy drawers on a toddler. Colt was silently cool as a cucumber, which had me wondering. Puddles was yipping up a storm so Maxine had to move along. "Listen," she said being tugged away, "there's not much more I can tell you, but honestly, be careful. My suggestion is to leave well enough alone. Drop the whole thing. Forget it ever happened. The stuff I've heard was through the grapevine, but I never thought it was idle rumor. People were scared – for real."

We thanked her for the information.

"Wow," said Roz.

"Holy cow," I said.

"Mama Mia," said Colt.

I started shivering again. Colt peeled off his leather bomber jacket and slipped it over my shoulders.

We stood in the middle of White Willow Circle, stupefied. Honestly, I couldn't get my mind around the idea of the Mafia in sleepy little Rustic Woods. It seemed too absurd to be true – as if someone had just told me Arnold Schwarzenegger was set to play the lead in Brokeback Mountain II. The two just didn't go together. I was about to express my doubts when I caught sight of Howard's black Camry rounding the corner. It moved slowly toward us. Lovely, I thought. The last thing I wanted to witness was a sequel to the Battle of the Manly-Men played out in the middle of my street. I wasn't in the mood. I turned to Colt wagging a harsh finger in his face. "Don't tell him what Maxine just said, okay? He'll get all weird – weirder than he's already acting. I'm just not up for it." Frankly, I was seething mad that he was ignoring my edict from last night. He sure had a lot of nerve.

"Sure. Whatever you say," he said seriously. Geez. He wasn't even smiling. Colt would smile through a 9.0 earthquake that was happening in the middle of a category five hurricane during a nuclear meltdown. Something wasn't right.

Howard pulled the Camry into our driveway, got out of his car and moved intently toward our little huddle in the street. I knew this was a visit with a mission – he wasn't just in the neighborhood. This was fishy behavior – the middle of the day? I looked at my watch. Ten forty-nine. Still morning, actually. Too early for lunch. Howard never left work during the day. To be sure, the bugger was up to something.

He walked right up to us, barely acknowledged Roz, much less me, his wife. Today must have been a no-suit day because he was decked out in his jeans and tennis shoes, topped off with his ratty Redskins sweatshirt. Some days Howard had to sport a suit to work, and others he was able to do the casual jeans thing. I was never privy to the whys of suit-day or no-suit day.

I got a grim look and terse nod of the head. He was still mad. Whatever. I had Mafioso problems. He could go fly a kite for all I cared. He held his hand out to Colt for a friendly shake. "Hey buddy, I want to apologize about last night," he said. *What?!* He hadn't called Colt "Buddy" since 1983. Asshole, maybe. Peckerbrain, possibly. Definitely not "Buddy." Fishy had just got a whole lot fishy-er. I crossed my arms suspiciously.

"Sure, dude," replied Colt in kind. "I understand. No problemo."

"So, can I talk to you for a minute?" Howard asked him. "In private?"

"Sure," answered Colt. "Step into my office." And he pointed to my backyard! Off they walked, like I wasn't even there.

"Hey!" I shouted. "What about me? Don't you want to talk to me?" Howard looked back and answered without batting an eyelash. "No."

I threw up my arms.

"I thought you told me they didn't even like each other," said Roz. "Doesn't Howard, you know . . .hate Colt?"

"He sure did last night!" I said.

"Maybe it's a trap. Maybe Howard's planning on jumping him when they're alone. Should we call the police?"

"And say what? That two men are being civil towards each other in my backyard? I don't think so." Besides, with my luck, Officer Brad would show up again. And quite truthfully, I'd had enough of police and FBI agents in the last few days to last a lifetime.

Roz and I stood like goons in the middle of the street while I pondered possible reasons for the frat boy reunion. Curiosity eventually got the better of me, and I left her to wander around the side of my house just enough to peek at them, hopefully without them seeing me. There they stood. Colt with his hands in his jeans pockets, nodding, while Howard seemed to control the conversation. He wasn't yelling or moving his arms around wildly like a madman. It was, in fact, two men, acting civil toward each other in my backyard.

I looked back to Roz. She had moved to the side of the road because Peggy was pulling up in her van. I walked back to where they had convened, Roz talking to Peggy through her rolled down window while her engine idled. Peggy's red hair was pulled up haphazardly in a high of pony tail that sort of flopped to one side and I could see through the window she was wearing her favorite sweat shirt declaring, "*Kiss Me, I'm Italian.*"

"Holy canoli!" she cried when she saw me. "I was just telling Roz – you're not going to believe this! I don't have long – gotta run and get my dry-cleaning and supper for tonight before the kids get home – but I just had to tell you!" She was revved up in major excitement mode. "So," she continued, "I was talking to my sister, whose cousin-in-law was the maid-of-honor for the Rhinehold's daughter."

"Who?" I asked, my head swimming from trying to connect the dots.

"Which one? My sister or her cousin-in-law?"

"The Rhineholds."

"Oh, them," she said. "They used to own your house!"

"That's not who we bought it from," I said.

"That doesn't surprise me. They moved out, according to my sister, a really long, long time ago."

"You mean, like maybe twenty nine years ago?" Roz asked.

"Si, Signora! So anyway, Annie – my sister – says that her cousin-in-law – Mary Alice I think her name is – told her that the old lady Rhinehold got really drunk at the wedding and started burbling something about moving to White Willow Circle was the worst mistake they'd ever made, and she was rambling on about crooks. She kept repeating it, crooks, crooks, crooks and about how everybody's lives had been ruined "that night," and she had to move all those years ago because of "that awful night" and "that awful man." They had to sedate her and carry her out of the wedding reception. Poor Maggie." She shook her head.

"Who's Maggie?" I asked

"Maggie Rhinehold – the bride. So anyway, it gets better. I know Maggie because we went to school together and she used to date my brother's best friend, Leo, until Leo went to juvy for trying to rob a hot dog stand . . . or was it a drive-thru photo mat?" Peggy had her index finger on her chin, attempting to sort out her own confusion, while Roz and I tried our best to be patient with her. Finally she shook her head and waved her hand as if ridding herself of that thought. "Anyway, this was too good to pass up, so I called her. Maggie, I mean. Although she's Maggie Temple now." Leave it to Peggy. No story left un-turned. "Well, she started crying as soon as I asked her about it because I guess it was like opening old wounds. She said her mother told her years later that they left this neighborhood because something 'scandalous' and 'dangerous' happened over there one night at your Boney House. Something no one will talk about, because the next day, a bunch of sleazy, mean Italian-looking guys came around threatening them that if they said anything, bad things would happen. She said she was standing back in the hallway where her parents couldn't see her while these thugs sat in her living room talking to her parents. She said her mother was crying when they left."

"Wow," said Roz.

"Holy cow," I said again. "Does she know who they were?"

"She said vividly remembers the face of the head honcho – and that she saw his picture in the paper a few years ago as part of an article about infamous men in the – get this – the Mafia. Some guy named . . . oh, geez, what did she say his name was . . . Jackson Five." She clicked her fingers as if the name would magically appear. "It was like one of the brothers in the Jackson Five . . . Lito . . . Frito . . . ."

"Tito?" I asked, nearly ready to lose it.

"That's it! Yeah! Tito . . . Tito . . . Tito Buttaro! That's it!" She looked at the clock on her dash. "Oh no! Gotta go! I want to be home when the kids get off the bus and I've got so much to do. I'll call you later! Isn't this cool?" And she whipped out of my driveway speeding off to the dry-cleaners.

I felt a little dizzy.

Roz looked at me. "Are you okay? You're white as a sheet. What did she say?"

"Tito Buttaro," I said.

"Yeah, so?"

I gave her the low down on my morning visit from the lady FBI agent posing as a PETA rep. Roz stared at me gaped-mouthed as I reiterated the living room questioning and how Colt made his discovery that the lady wasn't on the up and up. "The last question she asked me, before she left was did I know about a man named Tito Buttaro?"

"Get out!" she shrilled. "This is . . . I mean . . . I don't . . . Omigod."

My thoughts exactly.

Roz and I didn't have time to ponder over Peggy's new boatload of neighborhood history since Howard and Colt were coming back from their male-bonding experience. They both had their hands stuffed in their pockets, heads dropped pensively examining the tops of their shoes. Serious was stamped all over their faces. They stopped in front of us and Howard looked up. He gave me a weary sort of tentative smile and then looked at Colt.

"So, it was good talking to you again. Have a good trip back and good luck." He extended his hand again for a final shake goodbye.

"What?" I asked. "What trip back?"

"Oh. Yeah, well it turns out," Colt stammered, "I have to go back. Just got a call on my cell while Howie and I were shooting the shit – there's a, uh, problem, sort of, on this case I was working on in Century City. Gotta get back." He put his arm around me, and shook me around like I was his little sister. "But it's been real fun, Curly."

"I thought you said anything you needed to work on there you could do here," I said. I didn't know if I was sad, or mad that Howard had obviously scared him off. I was enjoying having him around and we were really on a roll with our investigation. Things were shaking up.

"Yeah, I know. Not this though. Sorry," he shrugged. "I'd better go in and make flight arrangements." And he was gone. I crossed my arms and shot Howard the evil eye. It was the evilest evil eye I could muster. Beelzebub would have cringed.

"What?" he whined.

"You know what! What did you say to him?" I shouted. Roz, not wanting to be in the line of fire, excused herself. "Call me later, Barb! It was good seeing you, Howard." She scooted off.

"I didn't say anything to him. I mean, I did, but I was just mending fences. I felt bad. We were best friends once, you know? I thought it was time. He's a good friend to you, and so I decided to make things right. That's all. He got the call while we were talking, like he said."

"Set things right? At eleven o'clock in the morning? You just left work to do that?"

"I'm not going to do it this time," he said.

"What?"

"Get in a fight with you. Not gonna do it." Then he did that George Clooney thing he does, where he kind of tilts his head and looks all cute and everything, and he smiles a little, but not a lot, and then I get all melty and woozy. He leaned over and kissed me softly on my neck. He lingered there just long enough for me to start feeling warm and tingly.

"I want to take you out to dinner tonight. Fiorenza's? I'll pick you up at seven." Then he kissed me on the lips. Ay Carumba. My poop-or-get-off-the-pot ultimatum was losing its force. Could I be strong? More importantly, would he really kiss me like that if he was in love with some other woman?

"I might have something to do," I said. Of course, I didn't have anything to do.

"Seven. We'll talk. We won't scream. I'll set things right with you, too," he said with a smile as he got in his car. I watched him drive off while I stood, alone in my driveway in a neighborhood riddled with death and deception and God knows what else.

A warmer than usual breeze blew through, tossing the trees around ever so slightly. I looked at the sky – a few puffy, gray and white clouds were moving in from the west, adding texture to the clear blue sky. I wondered if rain might be coming.

I was startled by a vibration against my hip and the faint sound of The Mission Impossible Theme song. It was Colt's jacket pocket. His right jacket pocket. I had forgotten I was still wearing it. I reached in and felt the vibrating object. I was pretty certain I knew what it was, but I pulled it out for a look-see, just to verify my suspicions. Bingo! Colt's cell phone. Now, how could he take a call on his cell phone when he didn't even have his cell phone with him? The sneaky creep. What was he up to?

I slipped the phone, whose display now read "MISSED CALL," back into the pocket and was about to storm up the driveway to confront Colt and find out why he and Howard were lying, when a shiny black Lincoln Town Car crept onto White Willow. It moved slowly past me, nearly stopping, but then continued slowly on. The windows were tinted so black that I couldn't see in. I watched as it made a tortuously slow turn in the cul-de-sac and came back, stopping right beside me. The driver's side window came down, revealing a man in a black wool coat wearing black leather gloves. By the crags and folds of skin on his square face, I guessed he was easily in his sixties, but his hair was jet black. It looked unnaturally black, so I was guessing he dipped into the Loreal. The black hair was jelled back and up high onto his head in what appeared to be a failed attempt to mimic Elvis Presley. His dark, droopy eyes screamed Italian ancestry.

Get a grip, I thought – my heart pounding. Maybe he was just lost and wanted directions. It happened all the time. Of course, not in my neighborhood, but there was a first time for anything. I guess. I was working up the courage to say something cute and quippy so I could appear innocent, but he beat me to the punch.

"Hey you," he said. I looked around. Not seeing anyone else, I pointed to myself and mouthed, "me?"

"Yeah, you. You think I'm talkin' to the fuckin' squirrels?"

I wanted to run, screaming at the top of my lungs, but my legs were wobbling like over-cooked spaghetti. The palms of my hands were juicing up and my armpits began dripping like two leaky radiators. At this rate, I'd dehydrate in about five minutes. That, or die from fright.

"I got a little present for you. Come here and get it," he said, holding up a shoebox-sized package wrapped in brown paper. I do a lot of stupid things, but taking that box was not going to be one of them.

"Oh, no thanks. I don't really know you . . . and . . ." I found some strength in my legs and started to move backwards when a man with a pug-dog face moved into my view from the passenger's seat and spoke.

"Listen, Snoopy," said Pug Mug, "we can do this the easy way, or we can do this the hard way." I was guessing the hard way would be taking a bullet from the small black gun he had conveniently pointed at my shaking body. Easy was good. I leapt forward, snatched the box from his hands and took four giant steps backward without asking Mother May I?

"That's better," said the Elvis impersonator. "There's a message with instructions in there. If I was you, I'd follow 'em, strict like, capisce?" The window motored back up to black and the car crept back down to the stop sign and turned away.

There I was, standing in the middle of the road, wanting desperately to move, but my legs weren't getting the orders from my frazzled brain. The synapses just kept misfiring. My body kept shaking from fear, yet I couldn't help but thinking that if I had read the scene in a movie script I would have laughed at how cliché it was. *Great*, I thought – *things just keep getting worse and worse, and to add insult to injury, when my life starts to imitate art, it has to imitate BAD art.* Suddenly, without warning, the dam broke and a flood was unleashed. I started crying buckets. I had finally broken down. No more Sigourney Weaver. No more Lieutenant Ripley, Alien Killer. I'd wimped out, big time. Huge, uncontrollable sobs wracked my whole body.

Colt was suddenly at my side. How he got there, I don't know, because I had lost touch of the world around me. "Curly! What's wrong?" he asked, enveloping me with his arms.

"I . . . *SOB* . . . I . . . *SOB* . . . *SOB* . . ."

He saw the package in my arms. "What's that?"

"I . . . don't . . . .know . . ." I felt like I was choking. "Man. . . *SOB, SOB.* . . . gun . . .a . . . GULP . . . message . . . *SOB* . . look." My whole body was in a spasm. Colt grabbed the box and tore off the brown wrapping in one swift move. He pulled up the top to peek in without letting me see the contents. He threw the top back down fast and blew out a strong breath. The color in his face drained away.

"You don't want to see this," he said. Even though I was terror stricken beyond reason, some inner voice shouted at me "Get a grip!" I managed to stop the sobs and wipe away the tears. Then the voice – sane, or insane, I'm not sure which – told me that I needed to see what was in that box. If that message was for me, the voice said, then I'd better darn well see what it had to say. I grabbed the box from Colt and threw off the top.

"Indiana Jones!" I screamed, seeing the curled up, stone-like figure of my now dead cat. On his lifeless body, was a folded piece of paper.

Chapter 12

Colt said that I didn't faint, but I have no memory of the several minutes after seeing Inidana's body in the box. The next thing I knew, I was sitting at my kitchen table wrapped in my warm, red fleece blanket sobbing and wringing my hands. My vision had tunneled, the periphery black. I put my attention on the blurry mug on the table next to me, until the blackness faded and it came into focus. There were voices and I tried to make them out. Colt. Roz. I was disoriented and didn't remember how I got there.

"Are you okay, sweetie? Barb?" It was Roz' voice. I looked down. She was kneeling on the floor looking up into my face. "Barb? Do you know where you are?" she asked.

I scanned the room. The fog was receding and I became aware of my surroundings. I felt cold and could see steam rising from the mug so I grabbed it with both hands. Oh, it was so warm. I wanted to warm my insides too. "Tea?" I asked, inquiring about the contents of the mug. Roz nodded. I pulled it off the table and slowly toward my lips. Still shivering like mad, I could barely drink without spilling. While I sipped haphazardly, the image of my dead cat popped into my mind.

"Omigod! Indiana Jones! They killed him!" I screamed, standing up.

"No they didn't!" said Roz soothingly, coaxing me back into my chair. "It wasn't Indiana. He's safe here in the house."

"It's okay, Curly." It was Colt's voice. I had been aware that he was talking, but now I realized he was standing behind me with his hand on my shoulder.

"But . . . but, that cat!" I stammered.

"It looked like him, but it wasn't him," Colt said. I heard a mewing and felt a soft, furry, LIVE cat rub against my leg. I took a deep breath. Thank God. I picked up his fat, wonderful body and cuddled him good.

"I thought you were gone Indy." I sniffled into his fur. Indiana Jones, always the talkative feline, replied lovingly: "Mew, mew." Then he jumped out of my arms, having had enough human bonding for the day.

"But it's not all good news," Colt continued. "There's something you need to see." He handed me the piece of paper, which I now remembered seeing on top of the cat's body in the box. It was folded over two times and had small, smudged bloodstains on it. I unfolded it and attempted to read, but the words blurred in front of me. "Oh crud!" I snapped, expressing a very familiar frustration.

"What's wrong?" Roz was still worried about me.

"I need my reading glasses." The day I hit forty-four was the final death blow to my near vision. I couldn't read a thing anymore without my reading glasses. Soup cans, price tags, papers from school, threatening notes from the Mafia. My eye doctor was kind when he broke the news, but I did detect him raising his voice a bit when he spoke, just in case my hearing was gone as well. I scanned the room for a spare pair – I kept several pairs around since seeing is often important to me. Unfortunately, I didn't spot any.

"Use mine," said Colt. "My inside jacket pocket." I smiled at him, glad to know that men were not immune to the inconveniences of old age. I reached into his inside jacket pocket and pulled out a pair of smart looking rimless bifocals and slipped them on. The words came nicely into focus. The message wasn't so nice: *"Stop your snooping or you'll end up like the cat. Tell your friends too."*

The cream colored paper was the type that would have come from a telephone message pad. Slightly darker shaded flowers decorated the paper, giving it a distinctively feminine feel. Odd choice of paper, I thought, for two men of the criminal set. The writing, in blue ink, was odd as well – formal, long, elegant lines in cursive. It was a practiced penmanship and another feminine touch. Only the smudge of blood and the words themselves indicated deadly intent. I took a sniff – whoever wrote it was a smoker.

I cocked my head and looked at Roz. "Did you read this?" I asked. She nodded her head. Two little worry lines were furrowed between her eyebrows. I considered the note quietly for a minute, then asked Colt, "What does this mean?"

"Are you kidding me?" Colt said, raising his voice in a shrill tone that I'd never heard come out of his happy-go-lucky mouth. "What this means is, that you're going to do what they say, and stay the hell away from all of this. This is super-serious shit, Curly. No more playing fun little solve-the-mystery games."

"He's right," said Roz shaking her head. She got up and sat in the chair next to mine. "Who would've known this could happen in Rustic Woods of all places? We have our problems here, but I sure as heck didn't think organized crime was one of them. It's unreal."

"Well, they can't be very bright," I said. "I mean, they only thought they had my cat. Right? They weren't even smart enough to get the right pet. One of the guys had this wacky, ridiculous, Elvis-like hair thing going on. And look at that paper and the handwriting. I thought those kind of people were a little more manly, if you know what I mean." Was I actually mocking the mafia? Had the events of the past few days stripped me of common sense brain cells?

"They don't need to be bright to kill you," countered Colt. "Tell me exactly what happened." So I relayed the whole story, starting from the point where I found his cell phone ringing in the jacket that he had given me to wear. He winced, obviously chagrined that he'd been caught in a lie, but he didn't seem to be chagrined enough to explain the reason why. I continued on, telling him about the Elvis wanna-be and the pug-faced thug with the gun. Yikes, the gun. I shivered at the thought. I tried to repeat everything said to me verbatim, or at least as best as I could recall. Roz had her hand to her mouth, her blue eyes as big as dinner plates. Colt sat with his head in hands. He shook his head when I finished the story, and his blond locks shimmered. He took a deep breath.

"Here's what we're going to do," Colt said. I'll take you and the girls to a hotel. You'll stay there for a few days, lay low, be cool, until this blows over. Once they see you're staying clear, it should all be good."

Wow. This didn't sound like the Colt I knew. The guy who loved to jump head first into anything no matter how dangerous. Of course, there's dangerous, and then there's deadly. This was definitely deadly. I guess he had grown up a little. And I liked how protective he was being toward me. It made me feel warm and cozy and important. Roz suggested we stay with my mother in her condo across town. I shook my head violently at that proposal.

"Probably not a good idea," said Colt. "While it might be unlikely, these creeps could be capable of finding her. Which brings up a good point. Maybe she should go with you."

"No!" I screamed. Two hours in a twelve by twelve room with my mother and I'd be calling Elvis and Pug-Mug myself to come put me out of my misery. "No way, Jose! Colt, you know my mother – she'll drive me crazy before the girls can ask 'Where's the ice machine?' Besides, how do you suppose we even explain to her that she should come stay in a hotel room just five miles from her own condo? Bad idea. Bad, bad idea."

"Fine," he relented. "We'll table that one for now."

"You could stay at the Wildwood Suites in Herndon," suggested Roz. "It's not too far away, but it's out of Rustic Woods." I said that was fine. Colt asked me for his cell phone with a childish, guilty look on his face, still not offering an explanation. I took it out of his jacket pocket and handed it to him, frowning the whole time.

"I've got a couple of calls I need to make," he said, not willing to look me in the eyes.

"Important business in Century City? Any other lies you want to run by me?" I asked.

"Not right now." That was all he said as he walked out of the room with the phone. I heard his footsteps pound up the stairs.

Roz waited until he was out of earshot. "So his story about needing to go back to LA was a lie. Why?" she asked.

"Best I can figure, Howard must have said something to him to convince him to leave. They must have come to some sort of 'gentlemen's agreement.'" I said it out loud, but something about how they were both acting just seemed a little off. Or maybe a lot off. I was sure Howard was jealous that Colt had come to stay, and I supposed it was plausible that Colt might have agreed to leave in order to keep the peace, but the way everything was going down just smelled worse than rotten eggs.

Roz was at the kitchen counter making a cup of tea.

"You know," she said as she poured the water into the cup, "Don't you think it's strange that there's been nothing going on over at that house?"

"What do you mean?"

"I mean with crime scene investigations and . . . I don't know . . . stuff," she said, plunging the tea bag up and down. "Don't you think there would be people – police, CSI, ATF, FCC . . . Geraldo Rivera, anybody – whoever cares about this stuff? Wouldn't they be coming around, asking more questions, searching the premises for more evidence? It's been oddly quiet since the last official car rolled out of here Saturday afternoon."

She had a point. I hadn't given it much thought. But common logic would lead even an ordinary civilian like me to think there would be more investigations, given the strange circumstances.

"There was the illusive Marjorie from the FBI," I said. "Acting all PETA-like and asking me that question about Tito Buttaro."

"See? Now that's just plain weird. What's the big secret?"

"Yeah, I guess. I mean, I've never found a dead guy in a house full of dead monkeys before, so admittedly I'm a little inexperienced with the process, but you're right. Something just isn't adding up," I said. Roz nodded her head in agreement.

"Don't you wonder whose head that was you found?" She asked.

"Not really. I spend most of my time trying to forget what it looked like. Although, after today, my interest is rising."

"I'm so damned curious I could scream."

"That's not the only thing that's got me bugged," I added. "Something's up with Colt too. He knows something he's not telling us."

Roz leaned in, the excitement of conspiracy glowing on her face. "Certainly, I don't know him as well as you do to know about his quirks and such, but in my opinion, he was acting very strange. I happened to look out my window and see you two in the street – I couldn't really see exactly what was going on, but then you screamed so I ran out. Colt was holding you up when I got there – we both walked you into the house and the first thing he did was grab your kitchen phone and run upstairs to make a phone call. He wasn't on the phone long, because he was back down in less than a minute. I asked him if he called the police, assuming that's what he'd done. He just shook his head no. He didn't seem like he wanted to offer up an explanation, and I was more worried about taking care of you than I was about giving him the third degree. A few minutes later I suggested we call the police, but he didn't say anything – sort of pretended he didn't hear me." We sat and sipped our tea in silence. I was going over the events of the last few days in my head and I assumed Roz was doing the same.

Monkeys from an animal testing lab show up mysteriously in my trees. No one gives me a reason why. Rotting human head and three dead monkeys found in the basement of a vacant house. No one gives a reason why. House vacant for thirty years. People afraid to give a reason why. Neighbors fleeing faster than Gloria Allred chasing down another celebrity lawsuit. Colt suddenly needs to leave town and, oh by the way, he won't call the police when the Mafia threatens my life. Yup. Not my ordinary kind of week. I thought about the poor cat that really had been murdered. Some cat lover somewhere was missing their poor pet right now, not knowing it had met a grisly end. I looked at Roz. "Where did you put the dead cat?"

"We left it outside by the front door."

"Still in the box?"

She grimaced. "Yeah."

Knowing I would need to do something with the poor little fella, I got up from my chair. Roz followed me to the front door. We both gasped when I opened it. Right in front of us, the yellow tabby cat that we thought had been dead was lolling around lazily on the ground next to the box. Roz pulled the door closed behind us, while I stepped down for a better look. Upon closer inspection I could see he wasn't lolling lazily so much as rolling drunkedly. His eyes were sort of glazed and glassy. "Roz," I said, "I think he's drugged!" I searched through his fur carefully. There had been blood on that note, so I wanted to know why. I found the reason soon enough. A small, raised bloody spot, barely smaller than a dime. I had seen the same sort of welt left behind when our vet gave Indiana his yearly vaccinations. This cat had been given a shot of something, I was fairly sure. The question was, who was the perpetrator? Elvis and Pug Mug? Were they intending to actually kill the animal? Certainly, by the words in the note, I was meant to think he was dead.

While examining the cat's fur some more, I discovered something even more interesting – a tattoo on his tummy. The numbers 47592 were clearly tattooed in black ink on a shaved area of his upper stomach area, closest to his chest.

"Roz, look at this," I said, barely able to believe what I was seeing.

Roz bent down for a closer look. She blinked. She looked at me. "A tattoo? On a cat?"

"Who would tattoo their pet? I've never heard of such a thing. Do you think it's an address?"

"I don't think this is someone's pet," Roz said. "I'm thinking this cat and those monkeys shared a home, if you catch my drift."

I stood up and stretched my legs, since my forty-five-old knees didn't work well in the kneeling position. "Meadowland Labs? You think this is a lab cat?" I looked down at the pitifully stoned animal. He looked so helpless. Those goombahs were really starting to get my dander up. Drugging cats, pointing guns, calling me Snoopy.

Roz and I decided to move the cat to my garage, making a comfortable bed for him out of an old discarded gift basket and a handful of old rags. We closed him in to keep him safe. Then we stood, silently on my driveway, staring out at our once quiet and safe White Willow Circle.

"You know," I said finally, "It's like we've found a table piled high with a jumbled mess of puzzle pieces."

"Yeah," she agreed, "and we need to put them together to see what the picture is."

Life in our cozy neighborhood had gone scarily awry. An evil element had reared its ugly head and I had innocently put myself smack dab in the middle. Common sense would say I should be afraid, run for cover while criminals lurked in my backyard and the men in my life seemed to be going off the deep end. Of course, I had already determined that my common sense brain cells had hit the road – left me for dead. Besides, I had made a commitment. I was not going to be one of those wimpy women who run away and hide. There would be no cowering for this chick. I was going to pull myself together, be brave and fight. Problem was, I needed to know what I was fighting. So, while Colt was upstairs doing his own thing, Roz and I hatched up ourselves a little plan.

Chapter 13

By the time Colt came back downstairs, it was almost 2:15 in the afternoon. Roz and I had orchestrated a simple, but somewhat daring, course of action. One that did not include Colt. Correction. The plan included Colt, he just didn't know it.

"Okay ladies," he said as he sauntered into the kitchen. "Let's get this show on the road. Curly, we should call that hotel and see if we can get you and the girls a room. I'd like to see you settled before I head out."

Roz was sitting at the kitchen table sipping tea and munching on pumpkin shaped sugar cookies while I filled the dishwasher with the dirty breakfast dishes.

"It's done," I said. "I called while you were upstairs. Callie will be getting home soon, and then we'll drive over, pick up Bethany and Amber from school and head over to the hotel. I'm going to go pack some things when I'm done here."

"Good," he said rubbing his hands together. "I'll ride over with you guys, make sure you have everything you need. Then I can catch a cab from there to the airport."

"So," said Roz. "You're still going back to LA?"

"Oh, yeah. Definitely. So! Let me help you pack," he said evasively.

"I could give you a ride to the airport – then you won't have to pay for a taxi. When does your flight leave?" Roz offered, winking at me when Colt had his back turned.

"No! I mean, thanks, but no, really. I have no idea how long it will take to get them settled, and I don't want to put you out. Late too – the flight, I mean – it's a late flight out. Thanks for the offer though." Colt might have been an above-average detective, but he was a lousy liar. He turned to me. "Where do you keep your suitcases? I'll get a couple for you."

"Guest room where you're staying – in the closet," I said. He rushed off, avoiding further discussion. Just as we suspected.

"I don't think he's going to the airport, do you?" asked Roz.

"Odds a million to one that he's not."

"Let the show begin," she said, with a devilish grin.

Our plan had several layers. First, Roz would run home and check county tax records online to see if she could dig up a name for the owner of House of Many Bones. Colt told me that most counties were online with real estate tax records and at the very least, we might get a name. She didn't have loads of time for researching, however, since she was also involved in Step Three of our plan. Thank goodness, her husband Peter had taken the day off to fix a grumpy sump pump, so he would be home to watch her kids when they got off the bus.

The one thing we both agreed from the outset – no more snooping around House of Many Bones. Colt was right – these guys had guns and didn't seem afraid to use them. No reason to put ourselves or our children in harm's way. I had no intention of running into Elvis and Pug Mug, or their firearms, a second time.

We had reached Peggy, still running errands, on her cell. Her mission, which she chose to accept, was Step Two in the scheme. She would Google Tito Buttaro as soon as she got home and find out all she could, then wait for Roz to call her with further instructions. I was to get to the Wildwood Suites with my girls and stall Colt as long as I could, waiting for Roz, who would know I was there because I would text message her the moment we arrived.

That was the third part of our plan. Roz would get herself placed inconspicuously after receiving the text message, so that when Colt left, she could follow him and find out what he was up to.

I knew he wasn't leaving town – he was sticking around for some reason. Probably to do some investigating on his own. Based on what Roz had told me, I figured he was onto something, and wanted to continue on his own. My assumption was that Howard had convinced him to leave town, but he'd decided to stay after the cat and note incident. Maybe he had some inside info on the mafia that he could work with. I couldn't be sure though, because one never really quite knew with Colt, so we would follow him and find out for ourselves. Of course, we could be way off base, and Roz might just end up following him to the airport, but only time would tell us that. We considered the Colt surveillance to be the most crucial part of our master plan, assuming he'd be unwittingly dropping clues in our lap as we followed behind.

Last, but certainly not least, I was going to keep my dinner date with Howard. While pretending to be one of Charlie's Angels was jolly good fun, saving my marriage was definitely more important. That evening's romantic dinner at Fiorenza's could prove to be the start to my happy ending. I had packed his favorite dress just for the occasion – a silky little blue number that hugged my body in all the right places, and showed off my best asset – sexy legs. I was always guaranteed a night of bedded bliss when I wore it. Goodbye Marjorie Smith.

Timing for this plan was crucial because we all had kids arriving home from school and Roz had a cub scout meeting at seven. We had perfect faith it could be done however, because as mothers, we already knew the fine art of juggling soccer practices, with piano lessons, with Karate, with ballet, with after-school Spanish enrichment, with homework, with dinner and bedtime at a reasonable hour. This would be a piece of cake in comparison.

My stomach growled while I was packing Amber's and Bethany's clothes into the smaller of two black Tourister suitcases. I remembered that I hadn't eaten since breakfast. My body didn't like that. I didn't want to stop for a break though, since Callie would be off the bus any minute. I did not look forward to telling her about our short-lived move to the local hotel. She was prone to teen-age hormone attacks, the likes of which I'd never seen before.

One minute, an angel from heaven, and then KABOOM! At the least little change or unplanned upset to her routine, the claws would come out, her teeth turned into fangs and she would transform into the fire-breathing, teen-age girl from Hell. It was like watching Bruce Banner turn into the Incredible Hulk. I'm told I did the same thing to my mother. I don't believe it.

Colt had barely unpacked the few things he had brought with him, so his job was quick. I found him on his laptop at my kitchen table when I came downstairs declaring I was finished and almost ready. I had to put down enough food and water for Indiana Jones as well as the mystery cat in the garage and then all we had to do was wait for Callie.

"You know," I said, scooping dry cat food into Indy's dish, "I just realized, Howard is expecting to pick me up here at seven tonight for dinner. I can't have him meet me at the hotel. He'll get suspicious." I already knew that I was going to need to call him and have him meet me at Fiorenza's instead, but I just wanted to test Colt – to see if he acted weird or suspicious.

"Yeah. You should call him. Tell him you'll meet him there instead," he said, eyes still glued to his laptop. Okay, nothing suspicious there, I thought. Callie's school bus brakes squealed so loud I could hear them all the way down to my house, so I knew she was going to be walking in the door anywhere between one and five minutes, depending on if it was a fast-Callie day or a slow-Callie day.

I quick picked up the phone and dialed Howard's cell, to change the meeting arrangements. No answer. I left a message. I decided to call his office also. His office was a high security part of the contracting firm he worked for, so all calls went through an automatic system with a series of menus which then always put me straight into his voicemail. I've never been able to reach him at work immediately, which is why I always try his cell phone first. I had just left the message on his work voicemail right when Callie walked in the door. I heard the door slam shut followed by several loud thumping noises, which, from experience, I knew to be her backpack, her coat, her purse and her lunchbox all landing on the foyer floor. Right, smack dab in front of the door. Ten thousand times I've told her not to leave her things right in the middle of the floor, and ten thousand times she always leaves her things right in the middle of the floor.

After the thump, thump, thump . . . thump, it was quiet for about three seconds, then, "Mo – om! Why are these suitcases here? Has another one of your old boyfriends decided to drop in on us?" Oh boy. This was looking like it could be a teen-ager from Hell day. Damn! Why couldn't it be an angel-sent-from-heaven day? I brainstormed a last minute lie. "The heat is out and it's supposed to go down below freezing tonight. I booked us a room for tonight at the Wildwood Suites in Herndon. They have a thirty-two inch plasma TV!" I yelled from the kitchen. "Cool!" she said. Whew! Dodged that bullet. I had learned early in motherhood the deft skill of the spur-of-the-moment lie. They're really just little white lies – harmless – and they're essential to making a mother's life easier. All mothers know this, whether they admit it or not.

Colt put everything in the van while I did a last minute check of the house, leaving certain lights on to make it look like we might be at home, making sure all faucets were off and not leaking. Then I locked up and drove us to Tulip Tree Elementary to pick up Bethany and Amber.

Pulling into the parking lot at Tulip Tree, I considered myself lucky to find one of only three visitor parking spots available. Considering that a good omen, I skipped quickly up a short flight of concrete steps to the glass double doors that opened to the school lobby. Just to my right was another set of glass double doors leading to the main office. I pulled the door open, stepped in and was immediately greeted by my most favorite public school employee ever – Mrs. Sanchez. Mrs. Sanchez was the receptionist as well as assistant to the principal. She was probably also the happiest woman I have ever met. Her face was brown and perfectly round like a basketball, and her cheeks were chubby and rosy, almost like a Hispanic Mrs. Claus. I had never seen Mrs. Sanchez without a genuine and toothy smile on her face.

"Meesus Marr!" She called out when she saw me enter. "How are joo too-day"

"I'm good, Mrs. Sanchez. And you?"

"Oh, joo know me – I'm always joost fine. We already see your hoosband today when he came in for lunch weeth your girls! He's sooch a handsome man! Looks just like that George Clooney."

I was more than a little surprised. "Howard was here?"

She nodded her head to confirm. "Jess." She said, grinning from ear to ear.

I stood, confused for a minute, and considered taking a peek at the sign-in log for visitors, when Bunny Bergen floated by me. Bunny Bergen was a parent volunteer in the front office. Six feet tall, model figure, manicured nails, flawless skin that never went without being perfectly made up. What I found more disgusting than her perfect features was her name. I never understood how a grown woman could continue to go by the name Bunny. In fact, I found it so ridiculous that I never actually said her name out loud.

"Hellooooo, Barb!" she oozed.

"Hi . . . there. How are you?" I responded uncomfortably, wanting to get myself to that sign-in log.

"I'm soooooo sorry to hear about that problem of yours!" She ended her sentence in hushed tones like she was keeping a secret for me. I immediately assumed she was referring to the fact that Howard had moved out, which made my ears perk up, because the only two people that were supposed to know were Roz and Peggy. Not at all happy, I was about to be really rude and ignore her altogether, when she continued on. "It's really too bad about your Uncle Guido going crazy, but don't worry. We'll keep an eye out for him. We won't let him near those girls of yours!" *My Uncle Guido?* The bewilderment I was feeling must have been written all over my face. I couldn't even respond. *Who was Uncle Guido? And why had he gone crazy?* Mrs. Sanchez, observing the entire conversation, had her hands on her head while she shook it back and forth.

"Mees Boony, Mees Boony!" she said, trying to get Bunny's attention. "Shhh! I so sorry Meesus Marr." She got up from her seat, grabbed Bunny

Bergen by the waist – she barely came up to Bunny's middle section – and ushered her away from the front desk, whispering something I couldn't hear. I saw Bunny put her hand to her mouth, looking like she'd said something she shouldn't have. Still befuddled, I took two steps over to that sign-in log. There was his name – Howard Marr. Reason for visit: Principal. Howard came to see the Principal? My heart was picking up its beat, when I became aware of an increasing amount of activity in the lobby. I looked at my watch. School would be getting out soon and I had a schedule to keep. Mrs. Sanchez returned to her seat and smiled at me as if nothing had happened. "Can I help you Meesus Marr?"

"Um . . . yes, I'm here to get Bethany and Amber for early dismissal. Could you call them out of class please?"

She bobbed her head happily. "Jess, jess. I can do that for you!"

I waited in the lobby for Bethany and Amber. They arrived at the same time, happy, as I knew they would be. "Mommy!" She squealed with glee as she bounded down the steps to the parking lot. "Daddy came for lunch! Isn't that cool?"

"Yes, I heard. Very cool. Too cool." I wanted to tell Colt about Howard's surprise visit to the Principal, spreading rumors about my imaginary Uncle Guido, but I couldn't do it with the girls in the car. I pulled out of the parking lot just in time to miss the arrival of the school buses.

Fifteen minutes later, we arrived at the Wildwood Suites in Herndon and I parked my van. While I stood at the reception desk checking in, receiving keys and directions to our room, Colt and the girls sat on comfy pastel, floral sofas in the lobby. I was just getting the last of my vital hotel information when Amber shouted, "Grandma!" My head spun around so fast I nearly gave myself whiplash.

"Barbara!" My mother shouted from the hotel entrance. She opened her mouth, about to speak again, when her eyes caught sight of Colt. Her eyes squinted and fixed on him suspiciously. "Coltrane Amadeus Baron. What are you doing here?"

The girls giggled. "Coltrane Amadeus?" laughed Callie. "Your parents didn't like you very much, did they?"

Colt smiled. "It's a family name," he said.

"What – the Adaams Family?" she guffawed. The truth that very few people knew, because Colt didn't want them to, was that Colt came from old European money, reinvested in the California gold rush. The house he grew up in was actually a mansion near Santa Barbara complete with an expansive marble foyer, thirty rooms, Olympic sized swimming pool, and martini-drinking, charity-event-attending parents. He was the black sheep and my mother did not like him one bit. He didn't let that stop him. He picked himself up from the sofa and moved smoothly to my mother, taking one hand, kissing it gently and said, "It's wonderful to see you again Mrs. Pettingford. I'm here visiting your lovely daughter, of course."

"Don't waste your time, Coltrane," my mother hissed. "I got your number a long time ago, young man."

"Mom!" I shouted. "How do you do it?"

"Do what?" she asked.

"Show up, all of the time, even when I'm not at home! How do you do it?" I was practically shaking. The last thing I needed was my mother coming along to screw up our well-laid plans.

"Well, I was out and about running errands when I realized I was right behind you on Herndon Parkway. I can tell it's your van by that big dent on the right side of your bumper – you really do need to get that fixed you know. It will rust and then . . ."

"Mom! Did you have to follow me in here?"

"Why? Is there a problem?"

"Our heat is out," piped Amber. "That's why we're here. We're going to watch TV on a big screen and order in junk food! Isn't it cool?"

"Your heat is out? Why should that matter? It seems awfully warm."

"Nope," said Bethany shaking her head very seriously. "We will be having a freeze tonight – Mommy says."

"My goodness," my mother said, throwing a fist to her hip, letting me know I had failed in an obviously simple task. "Why didn't you just call me, Barbara? My man Jerry always comes right out – he'll be at your place in an hour. He's the best in town. I'll call him right now." She started digging in her purse for her cell phone. I shot Colt a panicked look.

"Oh! Mrs. Pettingford," he intercepted her search. "Can I talk to you for a minute?" He pulled her to the front of the hotel. The automatic doors opened, letting them out then closed again behind them. I could see them through the glass doors talking outside, and everyone once in a while, my mom would nod and look my way. She had her normal serious look plastered on her face as she looked down from her superior height to Colt, who stood a good four inches shorter than her. I looked at my watch. I was worried about time. We only had so much available to us. It was a good opportunity to text Roz and let her know we'd arrived. I had just sent my message, when I heard a familiar male voice behind me.

"Hello, there." I spun around, coming face to face with none other than Officer Brad. I smiled immediately, because his handsome face elicited an instinctual response. He wasn't decked in his usual policeman's garb – instead he sported khaki Dockers, brown loafers, and a blue and white striped long sleeved dress shirt without a tie. Easy on the eyes without a doubt. But the coincidence wasn't lost on me. I was beginning to feel like he was following me.

"Wow!" *Did I really say that? Wow?* I stumbled on, hoping to cover over the seriously stupid interjection. "I mean, well – well, imagine meeting you here." *Hmm, smooth and original.* I trudged on, sure I could come out of this conversation looking like only half an idiot rather than completely idiotic. "No uniform – you're not on duty today?"

He smiled. I had never seen him give a full on smile before. It was a VERY nice smile.

"Sort of," he said then leaned in for a whisper near my ear. "Hotel security. Moonlighting." And he put his index finger to his lips indicating I was supposed to keep that quiet. Having Officer Brad whisper in my ear had a hypnotic effect on me, almost causing me to forget I had a mission to accomplish, and that my mother and Colt were outside, possibly cooking up some scheme that would interfere entirely.

The automatic glass doors swooshed open once again. I looked up just in time to catch a smile cross my mother's face as she re-entered the hotel lobby. I realized, however, that she wasn't looking at me. She put her hands to her chest and called out in happy recognition. "Eric!" She was gushing like a sappy teenager. Eric? Where did I know that name? Suddenly I realized she was walking toward Officer Brad! Aha! That was his name – Eric. Still couldn't remember his last name though. How in the world did he know my mother? By the time I could construct an audible question, she had her long arms around him hugging him. Officer Brad was a tall man, himself, so she actually didn't smother him with her show of affection. He returned the hug and salutation, "Hello, Diane."

"Barbara, Eric is the officer who pulled you over yesterday," she said.

"Yes, I know. But you didn't seem to recognize him then. How do you two know each other?" I asked in awe.

"Tae Kwon Do," she said, as if that answered everything.

"We met last night – I'm a new evening class instructor there," Officer Brad added.

"We sparred," my mother gushed like a schoolgirl.

I cringed at the image.

She patted him on the upper arm. "He's quite good." He blushed and smiled shyly.

"Boy," I said. "Tae Kwon Do instructor. You do a little of everything, don't you?"

He seemed interested in changing the subject. "So," he said to me, "are you staying here?"

My mother decided to answer for me before I could even open my mouth. "She is – her heat is out. It's a shame. A darn shame. You know we called my repairman, Jerry, but he didn't answer. I will keep trying for you. In the meantime, you just stay right here, and enjoy the warm room and time with your girls. Mother will take care of everything." She was patting me and rubbing me on the back alternately with a maternal tone that was completely unnatural for her. I desperately wanted to know what Colt had said to her. I looked to him questioningly, but he only shrugged, as if he was innocent. He did help by breaking up the happy reunion and moving things along.

"Well, Curly," he said, "the girls look like they're getting antsy – maybe we should get you to your room and get you settled. What floor are you on?"

I looked at the information brochure with the cards keys in my hand. "Third floor. Room 312." I said. Colt took control of the suitcases while I rounded up the girls.

"Good bye, Mom," I said as we moved to the elevator. She waved, but was engrossed in her own conversation with Officer Brad. I didn't want to seem rude, not bidding him farewell. "Good-bye . . . uh . . um . ." I couldn't remember his last name, and I surely couldn't call him Officer Brad to his face, and calling him Eric seemed too familiar. I was at a loss – didn't know what to call him. He helped me out. "Eric." He said smiling again. "Eric." I repeated. "Nice seeing you again." We piled into the elevator and as the doors closed, I caught sight of Eric and my mother in a more serious conversation, with her pointing in my direction. I got the distinct feeling that I was the topic of their conversation. I looked at Colt. "That was weird."

"What?"

"That policeman – he's everywhere I go these days."

Colt just shrugged, saying not a word, and with the girls there, I couldn't force the issue.

The five of us hauled the two suitcases and varied and sundry personal pillows, bed blankies and ragged sleep-time stuffed animals into room 312 – a spacious, tastefully decorated suite-style hotel room with a kitchenette and the much-anticipated thirty-two inch plasma TV in a comfortable living area. A small balcony was accessible from the sliding glass door in one of the two bedrooms. It would work. If all went as planned, the girls would be munching on pizza in a couple of hours while I was on the phone in the other room learning from Roz what Colt was up to.

Bethany and Amber were jumping and giggling on the twin beds in the second bedroom and Callie was talking on her cell. Colt gave the room a visual once-over and approved. He talked in hushed tones so the girls wouldn't hear. "This is good. You'll be safe here. Remember: stay put and stay un-involved. UN-INVOLVED – do you hear me? Things will settle down in a couple of days, and then you can go home. I'll call you to see how things are going," he said, playing with one of my curls and smiling.

Callie, who had finished her call, spied the intimate scene and wasn't happy. "She's married, you know. In case you forgot," she sneered from across the room. Devil girl was back.

I gave Colt a sideways look, showing him I was onto his game. "How do you know things will 'settle down' as you say? You seem very confident. Like you know something I don't." I may not have known what his game was, but I was onto it all the same.

"Listen to me, Curly," he said, put his hands on my shoulder and looking me straight in the eye like an overprotective father. "Stay put. Just stay here and stay safe. I'm going to get on a plane now and leave you here. Be good." Wow. Mr. Immature was talking to me like I was a child. What a turn of events.

"Promise me?" he asked. Well, I didn't want to make promises. I had a plan, and my plan didn't involve staying put. "Curly," he pressed on. "Promise me."

Fine. I crossed a finger behind my back. "Promise." I said.

He opened the door to leave. "I'll call a taxi from the reception desk," he said, holding the door open. We locked eyes for a good long time, before he pulled lovingly on another curl, wrapping it around his index finger. "Do you ever think about what would have happened if we hadn't broken up all those years ago?" Holy cow. That wasn't the first time Colt had asked me that question. The answer, silently, was "yes."

The answer I had to give him was, "I'm married now. I love my husband. I can't answer that question for you."

"Yeah," he said, "that's what you always say." He kissed me on the cheek and opened the door to leave. I watched him get in the elevator then scooted across the room toward the sliding glass door to peek out. Luckily, I had a good view of the parking lot to the side of the building as well as a partial view of the circular drive that served as a drop-off and entrance to reception. I scoured the parking lot and spotted Roz's forest green Sienna. She had backed it into a parking spot and was positioned just right to see Colt exit the building. Perfect.

I went out onto the balcony and was hit immediately by a strong, warm wind. Damn! My whole our-heat-is-out lie required freezing weather to be believable. How would I explain this to the girls? I made a mental note to watch the weather channel next time before telling a lie.

The sky had filled with more gray clouds – darker gray now. Twisting my body as best as I could around the far side of balcony wall, I tried to determine if I would be able see Colt come out as well, but with only a partial view, I wasn't sure I would be so lucky. I was looking for the top of Colt's head. Sure enough, within just seconds, a shock of blond hair appeared. Definitely Colt. This was good. Things were going as planned. Next, I thought I might see a taxi. I moved my eyes in all directions, finally landing them on something I wasn't expecting at all – a black Camry pulling into the circular driveway. Wait a minute! That looked like Howard's car. My cell phone rang. It was Roz. "Is that Howard?" I asked immediately as I answered.

"Yes!" she screamed. "Can you see?"

"Not now – he pulled out of view."

"Colt just got in the car."

"You've got to be kidding me. What are they up to?"

"Do I still follow?" she asked.

"Of course! Go! Keep in touch," I said, trying to keep my voice down so the girls wouldn't hear me out on the balcony. Howard's car pulled out of the circular drive, his indicator blinking for a right hand turn, which would put them heading south on Herndon Parkway.

We really didn't expect this change of events. We thought we'd be following a shifty Colt, not Colt and Howard together. Roz pulled slowly from of her parking space, following them out. She was smart enough to keep a decent distance between them. Then my eyes landed on something I had failed to see before. A black Lincoln Town Car. Black tinted windows. It followed out right on Roz's tail. It was a damn convoy. Holy cow.

Another strong gust knocked over a small round table on the balcony. The sky darkened ominously. I began to quake in my shoes, fearful that I had just succeeded in getting Roz whacked.

Chapter 14

I had to think fast. I ran back into the hotel room, grabbed my purse, coat and keys. I thought better about the coat – too warm for that now – and threw it down. I scrambled in my purse, looking for the bluetooth headset. I'd need it now for sure. Not finding it quickly, I began to panic. I almost gave up my search when my fingers grabbed hold of something possibly the right size and shape. I pulled it out. Aha! Got it.

Luckily, all three girls had found a show they could agree on and were motionless and mesmerized in front of the plasma. Think! What to do? They would have to stay alone in the hotel room if I went out chasing after Roz. Callie was old enough, she babysat the younger girls all of the time. I must have looked like Ginger Rogers dancing around the room trying to decide what to do. Okay – Ginger Rogers on drugs – still, there was the dancing. My eyes landed on the mini-bar refrigerator near the bathroom. Suddenly, I knew what to do.

I snapped my fingers at Callie to get her attention. "Sweetie, I forgot something at home. I have to go back. If I'm longer than an hour, grab what you want from the mini-bar." I pointed to the refrigerator. "See that? Keep it as healthy as you can, though, please?" She nodded as if she heard and understood, then turned her eyes back to the enticing plasma screen. I was giving it a fifty/fifty that she actually heard every word I said. "Callie! Listen to me! This is important." She turned her eyes back to me with her practiced teen I'm-not-stupid-Mom eye-roll and follow-up glare.

"Keep the door locked. I'm serious! Keep it locked. Don't open it for anyone. Do you understand? I've got my cell – call me if you need me. If you need help immediately, call down to the hotel security guard. Kiss, Kiss. I love you!" And I blew them kisses while running out into the hallway. Deep down, despite her need to appear tough, Callie was a good kid and smart to boot. I trusted her to keep that door shut and locked.

An exit sign hovered over a door at the end of the hallway. I found that it led to a stairwell – I took the stairs three at a time, finally exiting through a door into the parking lot. I had no plan other than seeing if I could catch up with Roz and stop a possible murder. Thank goodness I had her on speed dial. I punched the "2" on my cell while running to my car and simultaneously snapping the new bluetooth over my ear. Turned out to be a handier gadget that I thought. She picked up right away. "Yeah?" she answered.

"Are you still behind them?" I asked, buckling up and turning my engine over at the same time.

"Yeah. It's pretty easy."

"Where are you?" I asked.

"We're on Fairfax County Parkway – they're turning onto Red Cedar – it looks like they're heading back to White Willow," she said. My car started and I peeled out of my space almost hitting some old man in a long boat of a car. He stopped his car, laid on his horn and gave me the finger. Pretty vulgar for a man who looked a hundred years old.

"Okay!" I screamed at the old man. "I'm sorry! Move it! Move it!"

"What?" I heard Roz ask in my ear. The bluetooth was working perfectly.

"Nothing. Listen – we have a complication. You've got a bogey on your tail," I said.

"A what?"

So, sue me, I love Top Gun. I just prayed that this didn't end like when Goose died and Tom Cruise felt all guilty because he killed his best friend, even though it wasn't really his fault and everyone said it wasn't, but he still blamed himself and quit Top Gun school. I really, really hoped this wouldn't end like that.

"You're being followed!" I screamed. "Look in your rearview mirror – is there a Black Lincoln Town car behind you?"

"No . . . I don't think so . . . OH NO! There it is! Is that who I think it is?" She sounded like she was hyperventilating.

"I don't know for sure, but the car looks the same," I said. "Just keep driving. Nothing can happen to you if you keep moving." *Theoretically.* I picked up my speed, trying to catch up to Roz and her pursuer. "Are you on Red Cedar now?" I asked.

"Yes, but their turn indicator is on. They're turning onto Thin Branches Road, so I was wrong – they're not going back to White Willow." She was silent for a moment. "Now. We're on Thin Branches now. Barb! The black car is still behind me! They are following me! I'm scared."

"It's okay. Don't worry. I must be close to you. I should hang up and call the police, don't you think?"

"Yes. No! No! Don't hang up! I'm freaking here!"

I had just turned onto Thin Branches myself and spotted the Town Car. Thin Branches is a low-trafficked, two lane road that starts from Red Cedar and winds its way through Rustic Woods, ending at Rustic Woods Parkway. The sun had long gone away behind storm clouds and evening twilight was setting in so I was having trouble seeing the black car easily. Since environmentally-friendly Rustic Woods doesn't allow street lights, my job was especially difficult. Eventually, I caught up and I could see both the black Lincoln and Roz' van ahead of it. The three of us were lined up at a four way stop. I saw that there was a car in front of Roz at the stop sign, but I couldn't tell if it was the Camry or not. If it was, this could be our saving grace – I was figuring that Roz could get their attention somehow – honk, flash her lights, rear end them if necessary -- and hopefully we'd be able to scare off her pursuers.

"Roz, is that Howard in front of you?"

"No! Some jerk pulled out in front of me and now he's stalled! Howard and Colt are long gone." She honked her horn. "Oh no! Maybe I shouldn't have done that," she said. The driver's side door of the stalled car opened. A man got out and threw up his arms at Roz as if to say there was nothing he could do. He started to signal to her with a wave that she should go around him, but then a car coming from the opposite direction got in her way. Just as that car passed, the Town Car jumped forward and rear-ended Roz hard. I heard her scream into the phone. "Barb! Call the police!"

Just then, another call came in on my cell – Callie's phone. I didn't intend to answer, but somehow the call came through anyway, and I heard Callie on the other end. "Mom?"

I was breathing hard and watching the man, Roz and the Town Car, assessing my options while trying to answer Callie. Talk about multi-tasking. "Yeah, honey, this isn't . . ."

"Grandma is here."

"What?"

"Grandma. She wants to . . . " I was too busy watching the man with the stalled car to hear what Callie was saying. Obviously angry, he yelled an obscenity and started back toward the Town Car.

Oh no, don't do that I thought. *No stupid man! No! Turn around!* Too late. The Town Car's passenger side door swung open fast and before you could say "Fugettaboutit," a gun shot was fired and the man went down.

I screamed. I thought I heard a scream from Roz's van. I could hear Callie screaming in my ear, "Mom! What's wrong?" Then another shot and a loud pop. Before I could make sense of what was happening, the face of Elvis the mafia man loomed large in my passenger door window. Knowing my cell phone would be my savior if I got thrown in a trunk and driven to the river, I quick snapped it closed and hit the mute button on the side, ensuring silence if another call came in. Silence in my bluetooth. Simultaneously, I was trying to lock my doors and make an attempt at slipping the phone into my jeans pocket. It was all too much to do at once and I failed at getting the car door closed or hiding the cell. Instead, the door was ripped open and I was being pulled out by my hair. Elvis ripped the cell phone out of my hands and shoved it into his coat pocket. Instinctively, I reached up while being dragged and grabbed the bluetooth, clutching it in one hand while trying to grab my kidnapper with the other.

I could hear Roz screaming. The next thing I knew, I was in the back of the Town Car, banging heads with Roz. We hugged each other and didn't let go. I could taste blood in my mouth.

"Are you okay?" I asked her.

"I think he broke my hand!" she cried. The car lurched forward, moving at a speed way too fast for the roads of Rustic Woods. I was thrown against Roz as the car careened around a bend and changed direction. I was trying to figure out where we were, without a whole lot of luck since my head was throbbing. "Do you still have your cell phone?" I asked Roz. "No." she said. "He took it and threw it in the bushes." Okay, so they weren't as stupid as I thought. It was so dark, I couldn't make out the other figure in the front seat. I assumed it would be the same pug-faced, gun wielding goon from earlier, but I decided to find out for sure. "Hey," I asked craning my neck, "where are you taking us?" The shooter in the passenger seat turned around. Yup. Same Pug Mug.

"You don't follow directions so good, do you?" he asked. "Dis is an unfortunate ting for you." Wow, I thought, they really do talk like that.

The car weaved up and down winding roads, leading me to believe we were leaving Rustic Woods, heading maybe into nearby Oakton or Vienna. It was hard to tell and my sense of direction was all out of whack. By looking out the windshield I could see very few oncoming headlights so it was likely that we weren't on any major roads. Roz and I shivered, still gripping each other for our lives. Literally, I think.

"Can you tell where we're going?" I asked her. She shook her head no. I couldn't see her face very well in the dark, but I suspected we were asking ourselves the same questions – will I ever see my kids again? Will I live to see another day?

"I should have listened to Colt and stayed out of it," I said. She nodded yes.

Outside, the dark storm clouds made the dark night even darker. I could barely make out a faint outline of trees. I tried to guess the time. Working my way backwards from when I left the hotel, I figured it must have been nearly five o'clock, maybe five-thirty at the latest.

Our speed had slowed from our initial abduction. From the feel of it, I guessed we were moving thirty to forty miles per hour and, of course, slower on the turns. My eyes had adjusted somewhat to the dark inside the car and I located the very vague outline of the door handle. I looked at Roz who was looking out the window. I tapped her on the hand. When I had her attention, I pointed to the handle and made a motion with my own hand. Without words, I was suggesting we try to jump out – attempt an escape. She looked at me like I had suffered brain damage and shook her head violently. I didn't think it was such a crazy idea. Bruce Willis did things like that all the time and he was still alive.

"Come on," I whispered. She kept shaking her head. I nodded. She shook.

"Hey yous," said Elvis, spotting us in his rearview mirror. "No use tryin' those doors – we got 'em locked. You think we're stupid or sumthin'?"

"No!" Roz and I shouted in unison.

"Just sit back and enjoy the ride. You ain't goin' nowhere except where we say you're goin'."

I fell back against the seat feeling a little nauseous and a lot defeated. Roz blew out a loud sigh and joined me in my misery.

Pug Mug turned around and faced me. "We watched your video on You Tube. Pretty funny shit."

Words escaped me. "What?" I managed to ask.

"What song was that?" He was looking to Elvis for an answer.

"Madonna – Like a Virgin," he said.

"No," I corrected him. "Material Girl."

"Yeah!" shouted Pug Mug. "That's the one. Very funny. You got talent. You oughta do more of those."

"Thank you." I said, smiling. Roz gawked at me. I shrugged at her. "They like my video."

"Do you mind me asking," I continued, curious, "how you found my video on You Tube?"

Elvis sneered in the rearview mirror. "We got our ways, little lady." Holy cannoli.

For some reason, I kept talking. "The last time I looked, I had like twenty-five views."

"Oh no," said Pug Mug with surprising animation. "More than that." He looked to his co-kidnapper once again for help. "What was it? Ten tousand – sumthin' like that?"

"Ten tousand?" I repeated stupidly in my excitement.

"Hey, you makin' fun a de way I talk?"

"No! I . . . I bit my tongue. It hurth." I touched my tongue to prove my pain and affliction. Roz looked disgusted. I kept talking, figuring maybe if we made nice with them, they wouldn't have the heart to kill us.

"I was thinking of making another one, you know."

"Yeah?" asked Pug Mug, leaning over his seat now with one elbow hanging over. "What song was you tinkin' of?"

"*These Boots Are Made For Walking.*"

"Good one! Nancy Sinatra!"

"Actually, I was thinking of the Jessica Simpson version."

"Jessica who? Naw! You gotta do Nancy! She's Frank's girl. Hey – you should do a Sinatra song – Frankie's the best."

Lordy. Could these guys get more stereotypical?

"Oh, yeah," I said, realizing too late that I didn't sound convincing enough if I wanted to create a strong bridge of affinity with this felonious fellow.

"Absolutely. Love Frank." Actually, I did love Frank Sinatra, so it wasn't a tough sell. Roz blew out another more disgusted sigh. Pug Mug didn't like her reaction.

"What? You don't like Frankie?" he growled. Roz froze.

"Are you kidding me? She loves him. She came over just last week and we watched her favorite – *From Here to Eternity.*"

"Yeah?" He smiled, content, I was guessing, that we weren't Sinatra-haters. He pointed at Roz's hand. "How's that hand of yours?" He asked. Roz opened and closed the fingers of her right hand a couple of times. "It's okay, I guess," she answered warily.

"That's good – sorry 'bout that. Didn't mean to be so rough." Roz's eyes opened wide like she couldn't believe what she was hearing. Elvis slapped Pug Mug in the chest. "Ay! Stupido! Put a plug in it!" Pug Mug plugged it and was quiet for the rest of our trip.

Finally, after what seemed like hours, but was probably only minutes, the car pulled onto a gravel driveway and crunched its way to a stop. Both back doors were opened and Roz and I were yanked out of each door respectively. I felt something hard in my back. Gun, I thought. So much for making friends. I had learned my first lesson regarding men of the Mafia: a mutual affinity for Frank Sinatra would not necessarily save your life. This couldn't be happening, I thought. Just a few days ago my biggest worry was Captain Crunch: with Crunch Berries or without? Now it seemed I was standing at Death's doorstep.

Large floodlights positioned on the garage illuminated the area so I was able to make out our surroundings pretty well. The car was parked at the top of a long gravel driveway that wound down a good four or five hundred yards taking a steep dive at the last one hundred yards where it met up with the main road. I couldn't see a street sign, so I didn't know the name of the road. A monstrously large, two-story brick house stood at the end of the driveway. A three-car garage was attached to the house. On top of the house was a unique sort of widow's walk with a wrought iron railing. It looked like a typical Northern Virginia McMansion with a Victorian twist. The front porch light was on, as well as the large floods from the garage to the driveway and I could see lights in a few windows here and there on the front of the house. The two thugs had brought Roz and me together near the front of the car and were beginning to walk us, side by side around the garage and to the back of the house.

"Barb!" Roz whispered. "I found this house when I was researching House of Many Bones. It's owned by the same person."

"Are you sure?" I asked.

"Pretty sure I saw it on Google Earth – I can tell because of the widow's walk and the gravel driveway. If it's the same one, then we're in Fairfax Station." That made sense, based on how long we drove and the number of twists and turns we took. Fairfax Station is a good ten to fifteen miles from Rustic Woods, and consists mainly of very large new houses or small old ranches on multi-acre properties. I estimated the land surrounding this house was at least ten acres. I couldn't see another house from where I stood.

"What's the name?" I whispered.

"Crooks. Fred Crooks. He owns ten houses in Fairfax County."

I felt a thump to the side of my head.

"Shut your mouths, hear me?" Said Elvis, shoving the gun harder into my back.

Crooks. Peggy's story about the crazy lady at the wedding was beginning to make sense.

As they brought us around to the back of the house, I saw that the gravel drive extended around behind the house, and parked there, parallel to the back of the garage was a tan Prius. Another floodlight illuminated this back area of the house. There was a single door with glass panes on the back of the garage and between the car and the garage were three large metal trashcans. In the back window of the Prius were several small stuffed animals. The car looked familiar to me – it seemed I had seen it before. I didn't have time to give it much thought because we were shoved past the car and through another door that led down some dark stairs into the back basement portion of the house. I stumbled and almost fell over because I couldn't see and Roz stepped on my ankle. "Ouch!" I yelled. "Sorry," she whispered.

"I'll live," I said. Or maybe not.

"I said to keep your traps shut!" yelled Elvis, pushing us both. We fell down three or four more steps onto a landing that opened up to an amazingly spacious, nearly empty recreation room. There was a lot of chattering and screeching. A sound I remembered very well. Along one whole wall to our left was a set of black metal cages. Monkeys. Rhesus Macaques. Four of them. Our arrival had seemed to set them off and the noise was intense. Roz and I struggled to our feet and as we did so, we both spotted the same thing at the same time. In the far corner to our right, was a body, curled up in a ball. Conscious, unconscious, dead, not dead – I couldn't tell. I saw the red hair and recognized the bright white and orange "*Kiss Me, I'm Italian*" sweatshirt.

They had poor Peggy too.

Chapter 15

Elvis and Pug Mug shoved Roz and me to the floor, threatening certain bodily injury if we tried to leave. Elvis took off across the expansive room, disappearing up a second set of stairs that I assumed led to the main level of the house. We were left with Pug Mug standing, arms crossed, to watch over us, his gun protruding visibly from the waist of his pants. This was the first time I had really seen him head to toe. He was actually quite short and solid. Not fat, but not thin. Bulky – muscular possibly. He wore a very nice black leather jacket and black dress slacks that I guessed had a designer label. He might not have been the prettiest guy in town, but he was a snazzy dresser.

The two of us crawled to the corner, keeping one eye on Pug Mug. Roz immediately put her face down close to Peggy's. "She's breathing," she whispered. Thank God. Roz shook her a bit and Peggy stirred then opened her eyes. She was slow to come around, but she eventually recognized us both and seemed to remember where she was. We warned her to whisper, putting our fingers to our lips – one stray vocal emission could mean the end of us.

"Holy canoli," she whispered back. "My head hurts." She rubbed her scalp.

"How did you get here?" I asked her.

"Oh man, it really hurts." She rubbed her fingers through her red locks then tipped her head to toward us. "Do you see blood?"

Roz poked through her hair briefly. "No blood. You have a nice welt there though. What happened?"

"Give me a minute," Peggy said, "I'm still really woozy. Is the room spinning?" She laid down on her back and closed her eyes.

I took a moment to scan the room while she rested. There wasn't much to see. The walls were white and bare. Not a picture. Not a clock. Not even a poster of Frank Sinatra. The carpet we sat on was a tan Berber that appeared brand new. The room was vast – probably large enough to fit two pool tables easily, together with a dreamy personal theater – yet there wasn't a lick of furniture, with the exception of one lone black barstool which stood near the wrought iron monkey cages. Pug Mug caught me scoping out the place, but he didn't move.

Finally, Peggy sat up, ready to talk. "So I did that research you asked me to do. I was on the Internet waiting for the kids to get off the bus. Almost the first thing I find, when I search on the name Tito Buttaro, is that he's been missing for fifteen years. Maybe it was thirteen. Fifteen. Thirteen. Something like that. Anyway, they called him Tito 'The Butler' Buttaro. He was some Mafia big wig but I don't think he was what they call a 'boss'. . . ." Peggy was getting excited and her voice raised a couple of octaves in her frenzy. We put our fingers to our lips again, warning her to keep it to a whisper. Every once in a while, we'd peer over at Pug Mug to make sure we weren't being too loud for him.

Quite frankly, the monkeys were so loud they could have drowned out the Boston Pops. This appeared to get under his skin, because once, he yelled out, "Shut up, ya damn apes!"

"Anyway," she continued, barely audible now, "his wife, Viviana Buttaro, has become semi-famous. She wrote a book and she's been doing the media circuit. She claims some guy – I forget his name – whacked Tito. Boy, I just love that word, don't you? Whacked. Whacked. By the way, did you know there's a *Mafia for Dummies*? I found it on Amazon."

Peggy's inability to stay on topic was driving me crazy. "Peggy, what about Tito and his wife?"

"Viviana. I found two different video interviews with her promoting her book – they were probably done five or six years ago – she's kinda looney. She rambles on a lot and doesn't really stick to one story."

"But how did you end up here?" Roz pressed.

"That's what I'm trying to tell you. So I'm finding all of this really cool information, there was a lot of stuff – you know, it's really creepy how real it all is. These aren't very nice people. But anyway, my doorbell rings and it's Maxine," she said.

That was it! I knew I recognized that Prius. It was Maxine's. The stuffed animals in the rear window were poodles.

"Maxine?" asked Roz.

"Yeah, that's what I thought when I saw her on my front step. She's not someone who usually just stops by my house for a chat or anything, right? I know her, but not that well. She said she was just taking Puddles for a walk and was interested if I knew anymore about what you two had found out about the vacant house. So, I tell her all about what I found on the Internet, about Tito and Viviana Buttaro . . ." she stopped talking abruptly because we heard movement on the stairs. I was quickly coming to the conclusion that somehow our mobster friends must have scooped up both Maxine and Peggy. But that didn't explain why Maxine's car was outside. They must have kidnapped her in her own car.

Then I heard the barking. I'd know that ear piercing yap anywhere – it was Puddles the poodle. Just seconds after the barking started, Puddles came tearing down the stairs, with Maxine following behind. Puddles was dancing his poodle dance in circles around Maxine, who stood staring at us from across the room. She looked amazingly calm, I thought, for having just been kidnapped.

"Maxine!" I called out. "Are you okay?"

Peggy leaned into me and whispered in my ear. "Barb. Don't you see? She's one of them."

"Well, if it isn't the Trouble Triplets," Maxine sneered. "Puddles! Shut up!" She pointed a skinny finger to the floor. "Sit!" Puddles sat. "Good dog." She smiled. "Poodles are smart. You three – you're not too smart, huh?" She had traded her Canadian 'eh?' for a Jersey Italian 'huh?'

She was like Sybil, this woman. It was like aliens had come and traded her with a criminal look-alike. No more neighborly lady. This was Al Capone in a peasant skirt.

"She's kinda creepy, isn't she?" whispered Peggy.

"I'm really confused," said Roz.

"My knee-capping story was supposed to scare you broads. Normal people would leave well enough alone. What's up with you three anyway?"

"Well," I said, "I had monkeys in my trees. What would you do?" That didn't make sense when I said it out loud.

"That doesn't make sense," replied Maxine.

"She's right, Barb," whispered Peggy, "that doesn't make sense."

"Peggy!" yelled Roz. "You can stop whispering now!" Roz was getting testy. Understandably. A kidnapping at gunpoint will do that to you. We all heard the clanking of what sounded like high heels on hard wood floor, then a door opening and footsteps coming down the carpeted stairs.

Through the banisters, a figure revealed itself as it descended step by step. We saw the shoes first – three inch high red spikes; then the calves (I had better); the thighs (way too much cellulite); crimson mini-skirt, white low-cut silk blouse (I was guessing the boobs weren't real); the face (three inches of foundation, ultra-red rouge, fake eyelashes and probably at least three face-lifts worth of stretched skin); and finally a towering bee hive of platinum blonde hair (with black roots). This creature appeared oblivious to the fact that it was no longer 1965. She sucked on a Virginia Slim and blew the smoke out slowly as she sauntered our way. She stood close, looking down and contemplating us while taking another drag. She tapped one foot. The smoke came out through her nose.

"So," she said finally. "You know who I am?" Her accent was thick New Jersey and by the deep, coarse sound of it, I'd guess she sucked down one of those cigarettes about every three minutes. She was a walking lung cancer ad.

"No," I said.

"Oh! I do!" Peggy raised her hand exuberantly in the air like a kindergartner on caffeine. "You're Viviana Buttaro!"

"Give the girl a cookie," grinned our new smoking fiend friend. She had one hand on her hip, and motioned with the other while she talked, the cigarette just along for the ride. "I'm Viviana Buttaro. I ain't had an easy life. You ain't makin' it any easier, you understand?" I didn't understand, but again, I wasn't going to tell her that.

"Frankie," she said, not taking her eyes off us, "get me an ash tray, will ya? I don't want to make a mess on my new carpet down here." Pug Mug moved out of the room obediently, so I took that to mean that his real name was Frankie. Original. I got the distinct impression, from his posture, that the Sinatra-loving goon wasn't too happy about being ordered around. I filed that observation away in my memory bank.

"It is a very nice carpet – I love Berber!" gushed Peggy. Roz shot her a look that basically said, "If they don't kill you, I will." Peggy moved back against the wall and shut her trap. Viviana sashayed leisurely to the monkey cages. "Hello babies." She made kissing noises at the chattering primates. "Give mommy some kissums?" She made more kissing noises, eliciting shrieks from the caged animals. "See," she said, turning her attention to us humans, "you've become a real pain in my ass. What's the fuckin' deal? Things was goin' real good, except for a mistake here and there. I coulda cleaned things up and moved on just fine – this is what I do, you see. Except for you three bitches."

Okay. That was it. I hadn't eaten since breakfast, a man who used three tubes of gel in his hair had thrown me into a basement, and now this ridiculous woman who growled like a man, had the nerve to call me a bitch.

"That's what I want to know," I said putting forth my best bitch attitude. "What's the fucking deal with these monkeys anyway? Are you smuggling them into the country?"

Viviana just smiled. No answer. Peggy gasped, covering her mouth in horror. I could hear her whispering to Roz, "I've never heard her use that word."

Moving back over to me, Viviana bent her knees until she was looking me in the eyes, then exhaled her smoke slowly, right into my face. "Don't get fresh, bitch," she said, getting herself back to a standing position. "I'm menopausal. And I've got a gun."

Frankie returned from another room with a green glass ashtray. He thrust it at Viviana, who took it without any acknowledgement. It fit easily into the palm of her hand. She flicked her ashes into the glass object while Frankie returned to his station as hostage-guard. At the same time, there was crashing as if someone were being thrown into the door upstairs. There was shouting and then the sound of multiple footsteps. We could hear a, "Come on buddy, move it. Move it!" as if someone were being forced down the stairs. It sounded like our friend, Elvis. But who did he have with him now?

Sure enough, Elvis appeared, shoving another body into the room. He seemed proud of his most current prize, presenting it to his spiky heeled boss. "Viv, lookie here what the cat drug in!"

I was shocked. Stupefied. Beyond stupefied. Aghast. Could this really be happening? It was more than I could handle. I let out a scream as he looked at me with his puppy-dog eyes.

It was Howard.

Chapter 16

Howard held his hands behind his head, elbows in the air, while Elvis held a gun to his back. He pushed the gun hard, forcing Howard further into the room. Howard didn't say a thing.

"Well," growled Viviana, "if it isn't our favorite friend from the FBI."

FBI? This woman was very confused. Howard rolled his eyes. I couldn't understand why he was only rolling his eyes. Why wasn't he defending himself against the obvious misunderstanding? Certainly a huge mistake had been made and I needed to set things right.

"He's not FBI," I cried, trying to explain my poor husband's innocence. "That's my husband, Howard."

Viviana and her crew laughed.

"Why are you laughing. He's an engineer. Tell them Howard." While words tumbled out of my mouth, I started putting two and two together. Very possibly, they equaled deception. I looked hopefully to Howard, praying that he would jump in and verify that I wasn't the stupidest wife alive. His eyes drifted guiltily to his shoes.

Viviana grinned again, blowing smoke out of her nose and snuffing the remaining little bit of cigarette out in the ashtray in her other hand. She handed the ashtray to Frankie, who took it like a good servant as she did her slow stroll over to Howard.

"Where is it honey?" she asked. Howard rolled his eyes again.

"Back pocket. Right," he said. She moved her hand slowly around to his back pocket, keeping her face close to his and smiling. "Nice ass," she said, as she pulled out a black leather wallet. He coughed. "You need to quit smoking, Viv. It's gonna kill you."

Hold on! What was going on here? Howard acted like he knew this flagitious floozy. Roz and Peggy looked like two chickens ready to lay eggs. Viviana flipped the wallet open and shoved it in my face. In fact, she had it so close I couldn't read it – I could see that it was gold and it definitely looked like an official badge – but, of course, the words were a blur.

"I don't have my reading glasses – would you mind backing it up a bit?"

"It says Federal Bureau of Investigation. Department of Justice," whispered Peggy in my ear.

"I think I can figure that much out, Peggy!" I screamed, surprising, even myself as I started to lose it. "Do you think I'm stupid?" Peggy cowered against the wall again and Howard warned me, "Barb, calm down. Be careful."

I glared at Howard. How dare he tell me to calm down. My temper was boiling over. "Calm down? Did you just really say that to me? I . . . I . . . I don't' even know how to respond to that! My blood sugar tanked out two hours ago, I've had huge wads of hair pulled out of head, and now this fire-breathing, monkey-killing reject from the sixties tells me you've been lying to me for our entire married life – maybe longer? Calm down? Did you really say that?" Howard started the eye roll, but I intercepted, quick on the draw. "Don't you ROLL your eyes at me!" I was shaking and realized that during my rant, I had stood up. Everyone was quiet as lambs. Even the chattering monkeys were silent. Viviana just smiled and tapped her foot. She evidently thought I was a hoot. A quick "Psst" from the floor brought me back down to earth. It was Roz, trying to get my attention and patting the floor next to her. "Maybe you'd better just sit back down," she said soothingly.

I looked around the room and realized why she was making the recommendation. Pug Mug had moved his hand to the butt of his gun. He looked ready to pull it out and whack me at a moment's notice. Sitting, I decided, was a good idea.

When I sat back on my rump, I looked at Peggy. I felt terrible for yelling at her. "I'm sorry Peg," I said, feeling my face get hot and my eyes fill with tears, "I'm just . . . . having a really bad day." I was trying to choke back the tears, because, obviously, bravery was something we all needed at the moment, but then I started to realize that not only had my husband of seventeen years been lying to me for at least that same amount of time, but now it was very likely that we had just succeeded in orphaning our three beautiful daughters. I thought of my precious little bouncy Amber with her gorgeous red head of curls, my more serious Bethany who always had to act like she was in control, and my dear nearly-a-woman Callie who would likely grow up to marry a Japanese man, and I wouldn't be there to drink sake at their wedding. No Howard to walk her down the aisle. All because I watched too many action movies and thought I had become a character in one.

Which caused me to think. My eyes stopped filling up with tears. I sniffed a little. What would one of my action heroes do in this situation? What would Mel do? Or Bruce? Chuck? Stall. That's it. Stall. Hold them off then catch them off guard. I looked at Howard. Was it possible he had reinforcements coming in? He worked for the FBI, after all. Maybe a SWAT team would be dropping on the roof any minute, and all we had to was stay alive long enough for them to arrive. Think. Think. I needed a plan for stalling a bad guy. Talk! That's how they always stall in the movies. Keep the bad guys talking. Evidently, criminals love to blather on and on about their ingenious crimes.

The room was still quiet and everyone's eyes were on me – probably waiting for another freak-out. "I'm okay," I said, looking to my two friends with me on the floor. Then to Howard – "And I'll be careful."

Finally, I proceeded with Operation: Stall the Bad Guys. "So, Viviana," I said, pulling myself together, "I think you were about to tell me about the monkeys – you said you were smuggling them into the country. . . ."

"You ain't too smart, are you?" Viviana sneered, lighting up again. "Elvis, let Agent Marr here join his friends. So, you wanna explain things to your snoopy wife here?"

"His name is really Elvis?" I cried. Wow. That was kind of cool.

"Joey 'Elvis' Scarletti." said Howard as he hit the floor next to me.

"It's my hair," smiled Elvis. "You like?"

I grimaced inwardly.

"I saw a picture of him on the Internet too," said Peggy. "He worked for Tito Buttaro – he's a hat."

Everyone, including Howard, looked puzzled.

"I'm a what?" asked Elvis. He looked like he didn't know if he should be insulted or not.

"A hat," she repeated.

Howard gave her one more quizzical look, shook his head and dismissed her. "Elvis is a soldier – he worked under Buttaro – Tito "The Butler" Buttaro. Butarro was a capo."

"That's the word!" Peggy said pointing her finger to the air. "I knew it was something you put on your head."

"The Butler?" I queried.

"Wise-guy rumor has it that he whacked Jimmy Hoffa. The name is a sort of code."

"I don't get it," I said.

"The mystery of who killed Jimmy Hoffa . . . "

"Oh! I get it!" cried Peggy. "The Butler did it! Cool." She smiled and sat back again, satisfied she'd made up for the hat comment.

"So, getting back to the capo thing," interrupted Roz, "is a capo the same as a boss?" I answered that one. I knew my mafia movies.

"No," I said. "I'm pretty sure a boss is at the top of a family. A capo works for a boss and a soldier works for a capo. Money flows uphill to the Boss."

"Whoa," said Elvis. "She knows her shit. She musta read *Mafia for Dummies*."

"Yeah," agreed Viviana. "Let's open up a school and let Snoopy be the Professor of Wise-guys." The four of them laughed.

"Except in this case," continued Howard seriously, "maybe the money flows a little differently. Right, Viv?" Viviana just shrugged. She wasn't giving up a lot of information yet, but at least we appeared to be stalling okay. I took a moment, watching Howard, considering him nearly a stranger as he talked so knowingly about these gangster hosts of ours. Unfortunately, for all of my upset, I didn't have the luxury of pondering my husband's deceit. I was keeping my ears alert for the sound of those SWAT helicopters landing on the roof.

"Well, I'm confused," I said, working to keep the conversation going. "I thought Tito has been missing for a few years."

Howard nodded affirmative. "Oh, he's been missing alright. Dead missing, we're pretty sure. According to one of our informants, Viviana 'Smoky' Buttaro had her own husband killed, chopped into little pieces and fed to the sharks."

Viviana smiled, so I assumed this to be at least in the ballpark of the truth.

"Why?" I asked.

Viv didn't miss a beat to answer. "He was a dumb-shit. Plain and simple. Didn't know his head from his ass. I should-a had him whacked sooner. Shit-For-Brains nearly broke the Crooks operation right from the beginning. I kept him around anyway. Thought he had potential. I was wrong."

"What's the Crooks operation?" Roz asked. She was taking quite an interest.

"Should I tell them," Howard asked, "or would you like the honor, Viv?"

Viviana waved her nicotine-stained hand in the air. "Oh, you're such a good story teller. Go ahead. None of you assholes is gonna live long enough to tell another soul anyhow. Spill it. Let's see if you know your stuff, Signor Federali."

Howard went on to explain that twenty-nine years ago, Tito and Viviana Buttaro had grown tired of sending all their hard earned money up to the Boss who was then Vinnie Cuccinelli of the Cuccinelli family out of Philadelphia, and devised their own money making scheme. The problem,

Howard said, was two-fold. Tito really was a dumbshit. Turns out, Viviana was the brains behind the capo. That was number one. Number two: if Cuccinelli found out that Tito had a secret profit venture on the side, and put a woman in control, both Buttaros would end up with egg on their face and bullets in their backs. Cuccinelli, along with a majority of the mobster world, did not agree with the ideas of self-employment or feminism. Bottom line, they had to be stealth. According to Howard, stealth wasn't Tito's strong suit.

"So what was the scheme?" I asked.

"Real Estate. It's the place to be," answered Viviana, who was clearly enjoying the story of her life in crime. She was basking in self-regard.

Howard went on. "Tito and Viviana created a man named Fred Crooks, but he only existed on paper. Crooks was really just a front name for the Buttaro alliance," he said.

"Bull-shit! No alliance!'" shouted Viviana. She defiantly cocked her thumb toward her chest. "It was me! All me! I was Crooks. Alliance my ass! I came up with the name, I arranged the hijackings that got us the investment money, I did the research and the fucking leg work. All me baby! He was just a grunt – a stupid, fucking grunt. He worked for me. Don't you forget that."

"I won't," smiled Howard. I knew that smile. He just got something he wanted.

I was beginning to understand, to some degree, what Viviana had been up to. One of my favorite movies was *Donnie Brasco*, so I knew when she mentioned "hijackings" that she meant she was sending her thugs out to stop freight trucks by force, and steal the goods being transported. Those goods were then sold to any number of places for cold, hard cash. Evidently, she was reinvesting that money in real estate, rather than sending it up to Cuccinelli. A big time "no, no" in the world of organized crime.

"Who is Grumpy Lawnmower Guy? How does he play out in all of this?" I asked.

"Hired worker. Simple enough." explained Howard. "He takes care of all of the properties. Turns out, over the years, Viviana's enterprise had acquired over twenty properties, mostly in Northern Virginia, and then a couple in the Western side of Pennsylvania. Northern Virginia was prospected by analysts in the seventies to be ripe for real estate growth and they were right. Viviana chose the right money train."

Roz shook her head as if she didn't understand. "How do you make money buying houses that stay vacant?" Roz asked.

"Most are rentals, paying for themselves legitimately. Only three are vacant and come into use whenever Viv needs them."

"To smuggle monkeys?" I asked. Viviana looked disgusted throwing up her arms and sending ashes flying.

"Where does she get this monkey smuggling thing from anyway? What? You think I'm really this stupid?" She took a deep, calming drag on her cancer stick.

"Oh, they're not smuggling," corrected Howard. "They're disposing." Viviana smiled big and blew out a puff of smoke. I was beginning to think my demise wouldn't be by a gunshot to the head, but by second-hand smoke.

"Yeah. It's been my best and smartest financial venture. Better than the real estate. Quite a nice set-up, if I do say so myself," She replied. She was a proud criminal.

"I don't get it," I said.

"Oh!" Roz lit up – figuratively, not literally – "I get it! The testing lab – Meadowland has been paying her to dispose of their testing monkeys. Am I right?"

"Wrong," said Viviana. "You gotta think bigger baby. See, this is why I'm a Wise-guy – emphasis on WISE – and you're just a stupid little housewife. No offense. Meadowland is a nothing company. They can't pay the big bucks."

"Who then?" I asked Howard.

"Pharmaceuticals," he replied.

"Biggest industry in these fifty-one United States outside illegal drug trade," said Viviana, stamping out another ciggie.

"Fifty," said Peggy.

"What?" asked Viviana.

"Fifty. It's fifty states. Not fifty one."

"You sure?"

"Yup," quipped Peggy.

Viviana pointed her finger at Peggy. "You! Shut up. You're makin' me mad," she said.

Howard went on to tell us that Viviana had shown up on the FBI radar a little over five years ago, after an informant had mentioned there was a lady wise-guy operating on her own and doing business with at least two different pharmaceutical companies. She supplied the means to discreetly dispose of primates that were used in the testing process of all sorts of drugs, but, in the case of Meadowland, mostly new and improved anti-depressants, sleeping aids and other mind altering drugs that were currently Pharma's biggest source of income. In return for the favor, the pharmaceutical companies supplied her with brand name drugs to sell for profit. Big profit.

"We planted a guy on the inside of Parks and Rowe," said Howard. "They were one of the companies cited by our informant. Our undercover guy was gathering evidence against both Parks and Rowe and Viviana and her mini-mob. We were making good progress, but then he got found out."

I put my hand to my mouth, suddenly realizing something. "Was he . . ." I started to say.

"Yeah," he nodded, his face grave. "The guy you found in the house."

I started to feel sick again, remembering the grisly scene. Luckily, there was no food in my stomach to throw up.

"Who found him out?" asked Roz.

"That'd be me, sweet cheeks," answered Maxine, breaking her silence from across the room. She had been sitting on the stairs the whole time, keeping mum, save a chuckle here or there.

"As it turns out," said Howard, "Big Pharma keeps their own undercover henchmen – henchwoman in this case – on the payroll. Her cover was as a receptionist for Parks and Rowe. Their local Tysons Corner office. We didn't figure it out until it was too late."

"That's because I'm good," said Maxine, letting the pride in voice roll off her tongue slowly. "Real good."

"But wait," I said. "You skipped over the messed-up operation twenty-nine years ago. What happened? Why did Tito terrorize our neighbors?" Viviana didn't like that question. I detected that I'd hit a nerve. She waved one hand dismissively and strolled back over to her monkey cage. The critters began chattering up a storm again.

"All this talk is starting to bore me," she said. "It's time to get this show on the road." She looked at her watch. "I don't want to miss Survivor."

Suddenly, the lights flickered then went out for about ten seconds. I could hear Peggy wimper. When the lights came back on, I saw that Howard must have been trying to take advantage of the power outage, making a move toward Elvis, but he hadn't made it. He was sitting on top of Peggy, hence the wimper.

"Shit!" yelled Viviana.

"It's those storms," said Maxine. "News says there could be tornadoes."

"As long as it don't interrupt my show," said Viviana motioning to Elvis, who had put his gun to the ready during the brief outage. "Take him. You know what to do. Make it quick."

Elvis moved our way and grabbed Howard's arm, jerking him hard. "Move asshole. I ain't got all day." He pointed with his gun in the direction of the stairs to the main level. I gasped. Howard looked back at me and gave me a sad sort of smile. *I love you,* he mouthed. Then they ascended the stairs and he was gone. My heart was pounding and my head was swimming. It felt like the room was spinning.

"I remember him when he was just a little boy," said Viviana.

What was she talking about?

"Elvis?" I asked, trying to get a grip.

"No – your husband, stupid." She smiled an evil, Grinchy smile. "You don't know, do you?"

"Know what?" I asked.

"He changed his name years ago – when he was a teenager. He used to be little Sammy Donato. Tito whacked his pop, Mario."

Well, the punches just kept coming, didn't they?

Then I heard it.

Gunshot.

Chapter 17

The shot sounded from outside. I screamed. The monkeys screamed. Roz and Peggy screamed. We were all screaming.

"What's wrong with you?" scowled Viviana.

"You just killed my husband! What do you think is wrong with me?" I screamed, half crazed.

"Jesus, you're a pain. That wasn't a gunshot." She made kissing sounds to the monkey cage again. "Shhh, babies, shhhh. Everything's okay." When the monkeys finally reacted positively to her soothing mommy talk, she turned back around. "That was thunder."

"Didn't sound like thunder to me, Viv – sounds like the raccoons are in the trash cans again," countered Maxine.

"Frankie – go check it out," ordered Viviana

"Do I have to?" Frankie was actually whining. I was surprised. "You know doze raccoons freak me out." His body shivered involuntarily.

"Move your ass stupid!" she growled at him, pointing in the direction she wanted him to move.

"*Strega*," he grumbled under his breath as he ascended the stairs to the back of the house, slump-shouldered like a pouting child. Peggy whispered in my ear. "He doesn't like her very much."

"What?" I whispered back.

"*Strega* – it's Italian. He just called her a witch." Now there were other crashing sounds, although it was hard to tell where they were coming from.

Viviana snuffed out yet another cigarette then pointed to us. "You three – don't try anything stupid." She motioned to Maxine. "Follow me." They disappeared up the same set of stairs as Elvis and Howard. No sooner had they gone out of sight, than we heard a tapping on the basement window above our heads. At first I thought it was hail, but then realized there was a pattern to it. I looked up and thought I saw a face in the window. More tapping. Someone wanted our attention. Ignoring Viviana's threats, I stood up to see who was tapping. It was Officer Brad! He motioned for me to open the window.

Luckily, the latch turned easily and the window, which was at ground level, was open in a flash. Rain trickled in. Officer Brad was on his stomach and protected by a dark, plastic poncho. His face was still glistening with a heavy coat of rain water. He took a quick swipe at getting water out of his eyes before speaking quickly. "Get yourself upstairs. There's a guest room in the back of the main level – it has a bathroom. Get to that bathroom. Take this with you," he whispered. He threw in a small, cloth wrapped bundle that landed with a muffled thump on the carpeted floor. He must have been hiding it under his poncho, because it was barely wet, probably only catching some droplets on its trip from his hand to the window.

"I can't! They'll kill us!" I whispered in a panicked tone. Personal extinction was not the plan I had for myself right now. I was going to live to raise my children and rescue my husband. There was also that little dream to be invited to the Academy Awards after my website and movie reviews win countless accolades of their own. Putting myself between a gun and a known killer seemed a sure way to miss it all.

"You need to do this. Figure something out," he whispered with more urgency.

I thought for a moment. Staring at the handsome police officer, for some strange reason, I was reminded of the time he stopped me on the way back from the museum. Aha! An idea clicked in. I didn't know if it was a good idea, but it was the only one I had, so it'd have to suffice.

"Does it have a shower?" I asked

"What?"

"A shower! Does the bathroom have a shower? Or a bathtub?"

"I don't know. . ." Suddenly, Officer Brad rolled away from the window. Afraid we'd been caught. I quick shut the window, making sure not to lock it, and plopped back down next to Peggy, who had already slipped the bundle under her leg for safe keeping. My heart was pounding so hard I could hear it in my ears.

"Who was that?" asked Roz, whose face was noticeably losing its color. She was starting to look like Edgar Winter. Her generally perfect golden bob of shiny hair was tossed every which way, as if she'd just slept on it for twenty-four hours and her hand was swelling badly. Stress was showing all over my petite friend.

"Officer Brad."

"Who?"

"I've forgotten his real name again – the cute cop that looks like Brad Pitt."

"What's he doing here?"

"Looking for a game of Parchese," I said throwing up my hands. "He's here and he's got a plan. That's all I know."

"What kind of plan?" asked Peggy.

"I've got to get to a bathroom upstairs."

"Then what?"

"I don't know."

"So where's the plan?"

"I told you he HAD a plan. I didn't tell you I understood it."

"This sounds bad," said Roz. "He's the police for crying out loud – why doesn't he just call in the squads? Or the troops." Poor Roz could barely hold her head up. I was worried about her. I noticed she had taken to a nervous habit of rubbing her good hand along her thighs, smoothing out the fabric of her floral rayon skirt. She was right. Why couldn't he just come in with his comrades, take over the place and save us all? I kept listening for that thwump, thwump, thwump of the Swat helicopter, but all I heard was intermittent thunder. It seemed that any large sweeping rescue from law enforcement was not going to be forthcoming.

"How do you think he found us?" Asked Peggy.

"I don't know – good question. Howard maybe?"

Peggy shook her head. "That doesn't make sense. Why would he bring in one lone policeman?"

"Sense? None of this makes sense! It's freakin' insane! I go out in my van doing a crazy Nancy Drew imitation to follow your surfer dude friend around town, and end up in some Italian-American lunatic asylum!" Roz was losing it. I reached over and placed my hands over hers, hoping to comfort her. Strange, I thought, how taking the time to comfort someone whose fate was just as tenuous as my own, actually brought me a moment of peace. The peace didn't last long though, because down the back stairs came Frankie, mumbling something about raccoons and bitches on spikey heels. He was shaking off water like a dog who'd just had a bath. I had to think quick. If Peggy was right, Frankie wasn't too happy with Viviana right now, and if we were lucky, the discord might be a chronic condition we could exploit.

"Hey Frankie, are you okay?" I asked, trying to get on his good side.

"Fuckin' raccoons. I tell you, I don't know how yous can stand livin' around here. It's like the Goddamn wilderness. As long as I been around here, I still ain't used to it."

"There were raccoons out there?"

"Must'a been. Trashcans were all knocked over, bags ripped, trash everywhere. Never seen 'em come out in rain like dis though." He said, trying to shake a leg dry. I suspected the "raccoons" looked a whole lot like Brad Pitt.

"So, that Viviana," I said to Frankie, "I noticed she kind of treats you like . . . well, she's not so nice to you."

"You mean she treats me like shit?" He looked around. "Where'd she go?"

"Upstairs – that way. How does that make you feel?"

"What?"

"You said she treats you like shit – how does that make you feel?"

"What are you, some kind of stupid, fuckin' psychiatrist?"

"Just looks to me like you are a little unhappy."

"You said it. I ain't a little unhappy. I'm a lot unhappy. I'm gettin' real sick of doin' all her dirty work and gettin' shit for it. Elvis too. I should just let you go right now. That'd show her."

My heart skipped a beat and out of my peripheral vision, I could see Peggy and Roz perk up a bit. We might have our ticket out of here. I felt an adrenaline surge as the thought of a possible escape might be imminent.

"Boy," I laughed, "wouldn't that be . . . why don't you?"

"What?"

"Show her. Let us go."

"Are you crazy?"

Well, it was worth a try anyway. But I still had another trick up my sleeve. "I was just joking. I know that would be too risky. Nonetheless, I've got this problem you might be able to help me with," I ventured further. "It doesn't involve anything as crazy as letting us go."

"What kind of problem?"

Okay, I thought, *here it goes. Hope it works.* "It's a little embarrassing."

"I ain't sayin' I'm gonna help you, but if you don't tell me the problem, I sure as hell can't do anyting."

I shifted where I sat for emphasis. "I have this condition called Irritable Bowel Syndrome."

"What the hell is that?" He cringed, as if he were afraid to hear the answer.

To be perfectly honest, I didn't know anything about it myself, except that I'd seen commercials advertising some drug to solve the problem – that is if the twenty side effects, including dry mouth, hives, dementia, and liver failure didn't kill a person first. In any event, Irritable Bowel Syndrome seemed like three good words to throw at this Neanderthal goon in hopes he'd take pity on me and help me out of the basement and up to that bathroom.

"Well, I sort of have these bouts where, I . . . well, I can't control myself . . . my bowels I mean. Especially when I'm nervous or upset . . .like I am now. I've sort of had," I winced for added impact, "an . . .accident."

"Oh! Jesus!" He put his hands out to stop me from talking. "Don't! I don't wanna know! Holy crap."

"Yeah. That's the right word." I lowered myself to a barely detectable whisper. "I really need to clean up, if you know what I mean. Could you get me to a bathroom?"

"Ah, Christ!" he muttered, pacing around the room. He seemed to be silently thinking the idea through. I looked at Peggy and Roz. Peggy motioned to the wrapped bundle under her leg and gave me a questioning look. I nodded. If all went well, we'd need it in a minute. Finally, as if having an epiphany, Frankie said, "What the fuck, let's go. He pulled open his jacket, revealing a gun in a holster. He pulled the gun out, pointing it at us.

"I'll have to take all three of ya. I'm not leaving anyone alone. Don't try to pull nothin'." We slowly got up from the floor. Roz' legs were shaking visibly. Peggy held the bundle close to her leg as she stood up. I was afraid Frankie would catch sight of it.

"Frankie?"

"What?" he sighed, obviously exasperated with me.

"I'm afraid there's a stain on my . . . backside. It's just embarrassing – can't you walk in front of us? We'll follow – I mean, what are we going to do? Honestly." For a moment he was silent, and I was afraid I might have blown it. Suddenly, he grabbed Roz by the arm, shoved her in front of him and put the gun in her back. "You two follow me close. You pull any funny stuff, your friend here gets a one way ticket to an audience with the Big Guy." Roz screamed and started crying. My heart ached for her, but we had to keep going. We were getting somewhere.

He pushed Roz up the stairs while Peggy tried to slip me the bundle. I shook my head furiously and motioned her to hide it in the front of her pants. Her sweatshirt was baggy and would hide it better than my thin t-shirt. By the size and shape, I suspected with uneasiness that it was a gun – the last thing we needed to get caught. I watched as she slipped it under her sweatshirt then put her thumb up behind her back, indicating success. My fingers were crossed that she concealed it well enough.

As we came out at the top of the stairs, we found ourselves in a hallway, standing on pristine wood floors. Directly across the hall from us was a closed door. Frankie motioned to the door.

"There. That's the bathroom." He opened the door. I moved to peek in, keeping my rear end from his view, working to keep with the pretense that I was experiencing bowel issues. It was a small half bath – no bedroom attached. I had to admit, it was tastefully decorated in classy reds and golds and the modern pedestal sink was to die for, but it wasn't the bathroom Officer Brad told me to find. My heart pumped double time. I resorted to prayers. *Dear God, please let him fall for this* . . . "This doesn't have a shower," I said. "Or at least a bath tub."

"What?"

"I can't . . .clean myself here." I winced again, expressing my point best as I could. I was beginning to wish this was being filmed, because frankly, I was turning in an Oscar winning performance. "I really need a shower or a bath tub. If you know what I mean. I'm sorry to be so much trouble." Then I put my hand to my stomach. "Oh!" I wailed.

"What?" Frankie asked.

"Oh, my God. Oh, this isn't good. I'm feeling another wave . . . ."

"This way!" Frankie moved faster than the paparazzi chasing Britney Spears down Sunset Boulevard. Following his lead down the hall, we found ourselves in what appeared to be the back of the main floor. We landed in front of another door, which Frankie threw open in haste. He shoved Roz in and pointed the gun at Peggy and I. "There! Get in!" We did as he said, and the door closed behind us. It seemed that Frankie had had enough of the three crazy ladies from the suburbs.

I flipped on the light switch. We stood in the middle of a nicely appointed, reasonably sized bedroom with a queen-sized bed covered with a black and tan bedspread. A sleek, modern black dresser took up a large portion of the wall across from the bed. Black satin curtains were pulled back allowing a view from both corner windows. The room had an obvious masculine feel, and I thought I detected a hint of a familiar male cologne.

"Did you really . . . you know . . . in your pants?" Peggy asked.

"No! Gross."

"Just wondering. Pretty inventive of you."

"I'm not so inventive – if you want to know the truth, I nearly had an accident in my van on Purple Poplar the other day. Chili dogs didn't agree with me."

"Oh." She bobbed her head with understanding. "Been there, done that. Has that ever happened to you, Roz?" We both turned to find Roz curled up in a ball on the bed, head in her hands, weeping quietly. Sitting down next to her, I placed my hand on her arm.

"Are you okay?" I asked. She nodded her head and sniffed.

"I've never been so scared. He had a gun in my back!"

"I know. Trust me. The gun thing is new to all of us."

"They're going to kill us, Barb!"

She had a point. "I know it seems that way, but let's look at this from the glass-is-half-full perspective. We're alive right now. As long as we're alive, seems to me like we have a fighting chance. There's at least one policeman out there, obviously working to save our asses, and my guess is the authorities are on their way. Roz, they've got Howard – he might be dead, but he might still be alive and if he is, I'm going to do anything I can to save him. We really need to pull ourselves together and figure our way out of this – now. We need to stay alive for our kids' sakes. Do you really want to leave your kids behind with Peter, doomed to Spaghettio dinners for the rest of their childhood lives?"

She wiped her eyes and sat up, sniffing a few more times. "Okay. Okay. You're right. I can do this."

Peggy had been checking the three different doors in the room. The first two had been closets. "Hmm," she said opening closet two, "men's clothes. He likes black." She opened the third door. Jackpot.

"Here it is," she said. "Now what?" Getting up from Roz's side, I stepped over and looked in. More black and tan. Black towels, black rug, tan soap dish and toothbrush caddy.

"I don't know. He just told me to get myself here. I guess we just sit and wait."

"We can't wait for too long," said Roz, the sniffles winding down. "You're just supposed to be 'cleaning up' – remember? That can't take forever."

I spied a small frosted window on the wall opposite the sink. "Maybe we aren't supposed to wait. Maybe we're supposed to go out that window." Moving to twist the latch open, my hands stopped mid-air at the sound of shouting.

"What's going on in there?" It was Frankie. Peggy closed the bathroom door, leaving me alone. I decided to lock the door for added safety. All I could hear was muffled voices.

"She's almost done." Peggy shouted back. Since they were the only words I could hear clearly, and since they sounded especially loud, I assumed she had meant for me to hear her. I put the toilet seat down and sat, my back to the black shower curtain. Muffled voices drifted through the closed door, but I couldn't make out clear sentences anymore. Suddenly, a crack of lightning lit up the frosted window pane, followed immediately by near deafening thunder that shook the house from its rafters. The lights popped off and women screamed. Definitely Peggy and Roz. Before I could jump up, the shower curtain behind me swung open and a strong, calloused hand grasped my mouth, squelching the scream that was about to escape.

Chapter 18

I was jerked into the bathtub. Animalistic fight-or-flight instincts took over, and I thrashed about wildly in the pitch-black room. My attempts at escape seemed futile since I was obviously struggling with a large, strong man. There was also that familiar cologne scent from the bedroom. I was beginning to wish I had joined my mother in her venture to master the martial art of Tae Kwon Do. A black belt would have been helpful in such a situation. It was times like this, I thought, that hindsight was definitely 20/20. I quickly calculated that the next best thing to a black belt was teeth – and I had those. I pulled at the man's hands as hard as I could, making just enough room to open my lips and go for a chomp. Unfortunately, the sadly weak bite only caused a temporary release in the strength holding me. Definitely not enough to allow me a chance to flee. I remained bound by his arms, one of his hands still cupping my mouth. He whispered in my ear.

"Lady, stop fightin' me!" It was Elvis! My panic quadrupled. Now I knew I was a dead woman, the first nail pounded securely into my awaiting coffin. He whispered in my ear again. "Listen, will ya? Settle." It was true what they say – your life does start passing before your eyes as you stand on the threshold of death. Mental pictures flashed like images in a slide show. Me blowing out candles on my fifth birthday; my dad pushing me off on a triumphantly successful glide when I was trying to learn to ride my shiny blue bike; my parents standing on either side of me, cap on my curly mess of a head the day I graduated from high school; my best friend, Julie, and me, holding up mugs of beers and smiling joyously the day I turned twenty-one; Howard and me on our perfectly sunny wedding day; me holding a newborn Callie in my arms; Bethany presenting me with her personal Mother-Of-The-Year Award at her preschool Mother's Day party; Amber beautifully costumed as Tinker Bell last Halloween . . . each new picture of my life seemed to bring me greater and greater strength to survive. I couldn't die. Damn it, I would live to see my children again! I must have slowed my struggle as all of the thoughts rushed through my mind, because Elvis whispered in my ear again.

"There. That's good." Everything seemed to move in slow motion. "Now," he continued in a muted tone, "I have a message for you from Sammy."

Who? Where had I just heard that name? Sammy, Sammy . . . . . I was running the name through my memory data bank. I wasn't registering that name. Then BANG! I got a match. I felt a loosening on Elvis' grip over my mouth and I pulled away enough to shout, "Do you mean Howard?" Another crack of lightning lit up the room for a second, sending another shock wave through the house.

"Shhhhhh!" Elvis cupped my mouth again. "You gotta be quiet. This ain't gonna work if you don't keep it down!" What was he saying? What ain't gonna work? I was confused, but he had my attention. I needed to hear what he had to tell me about Howard. "You gonna fight me? You gonna scream?" I shook my head no. He released his grip on my mouth. I was panting like a sheep dog on a hundred degree day. Elvis removed his arm from its hold around my body and it sounded like he was rooting around in his pants. The next thing I knew, the bathroom was dimly lit by the flame of his disposable lighter.

Our bodies were embarrassingly entwined in the bathtub with my legs sticking straight up in the air. I must have hit my elbow on the side, when he pulled me in, because it ached now. I rubbed it, becoming simultaneously aware that Roz and Peggy were calling out my name in loud whispers. Elvis put his finger to his mouth, letting me know I still needed to keep things mum, then whispered, "Tell 'em to keep it down, that you got you a plan." I nodded obediently, still not sure if this action would end in self-preservation or self-annihilation. I crawled out of the bathtub, moving toward the door on my hands and knees.

They were just on the other side of the door, whispering to me again. "Barb! Are you okay?" They were trying the door knob, but it was still locked.

"Keep it down!" I whispered. I actually didn't know why we had to be whispering, but that's what the man ordered, so I figured it was necessary for some reason. "Keep it down – I . . . I . . " I had a momentary lapse in memory, forgetting what I was supposed to say. *Oh yeah!* "I . . . I got me a plan," I whispered back through the door.

"What?"

"I mean, I've got a plan."

"Let us in." I looked to Elvis to see if that was allowed. He was having some difficulty extracting his large frame from the small tub and our meager light flicked out briefly every time his thumb lost contact with the lighter igniter. He shook his head, telling me they had to stay out.

"Why?" I asked him. Peggy heard me, and thinking I was talking to them, answered.

"Why not? Come on, open the door!"

Having successfully rolled himself out of the tub enclosure, Elvis got down on one knee, moved in as close as he could to my ear and whispered into it. "Ax 'em where's Frankie at anyway?"

"Where's Frankie?"

"We don't know." Peggy replied.

Elvis repeated his mouth to ear whisper maneuver, which was really starting to gross me out. "Ask 'em is da bedroom door open, or closed?"

"Is da bedroom door open or closed?"

"Why are you talking like that?"

It was a strange habit I had, picking up accents easily. The last time we visited my great Aunt Gertrude Fenstermacher in Sheboygan, it only took me ten minutes to start uttering, "yah?" and "Ach mein-Gott!"

"Is it opened or closed? Just tell me."

"Must be closed. It's pitch black, but I didn't hear anyone open it. Frankie told us to stay put when the lights went out and I think he went off somewhere. Wait . . . there's a little light . . . from under this door. Do you have light in there? Did you find a flash light?"

Elvis moved in again for yet another command, and finally, repulsion got the best of me. I just couldn't stand his slobbery lips tickling my ear anymore. Without thinking about the consequences, I shouted at him, and put my hands up to pre-empt the inevitable. "Don't do that again! Come on! Ask them yourself! And why are we whispering anyway?"

"We can't let Viv and Max hear – why you tink?"

Curiosity must have been getting the best of them because I heard them fiddling with the door knob. It sounded like they were trying to unlock it.

"Barb!" Peggy said. "What's going on?" Before I knew what was happening, the door was falling open and Peggy was tumbling into the bathroom and onto the hard tile floor with Roz falling on top of her. In Peggy's hand was a hair pin. Exactly at the same time, a strange rumbling, almost chugging sound, like the sound of a lawn mower being started, preceded the slow return of electricity to the house. Instead of popping on, like I'm used to after a power outage, the lights came on dim at first, then gaining in intensity, as if the electricity was getting to them slowly.

"Generator," Elvis informed us. "Frankie's the only one besides me knows how to start that ting." Wide eyed and startled, like two bush babies caught in the light of a nocturnal nature photographer, Roz and Peggy were frozen in an awkward pile on the floor. They stared at Elvis, then at me, and luckily, didn't say a word.

Elvis handed me my cell phone. "Here, call Sammy," he shook his head and corrected himself. "Howard. Call Howard. He wants to talk to yous." I blew out an exuberant sigh of relief, taking the phone from his hand. My Howard was still alive. There was hope. Maybe Officer Brad was with him. Maybe they had the place surrounded. Those SWAT helicopters were on their way after all.

While I touched the number one, then "talk" on my phone, connecting me to Howard's cell, Elvis reprimanded Roz and Peggy. "Yous two there – get in here and close dat door! Yous want to mess dis whole ting up?" He pointed to the bathtub. "In there." He said. I understood his point. Even though the house was massively large, the bathroom we were occupying was quite small. Roz and Peggy climbed sheepishly into the cramped tub, facing each other and hugging their knees.

There were two rings and then connection. "Barb?" It was Howard! The last time I remembered being so excited to hear his voice was the time he called me from the grocery store to tell me he was bringing home wine from a bottle instead of from a box. Immediately, though, I could tell the connection was bad.

"Howard?" Nothing. He was gone. I looked at the display on my phone. I'd lost the connection. I only had one little flickering bar. Damn! Not now! No, no, no!!!! I shook the phone, as if that would bring him back on the line. Getting an emotional grip, I touched one and hit "talk" again. Weak rings connected to a barely audible Howard. "crackle, crackle . .Bar, crackle, crackle . . me?" Dead again. "This isn't happening!" I whisper-screamed as I tried to strangle the poor phone's little neck. If my life didn't depend on eventually connecting to Howard, I am very positive I would have chucked the gizmo hard to the floor, smashing it into pieces.

Peggy broke her silence. "What's your network? If it's Phone-America, I have trouble with that one all of the time. I can't ever get a good signal. Maybe you should switch." Either Elvis didn't like her criticism of Phone-America or he just didn't want us bringing attention to our happy little convention in the bathroom.

"Yous." He whispered, pointing to her, his finger so close to her face she went cross-eyed, "Keep dat trap shut." Then he played charades, imitating a zipper being shut across his mouth. Peggy mimicked his motion, and nodded, expressing that she understood. I figured that might shut Peggy up for say, five minutes. Then he pointed to both of them and said, "Stay put – don't move from dat spot. We'll be back." Then he moved to the door, putting his ear close. His one eye that was visible moved around in its socket, as if its motion coincided with his thoughts of what he heard or didn't hear. Finally, he pulled his head away, saying to me, "We'll go out in da room – you go to da farthest window, hear? See if yous can call from there. I gots to stand at the door and be ready for Frankie – no doubt he's gonna be here any minute."

Elvis opened the door ever so slowly, peeking out to make sure no one was in the room. He motioned that the coast was clear, opening the door wide enough for us both to slip out. Two very large windows met in the far left corner of the room. Between me and those windows was the bed. To our left, about ten feet, was the door that opened up to the hallway. I crawled across the bed, then down on the floor to the corner where I crouched. The windows were quite large, nearly as tall as the wall itself, and probably four feet wide, making it nearly impossible to stay hidden from the outside. Rain pounded hard against them. I looked over at Elvis. He stood poised at the door, his gun now at its ready, pointed at the door. Was he going to whack Frankie? What sort of convoluted mafia mess had I gotten myself mixed up in?

I flipped my phone open, but before my finger could make contact, the phone started ringing. I must have inadvertently taken it off silent mode when I dialed Howard the first time. I touched "talk" without looking at the caller ID. "Howard?" The responding voice was distinctly feminine, and distinctly that of my mother.

"Barbara? Barbara? Are you okay? Oh my God, I've been so worried about you!"

"Mother! I can't talk now!"

Unfazed and talking a million miles a minute, my mother rattled on. "Barbara! I'm in the hotel room with the girls. There are men from the FBI standing outside our door and they won't let us out. And I'm watching the news! They're live at a scene – a man was shot at and he says the shooters kidnapped two women. There are two abandoned vans. One looks like yours! Callie said she heard you scream when she called. Did Eric find you?"

"Mom, I'm going to hang up now . . ." My phone shook alerting me that another call was coming in. This time I looked at the caller ID. Howard. I needed to make sure my mother didn't screw things up. "Mom, I swear, DO NOT call me again or you'll get me killed!" I pushed talk again, disconnecting my mother and bringing Howard to life in my ear.

"Howard?"

"Barb! Can you hear me now?"

"Yes, I can hear you."

"I can see you. Look out the window." I turned around, moving to half a standing position, scanning the expansive lot, only partially lit from the floods that lit up the other end of the house. But if he could see me, I must be able to see him. Then, way back by the tree line, I saw a small light flash on and his face was illuminated. He was holding a flashlight up to his face and wearing some sort of dark colored rain poncho, the hood pulled over his head. He was waving his left arm back and forth, high over his head to attract my attention. I smiled, jumped up and down and waved back. He was probably seventy feet from the back corner of the house and I noticed he stood only ten or fifteen steps away from a wooden, double-door utility shed.

"I see you! I see you!"

"Listen Barb, don't ask questions, just listen." It was very hard to hear him because the rain was so loud in the receiver. I could tell he was trying not to yell, but still be heard.

"This is very important. Elvis is working with us now. He's going to get Frankie on board. Once he does that, everyone is safe. Where are Roz and Peggy?"

"In the bathroom."

"Great! That bathroom has a window – tell them to crawl out and jump – it's about a five foot drop. We can get them to safety."

"What about me?!" I screamed.

"Do you trust me?"

I couldn't exactly answer that question immediately. There were definitely trust issues, given the fact that he'd lied to me for our entire married life.

For all I knew, he was really Sammy Donato, mafia mole, working within the FBI to uncover their methods of bringing down the mob. Howard correctly interpreted my silence.

"Let me re-phrase that – YOU HAVE TO TRUST ME. Are you listening carefully?" He asked.

Did I have a choice? "Yes."

"A plan is in place to sting Viviana. You're part of that plan. Keep this phone with you and do what Elvis says."

"Okay," I relented.

"Good. Now. . ." A loud pop rang out and simultaneously Howard flew backwards, as if being pushed by some strong force. The phone flew out of his hands, and he landed flat on his back. Confused, I thought the pop was lightning.

"Howard! Howard!" Our connection was gone. I shot an anxious look at Elvis, who had heard the pop and was already on his way over to the window. As we both looked out at Howard, sprawled on the ground, we saw a long legged male figure move in from the wooded area to Howard's left, limping as if unable to fully utilize his right foot. The man, soaked to the bone because he wasn't wearing a coat of any kind, bent over Howard's motionless body, apparently checking for vital signs. After the very brief check, he stood up, facing the house and bringing to view a long rifle or automatic weapon of some sort which he rested on his shoulder pointing into the air.

"Ah, Jesus H. Christ!" muttered Elvis under his breath, throwing us both to the floor. "He can't see us."

"Who is that?"

Elvis shook his head and rubbed his face with his hand. "That's No Toes. Dis ain't good," he said. "Dis ain't good."

Chapter 19

Quick mental re-cap: kidnapped by Mafia gang ruled by insane, chain-smoking reject from the sixties – female; discover husband has alias name and FBI badge that he's been able to keep hidden from me for seventeen years (reminder to self: get a clue!); follow half-baked scheme provided by Brad Pitt look-alike to make a quick get away through guest bathroom; wind up playing bad game of Twister in bathtub with Elvis Presley wanna-be; witness the whacking of FBI husband; hear Elvis Presley wanna-be proclaim, regarding husband's whacker: "That's No Toes" and follow up with obvious comment, "Dis ain't good." Would Al Pacino be caught dead in this movie? Definitely not.

I stood motionless in front of the window staring down at Howard's body. Who would play him in the movie? Duh! George Clooney, of course. Silly question, Barb. Silly question. How about Colt? He always strikes me as a young Robert Redford, but of course, Bob is way too old now to play Colt. Wouldn't want it to look like the time Clint Eastwood tried to play a forty-year old photographer in The Bridges of Madison County. Shirtless and flabby pecs. Nope. That was just plain wrong. Colt. Colt. Where IS Colt? Colt was with Howard in the Camry. Where is Colt now?

I must have been in shock. My thoughts were a frenzied attempt to distract myself from seeing my own husband shot dead before my eyes. Roz's voice calling from the bathroom snapped me right back.

"Barb! Barb! What was that?"

Gathering my wits about me, I wondered what to say. Elvis and I peeked out the window and watched while the limping, scarecrow-man grabbed Howard's arm and pulled him toward the shed.

"Barb!" Roz tried again. Elvis, definitely agitated, crawled across the room to the bathroom door.

"We got a problem here. Keep this door shut." Then he shut the door and returned to my side. By now, with great effort, the man had dragged Howard's body behind the shed. No longer able to see Howard, panic finally kicked in. Was he dead? I needed to find out. I turned on my stomach and crawled a couple of feet, then stood, ready to bolt for the door. Thoughts about how or where I would go were not formed in my mind at all – I was running on pure impulse. Elvis was up and stopped me dead in my tracks, holding me back far too easily with both of his arms. He seemed to know exactly what I was doing.

"You can't go out there," he said, his craggy face serious and stern. "You'll ruin everything."

"But he might be dead! We need to find out."

"If he's dead, he's dead. Ain't nothin' we're gonna do to change that. And right now, dead or alive, we got us bigger problems. From da looks a tings, I'm tinkin' No Toes ain't here to wish us a Happy Birthday."

Toes. Suddenly things made sense. "It was you," I said.

"Me?"

"Screaming that night behind the vacant house. You were calling his name."

Elvis nodded.

"For crying out loud, can't any of you have normal names? How about John or David or Michael. Does this freak have a real name?"

"His given name's Frankie. That's why we calls him No Toes. So's not to confuse."

I was really starting to have my fill. I wanted my Colt and my Brad Pitt policeman to ride in on their white horses and whisk me off to a safe place where I'd find Howard alive and happy, playing a mild game of Monopoly with my girls.

Elvis kept me pinned with his bear-hug, probably assuming I still might want to run off in search of Howard. The thought of running into No Toes and his very large gun, or Viviana, or worst case scenario – both – disabused me of that idea quickly.

"You can let me go. I won't run," I said, defeated. Depression and pessimism were taking over. My cheeks tingled – the feel of a cry coming on. I closed my eyes and pressed my palms into them, hard. Sniffing and breathing deeply, I worked to get a grip. Focusing on thoughts of my girls and making it through this to see them again helped. And then there was Roz and Peggy – this was all my stupid idea from the beginning. First, snooping at House of Many Bones only to discover finding death and rot, then this whole let's-follow-Colt-and-see-what-he's-up-to thing. I landed us here, so I needed to see us through safely. With my palms still pressing my eyes tight, I sat on the bed, expecting to take a moment and gather my strength. No sooner did my butt hit the mattress than the sound of footsteps outside the bedroom door shot me straight back up. I threw down my hands and pointed my eyes straight on the door. Would the person on the other side come bearing an instrument of death? Was this the end? It seemed like I'd been asking that question a lot the last few hours.

Elvis motioned for me to hide behind him while he positioned himself, gun ready. We both heard a light knocking on the door.

"Hey ladies! Yous okay in there?"

I blew out a sigh of relief so hard that it tickled Elvis ear – he swatted at me. Elvis tore the door open in a flash, pulled Frankie in, poked his head out, looking both ways then quick closed the door again. Frankie looked very surprised.

"Hey! What's da deal?"

"Shhhhh! Keep it down and don't talk. We don't got a lot of time – get it?" ordered Elvis, fast and furious. Frankie put up his hands and nodded, obeying his obviously superior co-worker.

"No Toes is here. He shot Sammy – Howard."

"Sammy? You were supposed to . . . you know – get ridda him."

"Yeah, well I didn't, okay? More about that in a minute. You see him?"

"Who, Sammy?"

"No!" Elvis was losing his cool. "Did you see No Toes?"

"No."

"He's got an AK. Like he's on a killin' mission. You know where Viv and Max is?"

"Sure – they're upstairs watchin' Survivor. Why you tink I had to turn on the generator? Can't miss dat stupid show . . ."

"You sure?"

"Sure I'm sure. You don't trust me?"

"Sure, I trust you. That's why I want you to listen. Sammy – Howard – before he got shot, he made us a deal. We help the Feds get information from Viv and Max, we get us a free ride. Better yet, Viv gets put away – for a long time."

"Yeah? What makes you tink he's on da up and up?" Frankie asked, not appearing convinced his welfare was protected with this scheme.

"He promised me on her life." Elvis looked at me while my eyes widened to the size of basketballs. Frankie seemed impressed, and I sensed he was taking to the idea, but he still shook his head.

"I don't know . . ."

I couldn't stand it anymore. I grabbed Frankie by the collar and put my nose up to his.

"Do it! Just do it! You've got his word for crying out loud! Just say yes and let's get on with this before that crazy toe-less creep finds us and obliterates us!" Frankie was obviously startled by my outburst. He also had my spit all over his face. I let go of his collar, thinking maybe I'd gone a little too far. Frankie grabbed a clean and nicely ironed white hanky from his inside jacket pocket and wiped his face silently. While replacing the hanky, he spoke.

"Fine. I'm in. But if Sammy is dead, how do we know the deal is still on? Where is he?"

I'd had enough of the Sammy talk. "Okay – time out!" I demanded. "Right here, right now: how do you know Howard is Sammy Donato? According to Viviana, he changed his name when he was a teenager."

Elvis was looking anxious. "We need to talk about dis now?"

"Now." I put my foot down. Elvis took another weary swipe over his face, shook his head and put his hands on his hips. "It's like dis – Tito whacked Sammy's pop, but felt real bad about it, leavin' Sammy fatherless. Tito didn't have no pop growin' up, so I tink he could relate – anyway, so he had us sorta follow Sammy and his mom over da years – slip her money on da sly. Stuff like that. Tito essentially paid for da kid's college."

"Did he know about the money?" I asked.

"Sammy? No. And Tito nearly lost it when Sammy – Howard by then – joined the FBI after graduating. Word on da streets was he had a vendetta." Elvis was talking fast and acting very nervous. "Frankie here nearly shit his pants when he seen that yous two bought that house on White Willow Circle. Needless to say, when Max caught that mole at Parks and Rowe and whacked him, Viviana had a little sit down wit Sammy. Told him yous and doze girls a yours would suffer if he got involved – and better yet, he should do everything possible to stop the investigation."

I finally had my answer. Howard moved out to protect the girls and me! He wasn't leaving because he didn't love me anymore. While I took a mental moment to rejoice, Frankie got back to business.

"Survivor's gonna be over any minute. We're runnin' outa time here – you didn't answer my question. Where's Sammy?"

"Could you call him Howard please?" I requested rather forcefully.

Frankie made a face. "Where's Howard?"

"Toes dragged him behind da shed," Elvis said.

"'Cuz if he's dead, we don't got no choice, Snoopy, but to let Viv have her way wit you and your friends. Can't take no risk if we don't got protection, y'know?" I understood that Elvis and Frankie were only friendly to me as long as they remained safe from the wrath of Viv, or incarceration by the keepers of the law. Frankie continued, "Of course, wit Toes here, this could all be moot."

Moot? A man who regularly butchered the English language actually used the word "moot"?

"Who the hell is this No Toes?" I asked, curiosity getting the better of me. "Does he really have no toes?"

"On one foot," Frankie reported.

"What?"

"He's got one foot wit no toes. His cousin ran over his foot." As usual, Frankie had to look to Elvis for assistance. "Ain't that it?" Elvis nodded an affirmative.

"So, he has some toes," I answered, pointing out the obvious.

"What?"

"Well, he doesn't have NO toes – he has some toes."

"He gots no toes on that foot, so he's No Toes. Do you really want to keep talkin' 'bout dis when he's 'round here somewhere's wit an AK?" Frankie made a very valid point. I remembered AKs from Bruce Willis' The Last Boy Scout. Bottom line: AKs are bad.

"What's his problem with you guys?" I asked, since it seemed important.

"Ah, geez, this guy has been trouble from day one, ain't that right Elvis?"

"Trouble," agreed Elvis. "He's da whole reason you got those monkeys flippin' around in your yard. We was supposed to teach him the monkey killin' ting – the whole show, y'know: getting 'em from the lab, stackin' the cages in the van, transportin' 'em to the house, injectin' 'em wit the sleep stuff. We been doin' this for too long – we told Viv we wanted someone else to do the dirty work for a while. Turns out No Toes has a queasy stomach, who knew? He goes crazy when we pull out the syringes."

"It was a mess," continued Frankie. "Elvis is in the other room choppin' up Max's dead Fed, and shovin' the pieces into bags, cartin' the bags to the truck. Meanstwhiles I'm runnin' Toes through the process. I show him on three of the stupid apes, and make him try on the fourth. What does he do? Idiot leaves the fuckin' cages open, couple of 'em get out, scare the shit outa the one he's snuffin', next ting we know, he's out the door screamin' and the damn monkeys is followin' him." My Italian buddies were shaking their heads in unison.

"Fuckin' mess," said Elvis.

"If you've been doing this for so long, how come I never saw your truck before?"

"We always used the Great Falls house, but the pipes broke. Place flooded. Had to move the operation to White Willow."

"Why did you leave the head and the dead monkeys behind?"

"We tried to catch those live ones outside, then it started to get light. We couldn't risk it, we got the hell outa there."

It all made sense to me now – the truck, the lights on in the house, the howl. The howl was No Toes. Still, the story didn't explain why No Toes had become homicidal.

"I don't understand, though, why you think he wants to kill you now."

"You saw dat AK." Elvis was indignant.

"Yeah, but why?"

"We put the word out on the streets – No Toes is a fanook," answered Frankie.

I didn't know that word. "Is that bad?"

"That's bad – means he's a pansy. Gay. No one likes bein' called a fanook – in our circles that is."

"I wonder where da fuck he is now," Elvis said, putting his ear to the door, while Frankie sat on the bed. I heard banging from the bathroom my two friends had been sequestered in. Moving toward the bathroom door, the banging increased, and along with the muffled voices of Roz and Peggy I thought I detected a male voice. My heart leapt, first thinking it might be Howard, alive. But I started sweating bullets when I considered it could be the AK-toting No Toes. I placed my hand nervously on the bathroom handle. Just then, it swung open and Peggy threw her face out. We were both startled, neither expecting to come nose to nose with each other.

"Barb! Oh! You scared me!"

"What's going on in there?" I asked, not sure I was going to like the answer. "You okay?"

"Yeah, yeah, we're fine. But you need to see this . . . ." She opened the door wide, allowing me to see Colt sitting on the vanity. He had a large black vest on his lap and he was unwrapping the cloth bundle Officer Brad had given us. He looked up at me, dripping wet, with a wide grin on his face.

"Hey Curly! How are you?"

Chapter 20

Stunned, I immediately looked to the window, knowing that was his only way in. The banging I heard must have been the opening and closing of the window, which was now very wet and very muddy. In fact, the bathroom had become the center of a virtual mudfest with Colt being the bearer of the brown slime. He was covered in it from the waist down. Miraculously, his prized bomber jacket, save some moisture from the rain, was untouched. Staring at Colt, I realized that I was becoming numb to emotion. I seemed to be operating on some sort of automatic survival mechanism.

"I think Howard is dead. A man named No Toes shot him with an AK," I stated matter-of-factly.

"So that's what happened," he said, understanding lighting across his face. "Well, I wouldn't worry too much." He held up a black and very heavy vest, as if to prove his point. I had never seen a bulletproof vest with my own eyes, except on TV shows and in the movies, but it looked familiar, and given Colt's statement, I assumed that I was now seeing one in real life. I smiled, relieved.

"You think he's okay?" I asked

"Darn tootin' I think he's okay. But we don't have a lot of time, Curly. I need to explain things and explain fast. We're up against the clock here. Bad weather's causing us *muchos problemos*."

Colt spelled things out very quickly. As it turned out, he and Howard saw Roz tailing them and knew I wasn't far behind. When they figured out we'd been kidnapped, they were able to locate Roz and me with the tracking device they had hidden on my cell phone. (I'd get my head around that one if we survived this mess. For now, I was thanking my lucky stars that Elvis hadn't decided to throw mine in the bushes to the same fate as Roz's.) Howard was waiting for his FBI team to arrive and position themselves nearby in a surveillance van, but he got himself caught by Vivian's gang on purpose – against orders to do otherwise – because he feared for our lives. He took advantage of his time alone with Elvis to arrange what the FBI had been planning an attempt at for some time: striking a deal with Elvis and Frankie to help bring in Viv and expose the Pharmaceutical execs involved. Howard had been given the green light to make such a deal with the two thugs in exchange for their amnesty. Colt acknowledged the presence of both Frankie and Elvis who were both standing behind me at that point even though Elvis kept a watchful eye on the bedroom door.

Colt got down to business. "Frankie – I can't say anymore until I know you're on board."

"How do you know me?" Frankie was giving him a grim look through suspicious eyes.

Colt stood up to answer. "Frankie, this is the FBI – you think I ain't seen pictures of you?"

"Who da hell are you?" Frankie sniffed suspiciously.

"Colt Baron."

"You don't look like a Fed."

"I'm not. In fact, I had a hell of a time convincing them to let me come in here instead of sending in one of their own. I was afraid Barb would freak if it was anyone but me."

I wasn't very happy with the characterization that I could just freak at a moment's notice. "Well I'm not that unstable . . ." I started to argue.

"I thought Sammy was runnin' dis, but he's stuffed away in a shed, dead for all we know." Frankie argued. "So how are we supposed to trust you?"

"Here's the skinny," Colt said directly to Frankie and Elvis, "there's an FBI surveillance van serving as central command for this operation – it's set up a half a mile down the road. There's an agent in that van ready to run this operation in Howard's place. She's offering the two of you full amnesty if you cooperate. She has that authority. I'd take it if I were you."

"Sammy was on da up and up, Frankie," said Elvis, still balancing between our bathroom talk and looking out for No Toes. "This is our way out."

"Fine," Frankie said, shaking his head and putting his hands in the air as if giving up a fight. "I already told Snoopy I was in."

"Great!" Colt snapped up in a flash ready to put the plan into action.

"Curly, you're key in this plan. Put this on," he said, holding up the vest for me to slip my arms in, which I did. "Good. Now put this in your ear." He handed me a small, black plastic device. "It's an earbud – a small speaker. Put it in your ear. There's a small, hairlike line attached – see that?" I nodded, seeing the almost invisible plastic thread. He continued. "Put that behind your ear – that's how you'll pull it out when you're done. Now you'll hear transmissions from Agent Smith in the van."

"Agent Smith?" I said with a hint of sarcasm. "This whole thing is feeling way too much like the Matrix." Evidently Agent Smith had a way of hearing me, because a female voice came alive in my ear.

"You think I haven't heard that one before?" The lady's voice said. The tight and testy voice was way too familiar.

"Do I know you?" I asked, looking around the room, as if to find her in some dark corner.

"You may know me as Patricia Webber," said the voice again.

"Oh my God! You're Marjorie Smith, aren't you? You mean you're not having an affair with my husband?" I said, trying to be funny. My eyes were still scanning the bathroom for a visual of her, not understanding how she could hear me, but I couldn't see her. Colt, seeing me riddled with confusion, held up a small gold item that looked like a decorative medal. "It's a bug," he whispered. He turned it around, and on the back I could see a small, round, black button about the size of a watch battery.

"No, I'm not having an affair with your husband," said the voice, with no hint of humor. "You ready to get on with this?" Evidently she was actually as surly as the Ms. Webber of PETA she had pretended to be.

"Sure," I said. "What do I do?"

"We don't have a lot of time to accomplish our task. Tornado warnings are posted all over the eastern half of Loudoun County and western Fairfax. We need to get in, get it done, get out. Do you understand?"

"Roger Wilco," I answered while Colt pinned the medal-looking bug thing to his bomber jacket.

Silence. No Agent Smith. I thought we'd lost contact. "Hello?" I called out loudly, tapping my ear.

"Are you through being funny?" asked Agent Smith.

"Yes Ma'am." Did Howard have to work with this lady? She had the personality of a tree stump.

Colt took off his jacket and held it up for me. "Put this on Curly. It hides the vest and I've pinned the bug here. They should be able to hear everything, as long as everyone is in the same room.

"What about Toes?" asked Frankie.

"He the guy that shot Howard?" Colt asked.

"He's da one."

"They can't offer him amnesty. Right, Agent Smith?" Colt talked into the medal on my chest.

"Right," she answered in my ear. I nodded affirmative.

"Just follow their instructions," said Colt, "and he'll go down with rest of them. He'll never know."

Elvis shook his head. "You don't understand. He's not with us. He's against us."

"What?" Colt didn't look happy when he heard that.

"We ain't hundred percent certain, but we're pretty sure he's here for blood."

"He's the guy that botched the job in the vacant house and let the monkeys out into my yard. They put the word out that he's a fanook and that wasn't good," I explained.

"Shit!" I heard in my ear.

"Shit!" Colt shouted.

"Excuse me!" Peggy was yelling from the bathtub where she and Roz had taken up residence. "If there's an FBI van out there, is there any way they can come and at least get Roz out of here? She's looking pretty bad."

We all looked at Roz who was curled up in a ball and shivering. She was white as snow and her hand was swollen as big as a melon. I made my way around Colt and bent over to feel her forehead. She was running a nasty fever. During my many years tending sick children, I had developed a very keen sense of guessing a temperature just by the feel. I was calling hers a 103 degree doozy.

"Boy, she's sick," I said. "Roz?" Roz looked up. She shook her head, but didn't say a thing, then closed her eyes and put her head back down.

"Can we get her out of here?" Peggy asked again.

"Negative," came Agent Smith's voice. "Too risky. Especially given these new circumstances. This idiot might have cohorts on the property that we don't know about. Better for your friend if we keep her where she is." Agent Smith was quiet in my ear for a beat, then, with a hint of compassion in her voice, said, "Hey, Marr."

"Yeah?"

"We're sending a man for Howard now. If he's hurt, we'll fix him. If he's not, he's in that house already coming to save your ass." That Agent Smith was a tough cookie, but I got the feeling she was actually giving her best shot at comforting me.

"Thanks for the kind words." I turned to Frankie and Elvis. "Do you think No Toes brought guys with him?"

They shrugged their shoulders.

Colt had been rubbing his hands through his hair and generally looking worried. By the change in his mood since learning that Howard's shooter was a disgruntled employee, I could tell he was having second thoughts about going through with this operation.

"No," he finally said, shaking his head. "This is a different game."

"Mr. Baron is right," I heard Agent Smith say in my ear. "This operation was meant to have no risk to civilians."

Suddenly, the lights went out again. Colt pulled a flashlight out of his back pocket, lighting up the bathroom. His face looked like stone in the shadow filled room. "Give me that thing." He was pointing to my ear.

"My earbud?"

"Yes! Give it to me!" I pulled the device out of my ear and wasn't even allowed the pleasure of handing it to him since he grabbed it so fast. He plugged it into his ear and grabbed the jacket I was wearing, talking right into the bug.

"You need to abort this mission and send in a rescue team ASAP!" he yelled. I was angry that he was having this conversation without me involved. I couldn't hear her answers. Part of me agreed with him, but part of me wanted to move on.

Meanwhile, Elvis was talking about the power problem. "That shouldn't be," he said, shaking his head. "That generator's full of fuel. We got enough to keep this house runnin' for two days easy."

"Do we still get our amnesty if they abort?" asked Frankie.

"Amnesty ain't gonna be any help to us if No Toes puts holes in our heads," Elvis said, stating the obvious.

Before anyone could comment, the sound of shouting distracted us all. It was coming from somewhere in the house, although it was hard for me to tell from where exactly. I was pretty sure it was Viv and she sounded mad-dog mad – probably pissed that she was missing the last five minutes of Survivor. The shouts were getting louder and closer. I held my breath, praying she didn't fly through the door, cigarette and eyes ablaze, only to subvert our sorry sting.

"Frankie!" Her gruff scream was followed by a nasty round of hacking and coughing.

"Where is she?" Colt whispered to Elvis.

"Sounds like she's on this level – she musta just come down from her room – she's got her own stairway up. Probably she's near da pantry or dining room." Puddles started yapping at such a fervent rate and high pitch, he nearly quelled the sound of pelting rain on the windows. He was worked up about something. I imagined him bouncing up and down like one of those hyper, yippy dogs on a Looney Toons cartoon. Suddenly, Puddles gave out a desperate, heart-wrenching squeal then went silent.

We heard Maxine cry out frantically, "Puddles!" Her second screaming plea for Puddles was drowned out by the deafening sound of automatic gunfire.

Chapter 21

"We've got gunfire here!" Colt was still yelling into my chest. "You need to send in support now!" he yelled over the din. He had fingers to both ears listening for a response. He shook his head as if he didn't like their answer. "What do you mean they're not here yet? What about you?" With the chaos around me, several things became very clear. A mad man was roaming the house with a very large, obviously functional gun; my husband was somewhere, possibly still alive; and none of us was going to get out of this thing alive if someone didn't start kicking some butt. As my mind raced, and images of Howard and my girls flashed before me, I looked over at Roz, huddled in the tub. She had a family too. And Peggy – what would her boys do without her?

I dug way down inside myself and found that inner Lieutenant Ripley – Sigourney Weaver – extinguisher of killer aliens. I found that steel-strong woman who wouldn't back down or run off screaming. I found that woman hiding like a scared rabbit way down deep, and I pulled her up by her quaking little bunny ears.

Okay, Barbara Marr, I said to her. *You are going to do this. You're no wimp. No wimp – do you hear? You can do this thing. Think of Howard. Do it for Howard. Do it for Callie and Bethany and Amber. Do it for Roz and Peggy. Do it for Puddles, even though you don't like the yappy mutt. Hell, do it for poor, misguided Elvis and Frankie. Maybe you can give them a second lease on life. Do it! Do it!*

Infused with courage and determination, I pushed Colt away, felt around his ear until I located the plastic thread, yanked out the earbud, reclaimed it as my own, and shoved it back into my ear. Colt was mad, but I didn't care – I was a woman on a mission. A woman to be reckoned with, damnit.

"Smith? You there?" I said into the bug.

"I'm here."

"I'm goin' in." I shot a determined and confident look at Elvis and Frankie. "You ready?" They nodded hesitantly, their eyes wide in disbelief. "Good. Elvis, Viv thinks you're taking care of Howard, right?" He nodded, stunned. "Good. Then you stay here. Frankie, put that gun to my back and make this look real. Let's see what the hell is going on out there. I'll act scared as shit. Won't be hard to do." I took a deep breath.

Frankie, evidently agreeing to participate, stuck the gun in my back and flashed his miniscule flashlight to guide the way as we moved to the bedroom door. Dizziness tried to overwhelm me, but I wouldn't succumb. I reached for the doorknob, and opened the door walking out into the hallway. The hallway lead in two directions – we could move straight ahead or to our left.

"Put that fuckin' thing down you gimpy nit-wit!" It was Viviana. We could hear her, but couldn't see her. She was seething.

"Don't talk to me like that. I'm in control now and I'm here to make things right."

I guessed that must have been No Toes. His voice was agonizingly high pitched. Like Barry Gibb with a stuck falsetto.

"Max!" shouted Viviana, "where the hell is your gun?"

"Viv – I was chasing Puddles. Where's Puddles? What did you do to my Puddles?"

"You mean that rat I stepped on?" sweaked No Toes.

"Oh, Jesus!" Maxine moaned. Their voices were loud and clear and obviously coming from the front of the house. Frankie pointed to our left, indicating we should proceed in that direction moving through a vast kitchen/great-room combination. As we passed a granite- topped kitchen island, Frankie motioned to me to turn right and move toward the front of the house leading us in the exact direction of the heated discussion. After six to seven steps, we arrived at what I guessed, from its proximity to the kitchen, must be the dining room. I could only surmise as much, however, because the room was void of any furniture that would speak to its purpose. We stood in one of three arched entrances to the room. Directly in front of us were four towering, curtained windows. To our right, standing in another archway were Viviana and Maxine. Maxine was holding a bright battery-powered lantern, which flooded the room nicely. I was happy for that, since I nearly stubbed my toe two or three times relying on the dim ray of Frankie's penlight. To our left was an extremely tall, nearly anorexic man with horn-rimmed glasses and a sad excuse for a goatee on his pointy chin. With dirty blonde hair, he didn't look very Italian. Despite his gangly stature, No Toes managed to hold that big gun with amazing ease. I gasped inwardly when I saw it.

Agent Smith's voice rang in my ear. "Marr – where are you? Let me know somehow if you can."

I looked around, wondering how in the hell I could let them know which room we were in. *Okay*, I thought, *here I go. This is going to sound stupid.*

"Nice dining room you got here, Viv," I said.

"What the fuck?" she whirled around.

"Nice dining room. I mean, I'm assuming it's the dining room since it's right off of your kitchen. Will you be putting furniture in here?"

"Who are you, Martha Stewart?"

Well, maybe it sounded stupid, but it seemed to work because I got a compliment from Smith. "Nice job," she said.

"Thanks," I said too quickly to take back. *Ooops! Well, now that wasn't very smart.*

"What?" Viv shouted. Holy cow. I needed to remember not to answer back to the voice in my ear or this operation was going to be the shortest in FBI history.

"Thanks!" I said again, back pedaling. "I was saying thank you – that's a compliment – I love Martha Stewart."

"Jesus! Shut up all of you!" shouted No Toes from his archway. "Who are you anyway?" His screechy voice was hurting my ears.

Frankie took control. "Listen, Toes. . ."

"Don't call me that! I hate that name. I have five toes. Besides, that's the name of that guy in . . . that movie."

"Huh?" Frankie didn't know what he was talking about, but after a moment, a light bulb went off in my maniacal movie mind.

"That's it!" I shouted snapping my fingers. "*Eraser*, right?"

"Yeah, that's the one!" He looked pleased.

"Two Toes – Tony Two Toes in *Eraser*. But it was Two Toes, not No Toes."

"Well, I still don't like the name. I have a new one now."

"Yeah, fanook, what would that new name be now?" Viviana teased.

Poor Toes started shaking with rage. He appeared to gain control over his upset long enough to bring his gun down from where it rested on his shoulder, aiming it directly at her forehead. From the angle, I was pretty sure that if he chose to pull the trigger, she'd have quite a nice hole between those heavy fake-lash topped eyes. The same thought must have occurred to her, because she shut up quick and I thought I saw her lip twitch.

Viviana Buttaro sure wasn't my favorite person, but I needed her alive to get the information that my FBI friends wanted. I decided to try a little peace, love, and understanding.

"Um, Mr. Toes – I'm sorry, but I understand where you're coming from. What's your real name?"

"Huh?"

"What did your mother call you?"

"Dumbshit." Well, that didn't work.

"How about your dad . . . or an Aunt. Did you have a supportive Aunt? Maybe an Uncle who took you fishing? Someone who called you something nice."

"My name is Frankie – but that guy there already has that name. Like there can't be two guys named Frankie – what's that all about?"

Agent Smith's voice rang up in my ear again. "Marr – head's up. A car just passed our location – its turn indicators are on. Looks like it might be turning into your driveway." I wondered what the heck I was supposed to do with that information. Couldn't she just let me do my job in ignorant bliss? While saying a little prayer, begging for just one thing to go right on this God-forsaken night, the lights popped back on. Well hallelujah!

Viviana, her sour mood not sweetened by the resurgence of electrical flow, snapped at Frankie. "What's wrong with that damn generator, Frankie? You told me that thing was gonna last two or three days on the propane we got."

Frankie shrugged. "How da hell should I know? Jesus, Viv, I ain't no fuckin' 'lectrician. Da guy on da internet said two or tree days."

A hideous cackle escaped from No Toes sickly thin lips. He looked like one of the emaciated apparitions from *Poltergeist* laughing his evil little laugh. I wasn't liking his attitude.

"Your power's back on now. But you can forget that generator of yours. I cut the fuel line. Smell that?" His skinny nose tipped up and sniffed in the air. "That's the sweet smell of propane."

Agent Smith was talking to me. "Marr, did we hear that a propane line has been cut? Cough once if that's a yes."

I coughed hard into the medal on my chest.

"Shit! Can you smell it? Cough once again if yes."

I coughed hard once again, but it must have been a little too hard, because my throat tickled and I started coughing uncontrollably. One of those never ending, gut-wrenching coughs. Water was streaming from my eyes.

"What the hell does that mean?" I heard her say. She was really beginning to piss me off, this FBI lady in my ear.

"Whoa there!" shouted Frankie, slapping me hard between the shoulder blades. I was shaking my head, trying to communicate that he should cease and desist. He was hurting me, not helping me.

"She's not choking," chided No Toes. "You – stupid coughing lady – put your hands in the air!" he said to me. Doing what he said, I was relieved when the coughing began to subside. Wiping the profuse tears from my eyes, I noticed that during my fit, No Toes had let his gun fall from its focus on

Viviana's forehead. This had not been lost on Viviana, who had started to inch backward, evidently attempting an escape.

Additionally, I suspected that no one had noticed the new development while I was coughing like a patient in a TB ward – the fact that a car had, in fact, pulled into the driveway. I had spied the headlights briefly in between gasps.

No Toes might not have been the smartest bully on the block, but he was keen enough to catch Viviana before she could make her disappearance final. "Where do you think you're going?" he asked her slyly, pointing the gun rightly again. "Get back in here. We have plans for you."

My favorite lady FBI agent was in my ear again. "Marr! They aren't giving us what we need. You need to get them talking." Boy, I thought, if this chick was standing next to me, I'd reach over and strangle her skinny little bossy lady neck.

"Yeah," snorted Viviana, "'We'?" She was mocking him. "Who's 'we' – you and what other morons?" She and Maxine were laughing, while No Toes sneered and held his aim on Viviana's head. Their laughter was interrupted by the sound of bells reverberating throughout the house in a very grand manner. Doorbell. The mystery guest had arrived.

"Oh, I wonder who that is at the door?" I quipped for the benefit of those hiding safely in their comfy surveillance van. The look on Viviana's face was priceless. Even though I was trembling, wondering what would happen next, I enjoyed the spectacle of Viviana taken off guard.

Everyone stood silent for quite some time. Finally, Frankie broke the quiet. "You want I should get da door?" he asked Viviana. I have no idea if she planned to answer him or not, but her reply, as it turned out, was unnecessary, because the door opened all on its own. Or so it seemed. While most of the foyer was visible to Frankie and me, our view of the door was obstructed by a part of the archway. We could only hear the thing swoosh open, followed the loud clicking of hard soled shoes on a marble floor, and swoosh again as it closed. No Toes was closest to the door, but his expression didn't change, leading me to believe he knew the owner of the clicking shoes.

More loud clicks on the foyer floor preceded the arrival of a wide, hulking figure in the archway, taking his place next to No Toes. The very tall and very round man was smartly dressed in a keen suit that I guessed to be designer, only because of the crisp lines. I shop at Target and Walmart so my only experience with designer is what I see on the Red Carpets of the Golden Globes and Academy Awards. This was the Pillsbury Dough Boy meets Giorgio Armani. Silver cuff links and a popping, glossy red tie finished off the ensemble. He patted No Toes on the back and smiled widely, revealing an enviable set of pearly whites. He appeared to be one happy and satisfied dude.

"You done good," he said to No Toes.

Another man, not so nicely dressed, but equipped with his own AK, a bushy mustache, and several coils of rope, stepped in as well, but all eyes were on the happy fat man. Maxine was gasping, both hands on her face like that kid in *Home Alone*. Viviana's eyes were bulging out so far I felt for sure they were going to pop right out of her head.

"Holy shit!" shouted Frankie. I seemed to be the only one in the room who didn't know the colossal person standing before us. Curiosity was getting the better of me, plus I had to let Agent Smith know what was going on.

"Who's that?" I asked, turning my bug infested chest back toward Frankie, ensuring the best reception.

The grinning man in the archway rocked back on his heels and answered in Frankie's stead. "I'm Tito Buttaro. Nice ta meet ya."

Chapter 22

Tito Buttaro.

"Aren't you supposed to be dead?" I asked the mightily rotund fellow, while his "assistant" took a place just behind him. He was significantly shorter, maybe five foot ten to Tito's six foot plus. His coils of rope looked like they were meant for hanging or tying. Or both. I gulped.

Tito, in response to my statement, fanned his arms out as if putting himself on display. "As you can see," he said with great fanfare, "da rumors of my death has been greatly exaggerated." Lovely. A missing killer who liked to butcher Mark Twain. In my ear, I could hear a great amount of gasping and chattering, as if even the Feds were shocked by this interesting turn of events. Tito tipped his head to Frankie.

"How you doin', Frankie?"

No Toes accidentally answered the salutation. "I'm fine, Boss. Thanks."

Tito grimaced and hit him in the chest with the back of his hand. "Not you, No Toes. That Frankie."

"I ain't feelin' so good," Frankie moaned. A woozy wave was beginning to wash over me as well. The propane fumes were getting stronger. I had the feeling that a certain amount of asphyxiation mixed with a larger amount of dread was having its effect on both of us.

No Toes tipped closer to Tito and tried to whisper. Tried being the operative word, because we heard him clearly. "Remember the new name, Boss?'

"What?" Tito was frowning.

"The new name. You know – Screech."

Not appearing so affected by the fumes, Maxine laughed. She had been as quiet as a church mouse. "That's your new name? Screech? You'd rather be called Screech instead a No Toes? You ARE a fanook."

"I'm not a fanook!" he squeaked, moving the aim of his gun from Viviana to Maxine.

Shaking his head, Tito dismissed the new name. "Nah," he said. "I like No Toes. You're No Toes."

Maxine laughed harder. Poor No Toes looked defeated.

"Come on, Boss, let me make the hit now! Both of them. In the head. Bang!." Tito waved his hand casually at his skeletal henchman. "In time, Toes, in time. Did you cut the line like I said?"

"Done, Boss. Can't you smell?"

Tito tilted his head back and sniffed the air with his bulbous nose. Another smile crossed his face. "Good job." He lowered his chin, bringing his dark eyes even across the room with Viviana, who had turned as hard and white as the marble he stood on. "You ain't greeted me wit a proper 'Hello' there, Viv. You okay?"

Instead of answering Tito, Viviana focused a seriously deadly stare at Frankie, whose gun, I had realized, had slipped from its position in my back. *Come on Frankie*, I thought, *don't lose it now. Too much at stake.*

"You didn't whack 'im?" she hissed like an angry viper.

Frankie stammered. "Viv, we . . . we tought . . ."

Tito stopped him quickly, holding up his hand and interjecting his own two cents. "No need to explain tings to her, Frankie. What's done is done, right? She don't need to know da details now – she's got no future where she needs to know these tings. Her time is, let's say . . . limited." Tito pulled open his very slick and dapper raincoat, pulling out a gun so long it looked like it could snake a toilet clog. He waved it in my direction and smiled. "In a minute here, I'm gonna ask you who dis cute little chickie is, but right now I want to know, where's Elvis?"

"He's out," lied Frankie quickly. *Good, Frankie, that a boy.* More than anything, I needed Frankie in charge of his wits right now.

"You lyin' to me, Frankie? That wouldn't be da right way to resurrect our friendship." Tito turned to his emaciated acolyte. "Toes. Take a look around." The scrawny soldier skipped down the hall, evidently excited to be on his boss's good side. In less than three shakes, he was back with Elvis, hands in the air. Thankfully, Peggy and Roz were not with him. I was hoping Colt had them safely hidden.

"There ain't no others in dis house, are there?" Asked Tito, his air of pleasure wiped from his face.

"No, Boss!"

"You sure?"

"I checked things out myself. We're good." He was bobbing his head frenetically like a bobble head on uppers. Tito sniffed the air again.

"We're runnin' outa time here, boys. Start tyin' these dopes up. No Toes, you do Elvis first, Joey, you get Viv then Maxine there. I'll keep an eye here on Frankie and his little girl friend."

I was at least comforted to know there were some goons out there with normal names. The silent man, evidently named Joey, tossed a coil of rope to No Toes, then made stride across the room, his gun held ready. Tito strolled over, turning his own long revolver playfully in little circles. As the two men made their moves, Maxine must have decided to make a run for it. Out of the corner of my eye, I saw her make a quick movement, but, sadly for Maxine, Joey was quicker. One pop of his gun and she went down like a sack of Idaho potatoes. An involuntary scream shot out of my mouth, piercing the air. Things were deteriorating too fast.

Tito swung around and pointed his finger at Viviana. "Don't you try da same ting Smokey, 'cuz your end won't be so painless. Joey's got orders to make sure you die a slow and painful death should you attempt any monkey business. Monkey business! Ha! That's funny! Ain't that funny, Joey?"

Joey laughed, reaching Viviana with his rope. "Yeah, that's VERY funny, Boss. I like that one."

Tito slowed his belly laugh to a self-amused chuckle then turned back to me. "So, Frankie, tell me now – who's dis little lady?"

I held my breath hoping Frankie would realize that the truth would expose our operation and ruin our possible chance for rescue. Frankie wasn't answering. Beads of sweat were forming at my hairline. I still didn't feel the gun in my back and my worries about Frankie maintaining his cool were growing. Thankfully, from years of practice with my mother and my own children, I spit out a lie in record time.

"Listen," I started, my voice shaking. "I don't know what's going on here, but my husband and I are with the People for the Ethical Treatment of Animals and we came over here when a worker reported seeing monkeys caged in the basement of this house. We were just doing a routine investigation when this man you're calling Frankie jumped me with his gun. My husband got away. I'm sure he's calling the police right now! This place could be surrounded any minute!"

With that, Frankie threw up all over my back. That's Karma for you.

Tito, disgusted by the expulsion, growled to express his displeasure. "Ah, Jesus! Thank God he missed my shoes! These is my favorite Ferragamos – four hundred bucks a pair."

Toes was unfazed and excited to relay that my story probably had merit. "Yeah, Boss, I forgot to tell ya – I shot a man in da back of da house. Tought it was Elvis in da dark, till I got close. Musta been the lady's husband."

"You kill 'im?"

"Yeah, Boss. He's dead."

He's dead. The words played over and over in my head. Was it true? I didn't want to believe it. Howard had a bullet proof vest, and this goon obviously didn't check closely enough to find that out, so maybe Howard was still alive. I tried to stay positive, but tears flowed down my cheeks anyway. The nightmare just wasn't ending

"Don't you peace, love, and granola types got anything better to do wit your time? Now look what your good deeds got yous." He was shaking his head. "Joey, get Viv over here, let's bring everyone close so I can have my say easy like. Toes, get Elvis over here."

Obeying orders, No Toes shoved Elvis to the floor near my feet.

"Good, now get to tyin' dese two together." Tito was pointing to me and Frankie, who moaned. It wasn't going very easily for him, poor guy. I knew how he felt. No Toes gave me a hard push, landing me hard on my rump, nearly on top of Frankie. He got to work coiling the cord around both of us, our backs together, our hands tight to our sides. I couldn't help but worry he'd do harm to the precious bug on my chest.

This whole Tito-is-alive thing had really thrown me for a loop. I had ventured out – a woman without wimpiness – ready to save the day, and I'd only managed to get myself bound to a repentant crook with a weak stomach. And I couldn't even wipe the tears from my face.

Agent Smith must have heard my sniffles, prompting her to whisper reassurances in my ear that it was almost over and help would be along any minute. We'd all be fine she said. She sounded certain, and her comments did make me feel better. In fact, she sounded so certain, that I began to wonder if Tito hadn't switched teams – maybe he was an FBI operative sent in to move this operation forward. That seemed very plausible. But then, things being what they were, anything seemed plausible.

Joey forced Viviana, wrapped tight like a mummy with the duct tape, over to our bound assemblage on the floor then pushed on her shoulder until she dropped to her knees.

Tito looked satisfied. "Good, Joey, now go find that dead guy. Make sure he's really dead. Where is he, Toes?"

"Behind the shed out back, Boss. Dead as a doornail," squeaked No Toes. Joey nodded and shot off down the hall to the back of the house.

Tito bent down on one knee coming closer to Viviana's face. His smile was so confident and controlled that it sent shivers down my spine.

"Surprised to see me, Smokey?" he said low and slow.

Viviana didn't seem in the mood for playing games. "Just spill da beans, Tito – why you here? Whaddaya want?"

Tito threw his head back and laughed a very hearty laugh. She had really tickled his funny bone. "I don't WANT anyting' Smokey, 'cuz see, I already got exactly what I want."

"What exactly, would that be now? Smarts was never your strong suit, Tito, so I can't think you got a whole lot, unless maybe you found God."

"You know, you's right 'bout one ting. Smarts was certainly not my 'strong suit' as you say, but that's all changed. You know what I did while I was hidin' out – when Frankie and Elvis here, stupidly, left me for dead – I got myself a college degree – they call that a BA. Then I got myself an MBA – that would be a Masters in Business Administration."

"Yeah?"

"Yeah – you tink I'm lyin'?"

"You don't talk no smarter."

"Dis is what educated people call a regional dialect – it don't mean I'm stupid."

"I still think you're stupid."

"Well how's dis for stupid then? Da name Robert Whittier mean anyting to you?"

Viviana's face blanched in a nano-second. Her smile gone. She didn't answer.

"Smokey? You know that name?"

"Don't know what you're talkin' about."

"Let me see if I can help you remember." He put his gun right up against her forehead. I could see sweat trickle down her temple.

"Fine, asshole. I know him, and you know I know him. So what about it?"

"Well, I had me a little talk wit Mr. Whittier – we had us some café lattes together – and he told me he wasn't too happy wit da way you was runnin' your business. Long story short – he was considerin' lettin' me take a crack at tings. He wanted to tink it over though." Tito stopped talking for a minute and just stared at Viv. He shook his head slowly, then resumed. "You tink that little mishap in Rustic Woods wit No Toes and those monkeys was an accident?"

My eyes widened. I was starting to see what he was up to.

"Toes has been workin' for me from da get go. He was my double agent, so to speak."

Elvis and Frankie groaned, realizing they'd been duped. Viviana scowled at Tito, but still didn't say a word. She had egg on her face, and I guessed she knew it. What was she going to do?

With his gun still aimed at Viviana's head, Tito kept talking. "Now here's da ting," he said. "I found Whittier on my own, but I'm a lazy business man, as you know, and I'd rather you just gave me da names of da guys you's workin' with at Wister and at Heaton Dalmer."

Viviana was indignant. "Why would I do that? What's it gonna get me?"

Tito laughed again. He looked at me and said, "The lady wants to know what's it gonna get her? What do you tink, Mrs. Savior of da animals? What you tink it's gonna get her?"

The question had a rhetorical feel to it, but I decided to answer just to be safe. "Her life?" I asked.

"Aha! What you tink, Smokey?" Tito laughed. He was one jolly fellow.

Viviana was wary. "You makin' me a deal, Tito?"

Tito ceased laughing and took on a more serious tone. "Da deal is dis: you give me da names, I take over da operation – it's only logical since I got da MBA – and you work for me. And, oh yeah, you get to keep breathin'. But you even try to fuck wit me once, I kill ya."

Wow, I was amazed at the way things were unfolding, not to mention relieved that these two Wiseguys seemed to be coughing up the goods the way we hoped. Of course, I was still tied up and could be whacked in a heartbeat, but I needed to validate my wins as they came.

Viviana stared hard at Tito. I assumed she was weighing her options. Although, if it were me, the options of dead or not dead seemed to make for a pretty easy decision. "Fine," she said finally. But we do away with those two stupid fucks." She said, pointing her head in the direction of Elvis and Frankie. They didn't look surprised.

"Was there any question?"

She didn't respond, staying quiet for nearly a minute, which caused me to worry. We needed to get this show on the road. The last thing we needed was the Emphysema Queen of Fairfax slowing things down. Finally, she gave it up. "Dennis Mowry at Wister and Janice Corbett at Heaton Dalmer. And if you want my opinion – your friend at Parks and Rowe, Robert Whittier – he's on his way out. We'll need to watch him."

Agent Smith went live in my ear so loud I almost screamed out in pain. "We've got it! Move out! Let's wrap this up and bring everyone in – no casualties!"

Suddenly, the doorbell rang again. Odd, I thought, that the FBI wouldn't just break down the door like in the movies. Or better yet, just open it, since it wasn't locked. Panic raced through me. Please let it be the FBI, I thought, and not Jimmy Hoffa . . . with a PhD.

Tito looked as surprised as anyone else, so I took that to mean it wasn't one of his compadres. He looked around. He motioned to No Toes. "Toes – look down that hall – you see Joey?"

Toes moved backwards toward the archway, peeked around the wall down the hall. "No Boss. Nobody there."

At that time, Joey showed up out of the other hallway, drenched and out of breath.

"Boss, I looked everywhere! There ain't no guy nowhere! Dead or alive."

Tito shot No Toes a nasty look. Toes cowered.

"Get over here, boat of you – keep your eyes on these guys. I'll check dis out." Tito slipped his gun back into his raincoat, then moved cautiously to the hallway and disappeared as he moved to the front door. I heard it open. A familiar male voice sounded.

"Good Evening, sir. I'm Officer LaMon with Fairfax County Police. Someone phoned in a report of gas fumes emanating from this general area."

"Why don't you got a uniform?"

"I'm plain clothes, sir. I responded because I was the closest. We take these reports seriously due to the potential danger involved. Sir, what is that I see at the end of that hallway?"

Tito must have looked behind him or been taken off guard somehow, because the next thing I knew, he was on the floor unconscious. Faster than I could say Operation Handsome Cop, Officer Brad made one swift step over

Tito, and called out "Marr!" I thought he was talking to me, but then realized he was looking above my head. Simultaneously, he was tossing Tito's massive gun across the room, and with amazing skill, Howard caught it mid-air, then instantly took aim at Joey, who was standing right next to Viviana. At the same time, Colt had his gun aimed right at No Nut's brainless head. It all happened so fast, I never even saw him come in.

At last! The thwump, thwump, thwump of helicopters sounded above the house. Search lights, which I assumed were coming from the helicopters, sailed across the floor as they shot in from various windows in the house. The air was as full of excitement as it was from propane fumes.

"LaMon – radio!" yelled Howard. In a flash, Officer Brad was tossing a black radio through the air, which Howard caught brilliantly with his other hand. I had to admit, I was getting turned on. My husband was turning out to be quite the action stud. Who knew?

Howard spoke into the radio. "This is Marr. The perps are contained, one is down. One civilian very sick, send in reinforcements and EMT on the double! We need to get these people out of here!"

A helmeted man decked out entirely in black maneuvered expertly through the front door, gun at the ready. Another followed right behind him. Howard motioned to the first. "Over here! Take this man!" Howard was referring to Joey. "You," he motioned to the second. "Take the skinny one. Colt, go check on Roz and Peggy."

"Aye, Captain." Colt saluted and was gone when relieved of his duty.

Once the FBI agent had Joey safely in his care, Howard kneeled next to me, laying down his gun and radio, and started cutting the ropes with a blade he had pulled out of his pants pocket.

"Are you okay?"

"Now I am. You?"

"Yeah." He was struggling to cut the fibers.

Frankie, evidently relieved that the tough stuff was over, looked to Howard. "Hey, Sammy – did yous know that Tito was alive?"

Howard stuck his finger in Frankie's face hard and furious as if he'd practiced it a thousand times. "My name isn't Sammy anymore – you got that? Sammy Donato doesn't exist!" he screamed, his face so red I feared he would stroke out. From the look on Frankie's face, I guessed he'd never make that mistake again. Although, his question was a valid one.

The ropes binding me to Frankie were loosened about the same time another FBI agent entered the door, slick and ready for action. He was low to the ground, pointing his long and sleek firearm in all directions. He was right behind Officer Brad, and moving forward, when without warning, I saw him go down on top of Tito. His legs, during the fall, must have knocked Officer Brad's legs out from under him, because he went down too. It all became a mass of pandemonium, with agents and Howard yelling.

From the moment I saw that Tito was conscious, everything moved in slow motion. Him reaching and snatching with unbelievable ease, the gun from Officer Brad's hand at the precise moment he lost his grip on its handle. My realization that Howard was standing, completely open and vulnerable. Seeing his gun on the floor next to me. Tito turning over his fat body from under the pile of men on top of him, and taking perfect aim at Howard.

Without any forethought, I picked up Howard's gun with my shaking hands and pointed it straight at Tito.

Chapter 23

"Don't even think about it you fat-assed, greasy goombah mother fucking son-of-a-bitch!" The words just spilled out of my mouth and boy did it feel good. Still on the floor, I gripped the gun with both hands and worked very hard to look like I knew what I was doing. Which I didn't.

"Marr! Tell me what's happening!" Agent Smith yelled in my ear. The scene was too tense to answer. She'd have to hear for herself.

Tito laughed. "PETA, huh? Nice one."

"Barb . . ." Howard started to reach for my gun.

Tito stopped him quick. "Wouldn't do dat, Sammy." He inched the aim of his gun to me and smiled.

"Don't, Tito. This is between you and me," Howard pleaded.

The agent who had been tripped by Tito started to crawl toward his lost rifle.

"Tell him to stop!" Tito screamed.

"Stop!" Howard obeyed. The agent went still.

"So it WAS a vendetta," said Tito, appearing precarious on the floor. "You know, I took care-a you good, Sammy. Dis how you repay me?"

"What?"

"Ax Frankie." Tito put a hand on the floor and pushed himself up slowly.

Howard looked at Frankie, who nodded. "It's true Sa-, I mean Howard. Gave your Ma money every month. Paid for your college."

Howard's eyes were darker than I'd ever seen them before, but he didn't bat an eyelash.

"But I got a proposition for you," said Tito, standing upright now.

Howard didn't answer.

"I know tings you don't. Tings you wanna know, trust me. I tell you these tings, you let me go."

Howard still didn't answer. It was an Italian standoff. Finally, Howard's radio buzzed live.

"Marr!" yelled Agent Smith. "Make the deal now. I'm ordering the choppers out of here. High winds and two confirmed tornado sightings. One in Herndon and one in Oakton heading our way. I've got more ground support coming in, but I want you to get those people out of there. NOW!"

"Howard," I said, panicked. "The girls are in Herndon. And my mom."

Howard didn't even look my way. His cold, icy stare was focused on Tito.

"You heard it," Tito said, "make da deal."

Howard looked ready to lunge when the engine of a departing chopper started to scream as if it was out of control. The screaming noise intensified as the thwump, thwump, thwump of the blades slowed but became louder and louder. Something was very wrong and it showed on everyone's faces. Even Tito's.

Suddenly it became clear the chopper was coming down, possibly right on top of us. "Brace yourselves!" screamed Howard as the house shook with an explosion that could have rocked the richter scales. The screech of metal against metal was so loud I had to cover my ears. Dust and sparks flew, pieces of the ceiling fell, smoke filled the air. It was like a scene out of a Michael Bay movie.

When the screeching stopped, I found myself on my stomach holding my head. No one was talking, but the coughs told me others were alive. Wind whipped through the house. I turned on my side just in time to see Viv unwrapping coils of rope from around her while crawling toward my gun which was now within her reach on the floor. Scrambling quick, I grabbed the gun but not before she did. I was only vaguely aware of others moving and yelling while I fought Viviana for the firearm. Her fingernails were lethal weapons, scratching my hands to pieces. I felt around on the floor with my other hand, and as luck would have it, found one of Viv's spikey heels. Grasping it tightly, I brought the pointy tip of the heel down hard.

"You Bitch!" she screamed.

It worked. With the gun firmly in my own hand pointed at Viviana who clutched her fingers in pain, I scanned the room. Dust and debris flew through the air on currents of wind. Officer Brad had a gun on Tito while struggling to open the door. No Toes and Joey were safely in custody as well, and Frankie was pulling a large piece of wall off of Howard.

"Marr!" yelled Officer Brad. "The propane!"

"I know!" said Howard, brushing himself off. "Frankie, help Elvis." He looked at me. "You good?" I nodded. "Everyone out of here!"

"The door is jammed," Officer Brad grunted.

"Out the windows," said Howard. Two of the three large windows had shattered. Officer Brad, moving Tito toward one of them, knocked remaining shards with his shoes, then pushed Tito through. They were followed by agents guiding No Toes and Joey, then Frankie and Elvis.

Howard was kneeling next to Maxine's body. "Barb, go now!"

"What about you?"

"I'll follow you."

"You heard him," I sneered at Viviana, my gun making its point. "Move."

Viv coughed and stood up slowly. "I'm movin', I'm movin'." I followed her through the window, stepping over sharp pieces of glass. The exit was difficult as I fought gusts of wind and rain while gripping Viviana and still trying to hold the gun steady enough to keep her from running. Once onto firm ground we moved quickly out onto the front, sloping lawn trying to get distance between ourselves and the house. Black smoke billowed out of the windows, but Howard hadn't appeared. The helicopter, which was engulfed in flames, had hit the house from the east side nearest the driveway demolishing Elvis' Towncar and half the garage. One of its blades had snapped free and pierced clear through Tito's car.

"Howard!" I screamed. The smoke cloud grew and a small explosion from inside shook me to the core. "Howard!"

Finally, out of the smoke, Howard appeared climbing through the window, Maxine's limp body flung over his shoulder. When he was a safe distance from the house, he laid her on the ground. I took a deep breath, relieved everyone had made it out safely.

Then I realized not everyone had made it out safely. My heart stopped. Agent Marjorie Smith appeared at my side, taking Viviana by the arm and relieving me of my firearm.

"My friends," I babbled as she dragged Viv away. "Howard!" I screamed. "Colt and Peggy and Roz! They're still inside!"

But my last words were drowned out by the explosion that ripped through the house, blowing out windows and sending glass, brick and fire in all directions. As I turned to shield my face, the heat from the blast felt like fire on my back. I struggled to remain standing through it all, and when it felt safe to turn back around, the devastation floored me. The house, the helicopter, tree limbs the size of trees themselves littered the land. The wind and rain had died down quickly, and I stood aching, wet and mortified that my friends were dead inside that roaring heap of rubble.

Falling to my knees, I was too weak to take anymore. The nightmare was too much for me. I covered my eyes and cried. All around me, people were yelling and sirens were blaring.

"Hey!" a shout rang out in the distance. "You guys forget about us?"

I didn't need to look up to know that voice, but I looked anyway. From the far side of the house, limping up an embankment appeared Colt, holding Puddles the Poodle in one arm, and supporting Roz with the other and Peggy holding her on the other side.

Howard smiled at me. "See," he yelled over the chaos, "I knew he'd get them out alive."

Emergency vehicles arrived by the second, filling the night sky with strobing red lights. Howard was waving someone official over to Maxine, when I became aware of a disturbance behind me. With the all of the pandemonium and thinking my best friends were dead, I hadn't been aware at all of what was happening behind me. I had no idea where Frankie or

Elvis were, where they had taken the motley crew of gangsters. I had been peripherally aware that people were behind me but that's about it.

Slowly, I sensed something was wrong. Still on my knees, I looked to Howard first. He was standing, talking to an EMT, but also keeping one eye on the activity behind me. With my danger meter registering above normal, I turned my head to see what he was looking at.

A black van had backed up onto the lawn next to the drive way, its back doors open. Frankie and Elvis were inside. A large man with FBI printed in white on the back of his jacket was guiding Tito inside, his hands cuffed behind his back. Another smaller FBI agent had a cuff on one of Viviana's hands but struggled to get the other on while she ranted wildly. Something about her shoe. With one spikey heel still on the other foot, it appeared she was asking to get it off. When the agent relented, she reach down with her free hand to grab the shoe.

By now, Howard was next to me and heading toward the scene. "No!" he yelled.

But it was too late.

Viv whipped that pointy heel right into the agents face and when another agent came in to apprehend her, she whipped it around and nailed him too. Two agents downed with a four inch heel. She grabbed the second agent's gun with one swift move, and screamed, "I'm gonna get that snoopy little bitch if it's the last thing I do!"

Howard moved in front of me, arms spread and posed to guard while shouting to Agent Smith. He had no gun, no vest.

Viviana was snarling like a rabid dog. It was all happening too fast. "Outa the way, Sammy, or I'll take you too!"

I don't remember taking the time to consider jumping in front of Howard to shield him. I don't even remember moving. But I must have, because the next thing I knew, I was standing in front of him, arms stretched wide.

I heard a shot and a scream.

Chapter 24

I was on a red-carpet. The Academy Awards. I was up for Best Director of the action thriller, *Terminated Mission to Die Hardly*, produced by Steven Spielberg and starring George Clooney, Brad Pitt, and Sara Jessica Parker as the heroine who saves the day.

Of course, action thrillers are rarely considered in these categories, but the beautifully scripted subplot about an AIDS-stricken, paraplegic orphan girl who wanted to save the world from global warming won the heart of critics and The Academy alike. It became the most talked about film in America.

A stunning, blonde, twenty-something woman with a microphone in her hand and a neckline plunging to her navel waved for me to come speak with her. "Barbara! Barbara Marr! Over here!" I moved to her side and she put a microphone in front of my face. "Barbara – you're the talk of the town! Soccer mom turned director – handpicked by Steven Spielberg. Now your first film is up for Best Director and Best Film! How does it feel?"

"Dreamlike," I smiled.

"And who are you wearing tonight?"

I looked aghast. "Holy cow – no one I hope! I'm not in the habit of wearing people."

She laughed a practiced, made-for-television-laugh. "You are just a riot, Barbara!"

"Seriously now," she continued, "who's the designer?" I looked frightfully, once more, down at my torso, arms and legs. What WAS I wearing? Jeans and a long sleeved t-shirt from the This Is Cheap and Will Suffice Collection at Target. Unable to answer her question, I realized that my apparel barely even met the dress code for the local Irish pub. Giving up on me, the beautiful woman guided me in the direction of the Kodak Theater.

"Good Luck!" she said, moving on to bigger and better stars.

The next thing I knew, I was sitting in the front row next to Jack Nicholson, sunglasses and all, who smiled at me and called me "Sweetie." Ordinarily, I'd be inclined to deck any man who dared refer to me as "Sweetie," but this was Jack Nicholson, so I laughed a jocular laugh and patted him on the arm. I realized the seat on the other side of me is empty.

Music started playing and the lights dimmed. I was so excited, I could barely contain myself. Billy Crystal made a grand entrance on the stage and I joined the audience in a standing ovation. Everyone was so excited that Billy was back to save the ratings. When we sat back down, Jack had turned into Meryl Streep. I was embarrassed because Meryl was up for Best Director also – her first nod in that category. I smiled sheepishly at her, thinking I really should be bowing or genuflecting. Meryl is a goddess, after all.

Turning to my other side, I also saw the empty seat was no longer empty – it was filled to the brim with my mother's hulking frame. Even sitting, she had to look down at me, which she did now, with an angry scowl.

"Barbara," she scolded me, "what are you doing here when you should be fixing that dent in your van? And what about your girls, leaving them alone in that hotel room like that. You're a very lucky woman to have me around – I suggested to Eric that he call his friend at Phone-America to track your cell phone location. How else do you think he found you? That is, of course, because I was the brainchild of the satellite and cell phone revolution."

I was speechless and angry that she made me miss Billy's monologue entirely.

Suddenly, Billy Crystal was morphing before my eyes – his body growing taller and skinnier. He was holding an uzi with one hand and a cigarette with another. Before I could register that Billy Crystal had transformed into Viviana Buttaro, Howard, Amber, Bethany and Callie appeared in front me of playing Ring-Around-The-Rosy. No! Viviana had a rocket launcher and was aiming it right at us! I needed to do something fast, before she killed us all – including Meryl. The world would never forgive me if Viviana Buttaro whacked Meryl Streep on national television.

Noooooooooooooo!!!!!!!! I yelled at the top of my lungs.

When I opened my eyes, my heart was racing and my vision was blurred. Someone was holding my hand.

"Howard?"

"Thank God," he said. He was rubbing my head and kissing my cheek leaving behind a few of his own tears. "How do you feel?"

"My chest hurts. And my arm feels like it's on fire."

"You took three shots to the vest at close range and another grazed your right arm." He was wiping tears away from his face, but they came faster than he could wipe. "I'm sorry," he sniffed. "I'm sorry. I'm just so sorry."

"You have a way with words," I mumbled, half-dazed. I really wanted to go back to sleep. "Howard?"

"Yeah?"

"I love you."

"I love you too."

"Howard?"

"Yeah?"

"Would Ripley be proud?" My mouth was so dry I could barely form the words and my eyes were drooping terribly, but I had to know.

"What?"

"Lieutenant Ripley. Sigourney Weaver in *Alien* – did I do good like her?"

He laughed. "Better, I think. If I remember right, she only saved herself and the cat. You came out with zero casualties."

That was the last thing I remembered until they wheeled me past a screaming Viviana strapped down to her gurney and flanked by two of the biggest men I had ever seen wearing jackets with the letters FBI clearly spelling out their duty.

While a motherly, little nurse cleaned the wound on my arm with tender care, I could hear someone on the other side of the curtain ordering an IV and Ibuprofen for Roz.

"Is she going to be okay?" I asked the nurse.

"Don't you worry about her," she said, patting me softly on the hand. "She's very dehydrated. The fever will probably come down nicely once she gets those fluids we're giving her. She'll be good in no time."

On the other side of me I could hear a woman consulting with Peggy on the dangers of Post-Traumatic Stress in situations like hers, and recommending an anti-depressant to stave off the inevitable. Peggy told the woman in no uncertain terms that the only anti-depressant she needed was the love of her husband and three boys and if the woman didn't let her see them, then and there, she'd have to sue for medical negligence. Besides, her mother's best friend's sister had taken those things and that was how she lost all of her hair. She also gave the nurse a quick education on the subject of corrupt pharmaceutical companies only caring about the holy buck and did she know those companies actually do business with the Mafia? Eventually, the woman acquiesced, calling in the Rubenstein clan, probably not convinced that Peggy still didn't have a few screws loose.

Howard stayed with me, sitting next to my bed, holding my hand. He told me that when Viviana unleashed the weapon on me, the only Agent able to react fast enough was Smith who wounded her with several hits, but not mortally. Viviana Buttaro would live long enough to die in jail from lung cancer. Maxine, on the other hand, was teetering precariously in the ICU. She had lost a lot of blood. Even the monkeys made it out alive, he said, after Colt and Peggy released them during their own escape. Although, according to Colt, they didn't go easily. The monkeys that is.

When he felt sure I was well enough, he said he really needed to get back to the scene – there were reports to make and interviews to be taken. He could be out the rest of the night.

"It's okay," I said. "Go get it done."

"You sure?" Guilt was still written all over his face.

"Does it matter if I'm sure? You'd have to go anyway, right?" I had a new understanding of our lives at present.

He nodded.

"So," I said, "I don't know which to ask first: How? or Why?"

Howard didn't blink. He also didn't answer up immediately. "They're both big questions with complicated answers." He finally said.

"Can you at least give me an abridged version of the 'How', just to tide me over? I feel like the world's most clueless wife here."

He pulled his hand away from mine and ran them through his hair like men do when they don't want to confront something difficult. He took a deep breath before speaking. "My mother owns a condo near our house. I use it to store my gun, my badge. Park a bureau car there if I'm driving one. If I'm on a tough case, I tell you I'm on travel and I stay there."

"Your mother?" I asked, unable to believe she had been in on the years of deception.

"That gets into the why – it's . . . can we do this later?" He looked at me ashamed, but at least he was looking me in the eyes.

"Obviously," I said, "we have a lot of talking to do. I'll see you when you get home?"

He smiled a very relieved smile. "See you at home." He kissed me tenderly on the lips and walked away, those letters again, FBI, now obvious on his back.

I called after him. "Hey!" He turned around with a show of concern on his face. "You look pretty sexy in that jacket. You should've let me see it a long time ago." He smiled brilliantly then disappeared behind the sterile curtains that separated me from the rest of the hospital.

Roz was admitted overnight for observation, Peter sitting vigil by her side. They released Peggy and me. Since I didn't have a husband available to take me home, I got the next best thing – Colt. He'd driven over in Howard's Camry after a de-briefing by agency officials.

"Your mother wants to see you," he said warily in the car.

"No! No, not tonight. I just want to sleep. Please."

"Got it," he said, relenting.

"How long have you been in on this?" I asked finally.

"Only since today. Swear. Howie clued me in at your house earlier."

"The backyard chat?

"Yeah."

"Have you known he was with the FBI all this time?"

He shook his head immediately. "No. Not until today. Really."

"So why did he tell you today?"

"He wanted my help keeping you safe. He was driving me to pick up a rental car when you and Roz got yourselves kidnapped. What the hell were you thinking?"

"Well, you weren't doing a very good job of keeping me safe now were you? Besides, why couldn't you just keep me safe by staying at the house?"

"Well, the original plan was to keep you from worrying by keeping a distance, watching the house and making sure Viviana's crew stayed away. But then when they showed up, we decided to stow you away at the hotel while I stayed at the house in case they came around again. You were supposed to stay safe at the hotel – remember?"

Embarrassed by my actions, I tried to explain myself. "We had a plan."

Colt didn't respond to my excuse.

We stayed quiet for a while until I decided to change the subject to Howard's alias. "How about his name – he's Italian? Did you know that?"

"We were very tight in college – he told me everything years ago. It's a wild story. His name, his old man."

"His dad was in the mafia?"

Colt shook his head. "He was an honest business man. Too honest, too much integrity for his own good. Tito, as far as I understand, was working under a guy who ordered him to make the hit."

"Frankie and Elvis told me that Tito felt bad about it and took care of him financially – even paid for his college."

Colt seemed impressed. "No shit! Really?"

"Did Howard know that?"

"I don't think so."

I grew quiet once more, exhaustion rolling over me like a tsunami. I dozed off in the car and had a vague recollection of making it as far as the couch once we reached home. The stairs to my bedroom seemed just too monumental.

When I woke up, my chest still ached and my right arm burned like someone had marked me with a branding iron.

"You okay, Mommy?" Amber's sweet voice whispered in my ear. I smiled and turned my head to find her, bedecked again in her fairy paraphernalia, waiting for my awakening.

"I'm okay, Sweetie. You?"

"Oh, I'm great! We're having tacos!"

The air was, in fact, filled with the aroma of Mexican spices, and my stomach growled an expectant growl. Food! Finally!

"Come on, Mommy. We're waiting." Careful to grab me by my good arm, Amber pulled me to a sitting position.

"What time is it?" I asked her with only a slight wince of pain.

"Daddy!" she yelled to the kitchen, "What time is it?"

"One forty-five!" Howard's voice rang back.

Bright, glorious sunlight streamed in from all of my windows. It was a new day, after the scariest night of my life. I pulled my sorry butt off the couch and made my way to find Colt had chopped and stirred up a fabulous mexi-feast. My stomach growled again at the colorful sight of it all – tomatoes, lettuce, guacamole, black olives.

Howard was sitting in front of a newspaper with a Corona, and the table was set for three. Looking out the sliding glass door, I could see Bethany and Callie setting up three places at the table on the deck.

"Who's eating outside?" I asked Howard.

"The girls wanted to eat out on the deck, but I wasn't really up for it. You okay in here?"

"Sure." I nodded, just glad to have him back again.

When I sat down across from him, he put his paper down and gave me a sort of hang-dog look. The atmosphere was awkward. I just didn't quite know what to say. Evidently, neither did he.

"So," Colt said, breaking the silent moment while pulling taco shells from the oven, "wild night, huh?" After another brief moment of silence, we all laughed.

"Hey," I perked up, remembering something that had been gnawing at me, "I still don't know what happened at House of Many Bones thirty years ago that had everyone so scared. Viviana wouldn't answer that question."

Howard explained that little story for me while Colt put bowls of taco condiments on both tables. As bad luck would have it, Viviana and Tito hadn't owned the White Willow house very long when Tito, a known philanderer, decided to invite a couple of paid girlfriends over for a kinky threesome. Unbeknownst to Viviana, he had outfitted it with furniture for just that very purpose. Only thing was, when the girls showed up they were men. Undercover cops, disguised as ladies of the night on a routine prostitution sting. The cops had no idea Tito was a Wiseguy. When the bust went down inside the house, all guns came out and while Tito only got grazed in the leg, one cop was shot dead. The other managed to escape out the back door, before Tito managed to bring him down with an axe.

Problem was, said Howard, several neighbors heard the gunshots and came out to investigate. No one had called the police, because Rustic Woods, being what it was in the seventies – quiet and practically country – they all thought it was just someone shooting at a wild animal.

"Needless to say," said Howard, "they were shocked to find Tito Buttaro holding an ax, standing over a dead man dressed as a woman. Tito, thinking he had no other recourse, told them who he was and what he did for a living and warned them if they wanted to live to see another day, they'd all go back to their houses and keep quiet."

"Which they did?" I asked.

"All of them. The Perkins, the Rhineharts, and the MacMillans. Tito and his soldiers came back the next day and made a personal visit to each family, just to push home the point. Don't talk."

"What about the cops?" I asked.

"Their bodies were found in a dumpster in Manassas a few days later. Investigations went nowhere. They never considered that Mafia was in this area at that time."

"Wow." The only word I could muster.

"That's about it," agreed Howard.

"What happens to Frankie and Elvis?"

"They're cooperating and filling in the gaps of information we were missing. They'll get full amnesty. A couple of funny guys – they've never liked killing. That's why Tito wanted them around – figured he was safe that way. When Viv gave the order to whack him, they cut a deal with him – he stays in hiding, they don't kill him. And they're telling us everything about Viviana, down to her shoe size." Howard laughed a weak sort of laugh, and shook his head lightly. "She was cooking up a half-baked scheme to sell her houses and bankroll the production of a screenplay she wrote about her own life." He started digging in his back pocket. "Here Barb, I wrote it down so I wouldn't forget – I thought you'd get a kick out of this." He produced a small bit of paper that looked as if it had been torn from a bigger piece. He read from it, laughing. "*Misunderstood – A Mafia Wife Unshackles the Chains of Bondage.*"

Colt had been sitting and feeding himself tacos by now. "Too bad she's going to jail for a long time – that sounds like a box office winner," he laughed.

"She claims she was on to us at the end – that's why she so easily gave up the names to Tito. She's asking for a deal as an informant."

"Will she get it?" I asked.

"Is the Pope Jewish?" Howard laughed, grabbing a taco and slapping on a dollop of guacamole. He ate half, then put it down. "I'm too tired to eat."

He did look done in. A day's worth of stubble had grown on his face and the circles under his eyes told me that he hadn't slept at all the previous night. His gorgeous hair looked like it had been through a car wash. He pulled his exhausted body slowly out of his chair. "I'll be right back."

"Wait," I said, "you owe me an explanation."

"Now? Can't we do this when we're alone?"

"Last night – if you had your vest on when No Toes shot you, why weren't you wearing it later?"

Howard smiled a weak, but satisfied smile. "After that numb skull pulled me behind the shed while I played dead, I waited until the coast was clear then crawled to the back of the house – I found a basement window unlocked, but I couldn't crawl through with my vest on."

"How did Officer Brad know to throw you the gun?"

"I lost mine crawling in the mud. I was able to access a land line in the house and patch through to Smith."

"Geezie Louisie – I'm married to a real life action hero, aren't I?"

He smiled again and walked out of the room and up the stairs.

"Boy," said Colt after Howard left, "you guys have been married, what? Ten, twelve years?"

"Seventeen."

"Wow, has it been that long? Well, anyway, I gotta tell you, after all these years, that guy is just as crazy about you now, as he was back our first year of college. C-R-A-Z-Y. You gotta love it." He said.

I smiled.

"Yeah," he said, nodding his head and finishing his thought, "I know how he feels."

"So," I said, deciding to move quickly away from the topic of long lost love, "do you have a return ticket to LA?"

"Of course not. In fact, do you mind if I stick around a little while longer? This place is starting to grow on me. Pretty exciting around here." He smiled.

"Sure," I said, "stay as long as you want."

I polished off at least six tacos and they were yummy in my tummy. Finally, feeling satiated, I decided to go see how Howard was doing. He had pulled the curtains shut and was under the covers of our bed, out like a light. I looked at his peacefully sleeping face. I wondered about the man I didn't seem to know now. How would we move forward from this? Could I forgive the years of lying? I didn't know. I decided not to worry. There would be the time for the questions and time for the answers. Time, possibly for understanding. Or not understanding. Another time, though. Another time.

I took off my shoes, crawled under the covers and curled up cozy like a spoon next to my husband, who was finally back where he belonged, in my bed. It felt nice to be safe again, basking in the warmth and comfort of a space that was ours and ours alone.

Chapter 25

Halloween came and went. I spent the first two weeks of November finessing ChickAtTheFlix.com, but was still working up the courage to put it up live on the web. Now, just two days before Thanksgiving, Roz, Peggy and I were sitting in chairs, dressed in white uniforms watching a master class at Master Kyo's Tae Kwon Do.

"Do your sides hurt?" Whined Peggy. "My sides hurt."

"Only your sides hurt?" I moaned in response. "My whole body hurts. My fingernails hurt."

"What are you all complaining about?" Roz piped up. "You should try this stuff with one of these on." She held up her right hand presenting a very fashionable plastic wrist guard. Turns out, Frankie hadn't broken her hand, but had wrangled her wrist into a fairly nasty sprain.

Having recovered from our various wounds, both physical and mental, we had resolved to learn ourselves some self-defense. We had strolled into our first class the previous week, full of excitement and eager willingness to tone our bodies and minds, while gaining the valuable skill of chopping a piece of wood in half with our feet. We figured if we could splinter wood with our feet, we could bring down any man, woman, or medium-sized animal that might seek to harm our middle-aged bodies. After two days at the back of the line as peon "No Belts" and suffering excruciating physical pain in every possible muscle in my body, my mind was now telling my body to skip this joint and go next door to Joe's Bar for a cold one.

"So," asked Peggy, "Have you heard anymore about Viviana? Is she being sent up the river?"

"What does that even mean?" asked Roz.

"I don't know. Don't they say that?" she said, grimacing as she lifted a knee to cross her legs.

"No," I said, groaning. "I don't think Howard is allowed to tell me anymore. Or else he won't. Don't know which. You know, we're all witnesses. We'll be required to testify against her in court." It was hard to tell if the worry on their faces was from fear of court, or fear of the upcoming hour of cruel Korean torture.

"What about Howard?" asked Roz. "Looks to me like he hasn't moved back in yet. What's the deal?"

I grinned an evil grin. "I'm making him date me again. Told him he had to work to win me back."

"Will he?" asked Peggy, "I mean, you will forgive him, right? Right?"

"Maybe . . ." I said.

"What about Colt? I saw him at your house yesterday – he hasn't left yet?"

"He's moving out here – says he likes the area. Evidently DC is a great place for PIs. Congressmen cheating on their wives and such."

"Where's he staying?"

"Howard's condo. They're roommates again." I couldn't help but laugh at that irony. Roz and Peggy bugged their eyes out in response. "Oh, yeah. It's very interesting. Funny too, because they have a new pet. A dog."

"A dog?" asked Roz.

I nodded, smiling. "Puddles. In a cast from the waist down."

Roz and Peggy laughed, both grabbing their waists, grimacing from the pain that even a mere giggle could cause after a week of never ending, sadistic sit-ups.

The master class had been dismissed, and energized boys and girls with important colored belts dashed onto the mat after making their requisite bows. I always forgot the bow. Certainly, the discipline and respect it represented was important. I didn't disagree in theory, I just always forgot.

Roz bravely stood up first, followed by Peggy. They looked at me, still sitting in my chair, every muscle aching and throbbing.

"Maybe we should bag this and learn to shoot a gun instead," I proposed. "It wouldn't hurt so much. And we'd probably all look really sexy holding one."

Roz shook her head violently. "Forget it. This was your idea, remember? Besides, I'd be afraid to tell your mother we were quitting. She scares the hell out of me."

I acquiesced and rose slowly from my chair, making ouchy noises with each pain. Hobbling to the mat, I made the same darn mistake I made every time. I forgot to bow. I cringed as my foot touched the mat, realizing too late that the law had been broken. A booming roar sounded from the front of the room. "Mrs. Marr! Did you fail to bow?"

Roz and Peggy hid giggles from our instructor who was reprimanding me. Damn!

"Yes, sir," I mumbled, ashamed and embarrassed while all of the obedient little boys and girls stared at me.

"Mrs. Marr! I don't think I heard you!"

I looked to the front of the class, finding my mother, the black belt instructor chiding me mercilessly. "Yes sir." I repeated loudly enough for her to hear.

"Eric," she said to the assistant standing next to her, "count for her while she does twenty push ups."

My handsome Officer Brad suppressed a smile as he met me in the corner where my punishment would be served. His left arm was fully encased in an orange cast resting in a dark blue sling.

"You know how to shoot a gun, right?" I asked.

"You're not thinking of shooting her are you?" he asked.

"Actually, no – I was thinking I needed to learn how to use one for protection, but your idea is much better."

"Okay, down on the floor for twenty," he said.

I almost responded with a quippy remark regarding the possible innuendo contained within that statement, but fought back the urge. I smiled anyway then took a deep breath. If I could take three bullets in the chest from a spikey-heeled lady mobster on a mission to kill, I could manage a push up or two . . . or twenty.

the end.

Were you entertained?
If so, check out Karen Cantwell's website
http://www.KarenCantwell.com
to learn more about her other books and short stories

Made in the USA
Lexington, KY
10 October 2010